when
strange
gods
call

when strange gods call

a novel

Pam Chun

SOURCEBOOKS LANDMARK™
AN IMPRINT OF SOURCEBOOKS, INC.®
NAPERVILLE, ILLINOIS

Published by Sourcebooks, Inc.
P.O. Box 4410, Naperville, Illinois 60567-4410
(630) 961-3900
FAX: (630) 961-2168
www.sourcebooks.com

Library of Congress Cataloging-in-Publication Data
Chun, Pam.
When strange gods call : a novel / by Pam Chun.
    p. cm.
ISBN 1-4022-0303-9 (alk. paper)
1. Chinese American women--Fiction. 2. Chinese American families-
-Fiction. 3. Conflict of generations--Fiction. 4. Women art teachers--
Fiction. 5. First loves--Fiction. 6. Hawaii--Fiction. I. Title.
PS3603.H85W47 2004
813'.6--dc22

                                                    2004013216

Printed and bound in Canada
WC   10 9 8 7 6 5 4 3 2 1

For my father, Kwai Wood Chun

Table of Contents

Acknowledgments ix

Author's Note xi

Demming Family Tree xiv

Ai'Lee Family Tree xv

Chapter 1:   The Lure of Ghosts and Gods. 1

Chapter 2:   Like a Moth to a Flame. 35

Chapter 3:   Beach Ghost Stories 49

Chapter 4:   The Demmings. 65

Chapter 5:   Lailee's Secret. 81

Chapter 6:   Family Ties and Curses 89

Chapter 7:   Reunion with the Past 107

Chapter 8:   The Cycle of Past and Future 121

Chapter 9:   The Ai'Lee Ladies. 131

Chapter 10: The State Capitol. 145

Chapter 11: Flying Through Water. 153

Chapter 12: The Lu`au. 169

Chapter 13: Ga Na Gnew, the Hawaiian 187

Chapter 14: Taiko Drum Beats 193

Chapter 15: Ginger Ai'Lee. 199

Chapter 16: Hurricane Warnings 223

Chapter 17: The Beginning and the End 241

Chapter 18: Aftermath of the Storm 249

Chapter 19: The Hawaiian Wedding 265

Chapter 20: The Tears of the Gods. 271

About the Author 275

Glossary of Hawaiian Terms. 277

Acknowledgments

Mahalo to my son, Ryan C. Leong, who loves ghost stories and encourages me to tell them. Fond Aloha to the best storytellers in Heaven: Popo Chun, Popo Lau, my mother Sara, and my brother Dale (who told the tallest tales). Mahalo to master storytellers Auntie Fannie and Uncle Bob Wong, and my father.

Deepest appreciation to my ku`u ipo, Fred Joyce III.

My fondest Mahalo to Jan Tyau Peterson and Auntie Blossom Tyau for including me in their `ohana. Thanks to my Maui cousins, Claire Crockett-Shaw, Ermine and Fred Gartley, and William F. Crockett for the inspiration.

My deepest gratitude goes to my guardian angel, Elizabeth Pomada, and Michael Larsen.

I owe an armful of leis in thanks to my editor Hillel Black who is the embodiment of gentlemanly scholarship and to Peter Lynch for his thoroughness. Thank you to the team at Sourcebooks for their support.

Mahalo to Maile Meyer, Beth-Ann Kozlovich, Brian Melzack, Les Honda, Ramsay Goldstein and the Ramsay Museum, Pat Banning, Wing Tek Lum, Professor John W. Conner, Dr. Carol Fan, Muffy Gushi, Wanda Adams, Nadine Kam, and especially to Jo Ann Tanouye Schindler and Joyce Miyamoto at the Hawaiian and Pacific Library Collection, Hawai`i State Library, for welcoming me "home."

Thank you to my special friends: Barbara Bundy, Muriel Kao, Genevieve and Paul Ong, Patricia Seid, Steve Chan, Carolyn Gan, May Louie, Susan Lin Shyn, Rena Young

Ochse, the Women's Roundtable at the University of San Francisco Center for the Pacific Rim, the Alameda Library Book Group, the Chinese Chapter CAL–Berkeley Alumni Association, and Dr. Franklin Odo of the Smithsonian Institute.

I owe my fondest Aloha to the University of San Francisco Center for the Pacific Rim for their support.

My deepest appreciation goes to the members of the Chinese Historical Society of America, Chinese Historical Society of Southern California, Chinese Women's Club of Honolulu, Associated Chinese University Women, Organization of Chinese American Women, Hawai`i State Society of Washington, D.C., San Francisco Chinatown Opti-Ms. Club, Chi-Am Circle, and the Chinese Historical Cultural Project for their generosity and support.

Special thanks to my fellow Storytellers at the Asian Art Museum of San Francisco for their inspiration.

Thanks to Paul "Doc" Berry and Winston Healy who set me on the path. My sincere thanks to my friends who cheerfully read the manuscript: Terese Tse Bartholomew, Mari Campbell, Sondra Coppersmith, Alberta Eckers, Muffy Gushi, Mindy Hart, Muriel Kao, Cynthia McCullough, Genevieve Ong, and Jan Tyau Petersen.

Author's Note

When I was a child in Hawai`i, whenever our family gathered, the evening would end with stories. My grandmother, aunts, uncles, and parents remembered the Territorial Days when life was simpler—planting taro in the terraced rows, running barefoot, and climbing trees after school. But when the moon mounted the warm dark nights, my cousins and I craved the ghost stories. In those days, gods and goddesses, ghosts and spirits were very much alive.

After a sunset swim and barbecue on the beach, all of us gathered around the glowing hibachi coals, knee to knee in the darkness. Did we know that a little boy had drowned right here at this beach, an uncle would ask with a glint in his eye. We shivered when we heard the tale of how this seaweed-dripping ghost haunted the sea waiting for an unsuspecting victim.

On the way home, we would pass darkened houses, supposedly haunted. My father would point out trees where ghosts could be seen luring drivers.

When my father turned onto our street we were instantly silent when we passed the three old cemeteries and four temples and churches—a richly fertile haunt for spirits. Early one morning, my mother's cousin had awakened us with her frantic pounding on our front door. On her way to work, traffic had slowed to a crawl. A man and woman, drenched in blood, beckoned to all the drivers from the wall at Kipapa Gulch, a treacherous road. The couple had been driving home from a school meeting and died in a car accident the night before at that very spot. Her cousin had seen the couple's spirits luring the morning commuters to "take their place."

While the Chinese and Hawaiian ghost stories—of which our family had an endless supply—shaped our imaginations, we were trying to be as American as the people we saw on television and in the movies. Our school curriculum covered American history, not Hawaiian history. Our teachers emphasized speaking good English, not the pidgin we used to communicate with our friends and neighbors who spoke dozens of languages. But we always remembered that spirits inhabit trees, rocks, mountains, and the wind. Ghosts return to homes and roadsides. Strange gods and goddesses take human form to confound us.

Hawai`i is a mix of many cultures and languages from ethnically diverse lands of the Pacific. Perhaps it is Hawai`i's tumultuous history—a Hawaiian kingdom overthrown by American businessmen, ruled by a provisional government and a republic, annexation, and statehood—that allows us to be comfortable with both the mystical world of Hawai`i and the logical Western world of America. It has taught us that what matters most are the people and our ability to get along and adapt.

According to the 2000 U.S. Census, there are more Hawaiians living on the United States mainland than in Hawai`i. Even though we keiki o ka `aina—the children of Hawai`i—have left the Islands for political, economic, or educational reasons, we have taken the tales and myths and legends of Hawai`i with us.

So now when the wind rustles the trees, we listen for the Night Whispers and teach our children to hear their stories. We teach the little ones the rituals and how to observe the festivals based on ancient ways. They hear chilling ghost stories from our childhood steeped in the legends of many. So when they inhale the humid air, hear the haunting voices, and listen to the Night Whispers calling, they will know that the spirits of all these ancestors belong to them.

When Strange Gods Call evokes these ghosts and spirits of Hawai`i. Names, characters, places, and incidents either are the product of the author's imagination or are used fictitiously. Any resemblance to actual persons, living or dead, business establishments, events, or locales are entirely coincidental.

The gods and goddesses, ghosts and spirits, however, are real.

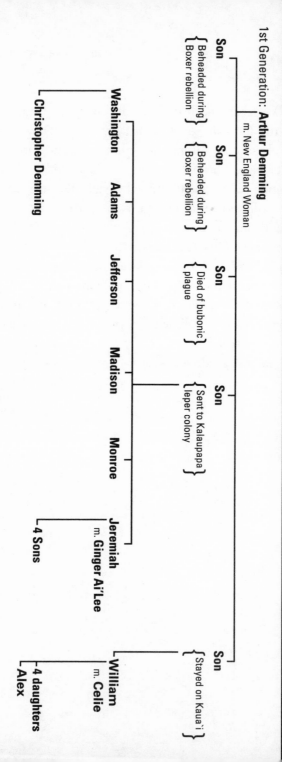

❧ Demming Family Tree ❧

1st Generation: **Arthur Demming**
m. New England Woman

Son
{ Beheaded during
Boxer rebellion }

Son
{ Beheaded during
Boxer rebellion }

Son
{ Died of bubonic
plague }

Son
{ Sent to Kalaupapa
leper colony }

Washington

Adams

Jefferson

Madison

Monroe

Jeremiah
m. **Ginger Ai'Lee**

Christopher Demming

4 Sons

Son
{ Stayed on Kaua'i }

William
m. **Celie**

4 daughters
Alex

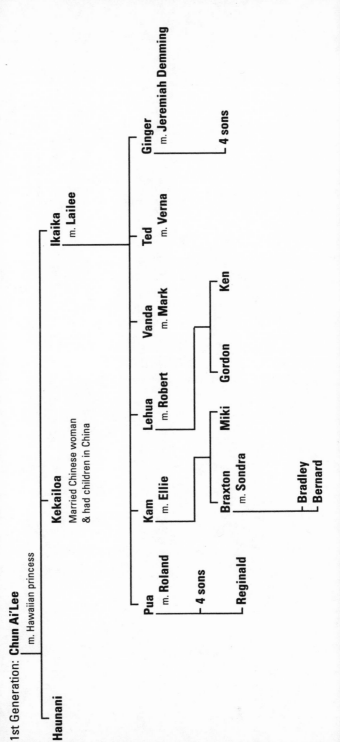

Ai'Lee Family Tree

1st Generation: **Chun Ai'Lee**
m. Hawaiian princess

Haunani

Kekailoa
Married Chinese woman
& had children in China

Ikaika
m. **Lailee**

Pua
m. **Roland**

4 sons

Reginald

Kam
m. **Ellie**

Braxton
m. **Sondra**

Miki

Bradley
Bernard

Lehua
m. **Robert**

Gordon

Vanda
m. **Mark**

Ken

Ted
m. **Verna**

Ginger
m. **Jeremiah Demming**

4 sons

when
strange
gods
call

Chapter One

The Lure of
Ghosts and Gods

Hawai`i, 1958

Millions of stars surrounded the cliff like a river of iridescent sand across the skies and spilled down to the sea
hundreds of feet below. Alex coasted to the edge, to
where we could hear the surf pound against the lava
rocks beneath us.

I turned to study his face, to see how he had changed.
He had traveled six thousand miles away and lived
where seasons changed from icy snow to dripping heat.
He returned from his first year of college taller, broader
in the shoulders, with an East Coast polish to his speech.
Since I had never left the Islands, I wanted to know
what he had seen, what he had felt.

Alex gripped the steering wheel of his '47 wood-
paneled Olds and stared into the darkness as if memo-
rizing the position and brilliance of each star.
"Hawai`i is a galaxy apart, a whole different world,"
he said with his old charm and confidence. The old
Woody was Alex's pride, one of the things he missed
the most while he was away. Its wood sides, stripped
by the sea air, worn to a patina by the sun, were
smooth to the touch. Even its interior scent, of wood

and worn leather, reminded us of the days we had spent as salty-haired teens.

The wind whistled in through the side windows that had never closed properly after we pried them open. It became our private joke, a reminder of our first date when he locked the keys in the car fifteen minutes before my ten o'clock curfew. Frantic, we had jimmied the lock with a coat hanger. Alex pronounced our success a good omen, despite our families' legendary rivalry. But his year away had been a year of silence.

Alex leaned forward and pulled me close. "Let me teach you what I learned on the East Coast," he said. His voice was throaty and his hands were smooth, hot, and silky against my throat when he kissed me. His shirt, a Hawaiian print that smelled like a sunny afternoon under salty skies, was soft against my bare arms.

I was breathless. I no longer heard the sea or the wind. The air was sweet with ocean spray and resonant with the boom of the waves

But when his hands slid up my bare legs, my fists were faster. His head flew back and smashed against the window with a resounding "Thwack!"

"Miki," he yelped in pain. He clutched the left side of his face and winced.

My fist and open palm were poised in front of me in the Crane position, ready to strike again. The Alex I knew was a gentleman; we had gone no further than passionate kisses in high school. He knew I was a fighter, the result of growing up in a clan of brawny male cousins. I took a deep breath, ready to bolt. Since we were students, I could forgive him for not calling. It was expensive—five dollars a minute. But to not write for a year, to not even call when he got back a month ago, then to drive straight to this lookout on our first date … the heat of his fingers burned my thighs.

Alex's lips twisted in a scowl. He huffed angrily. He started up the car and screeched into reverse. "This is 1958, Miki Ai'Lee. Girls on the East Coast know how to have fun. Stay an island peasant the rest of your life."

I swore at him in Chinese, Japanese, Hawaiian, and everything else I knew.

His cheek showed no evidence of my bruising punch yet. But I had hurt something other than his handsome face.

His eyes turned red as fire bolts when he floored the accelerator. Seconds later, his precious Olds Woody flew off the cliff and exploded into a sparkling shower of confetti that joined the millions of stars stretching from the sky to the sea. Alex opened his arms and shot across the Pacific like a meteor.

"Alex," I screamed. I tumbled end over end through the dark sky, hands outstretched. I felt the air suck from my lungs as he disappeared over the horizon. I rocketed through the darkness of night. Then I grabbed a moonbeam and slid back to earth in a shower of silver tears.

~❀~

San Francisco, 1970

It was dawn. The fog had crept in overnight and smothered the hills of San Francisco while the winds off the bay howled like banshees. When I woke, I yearned to breathe the misty clouds that wrapped the peaks of Nu`uanu at night, when the wind howled through the tree tunnels of the Old Pali Road and ghosts loomed in the darkness with outstretched hands.

My grandmother said that dreams are doorways to yesterday and tomorrow, that yesterdays become tomorrows, that dreams never lie. Alex Demming was my yesterday, a door slammed shut and bolted a dozen years ago, a friendship doomed a hundred years before a Demming and an Ai'Lee ignited a saga of mysterious deaths and deceit.

I had never dreamt of Alex before. It had been twelve years since I slugged him, twelve years since he stormed out of my life. Alex, tall and gangly, his brown hair rebelliously tousled, would have returned after college to run the Demming ranch on Kaua`i.

Twelve years ago I was a skinny eighteen-year-old with creamy skin that refused to tan. In those carefree days, my hair fell to my waist like an ebony waterfall or streamed behind me when I ran in the wind.

Now I am a professor of art history, thirty and unmarried. I wear sleek suits and carry a briefcase. While I built a career in San Francisco, Hawai`i became the nation's fiftieth state, a magnet for federal and international investments in tourism and business. Alex's family—the Demmings—tracks four generations upon the land that had once belonged to the Ai'Lees and is one of Hawai`i's most powerful landowners.

But in my dreams, I heard the voice of ancient legends, the Night Whispers, call my name from across the

Pacific. Miki Ai'Lee! Miki Ai'Lee! Their chants reminded me of ritual incense spiraling in neighborhood temples and coconut fronds rustling on a warm Hawaiian breeze.

Goosebumps prickled up my back and down my arms. Chicken skin, Hawaiians call it, when the hair on your neck tingles and shivers run up your spine. Chicken skin. Someone, somewhere, was holding me in his thoughts, remembering, pondering, reaching for me.

I dug in the darkness for the phone.

My father, Kam Ai'Lee, was already up, slicing a Portuguese sausage for his breakfast omelet. He didn't sound surprised that I had called before dawn. Hawaiians rise as soon as the night rains have stopped, before the morning has steamed the dew off the grass. Over the transpacific phone lines he sounded like he was sitting on the ocean floor, his words bubbling up one by one. He tried so hard to avoid the exorbitant per-minute charges that he usually hung up after three terse minutes.

"Miki! Good thing you called. Your grandmother fell and hit her head. Another dizzy spell. I found her lying on the kitchen floor yesterday. No broken bones but she has a huge lump on the back of her head. Dr. Lee is worried, considering she's ninety-one and with all those stairs! But she insists on living alone." He held his voice calm and steady, but I heard tears in his eyes. I imagined him standing barefoot on the green-flecked linoleum in the kitchen, the phone in his right hand, a dishrag in his left. He was a head taller than I was, with sinewy muscles and not an ounce of fat. At seventy, he had thick salt-and-pepper hair, angular cheekbones, and sharp, bright eyes. Since it was summer, he would be wearing shorts and a collared polo shirt softened by many washes.

I sat up and turned on a light. My grandmother was my kindred spirit, my surrogate mother. She hid her frailties with stubborn independence, a trait we shared. "I'm coming home, Dad," I said quickly. I grappled for a pen and paper and started clearing my calendar. I had three months before my university students returned for the fall. I could be on a plane tomorrow.

He was quiet, taken aback by my sudden offer, and obviously happy. "Thanks, Miki. You know how independent your grandmother is. She says she'll die in her own house when she's ready. But you're her favorite and she'll listen to you."

I imagined my father replacing the receiver, thin worry lines creasing his handsome forehead. He'd turn back to the wooden cutting board at the sink and pick up his knife, all the while counting the minutes until I returned.

❧ ✿ ❧

When I first left Hawai`i for San Francisco, I flew out of the old Honolulu Airport, the backdrop to the most dramatic farewells. One could look across the vast open-air terminal, which was one massive building, and see everyone who was arriving and departing the island of O`ahu. Everyone was engulfed in a scented sea of orchid, pikake, tuberose, and plumeria blossoms. No one left without friends and family descending upon them with armloads of flower leis and loud kisses. Loved ones walked across the tarmac loaded with leis up to their noses. At the top of the stairs, they turned, threw kisses, then waved through the little windows at their seats until the plane taxied out onto the runway. No one left the gate until the airplane lifted off and disappeared over the Pacific. Upon arrival, the pageantry of flowers and hugs and kisses was loudly repeated.

Now I returned to a new Honolulu International Airport that featured sleek jetways and air-conditioned gates far from the main terminal. The tourists jumped on the chilly wiki-wiki bus at the gates but the locals walked all the way to baggage claim to savor the warm humid air.

I joyfully inhaled the scent of home: flower-sweet, ocean-salty, fresh with the perfume of lush tropical forests. The long-sleeved silk blouse and slacks that barely kept me warm in San Francisco fluttered softly against my skin in the breeze. I felt the humidity slow me down to Hawai`i's pace until I, too, ambled like the locals. Above me, the coconut trees swayed against the shockingly blue sky. How I had missed the seductive rustle of fronds in the trade winds.

At last my white Samsonite, a high school graduation gift from my parents, tumbled out on the baggage carousel followed by a case of roast ducks from San Francisco's Chinatown, for one never visits family without bearing gifts.

A yellow Chevy convertible rumbled to the curb the minute I left the air-conditioned terminal. My cousin Reginald, in a tropical-weight suit, leapt out of his car with three plumeria leis swinging in his right hand and gave them to me one by one, with a kiss. "Howzit, Miki! I had to go to Ewa this morning, so I told your father I'd pick you up on my way into town. You've been gone too long. I haven't seen you since your mother's funeral eight years ago. Mazie and the girls made these leis for you last night. You look the same, except so pale. No sun in San Francisco?" He teased with laughter in his thick-lashed, large brown eyes and the whitest welcoming smile.

The last time I had been home was traumatic and depressing. The sweet yellow petals against my cheek softened the memories. I tossed my suitcase in the back seat and got in. "I don't get to go surfing every day," I retorted saucily, "to keep up my beach-boy tan and physique like you."

He slid back in the car with muscular ease. "Those days are gone," he laughed heartily. "I'm a working man now. Yes, still in juvenile probation with the courts." He nodded, noting my appraising glance. "Yes, turning white, too!" His short, thick hair had sun-bleached to brown with distinguished white streaks. He pulled out and headed towards Honolulu.

Reginald nodded at my taped cardboard carton he had shoved into the back seat. "Looks like you brought a case of roast ducks for me." He smacked his lips.

"Filch them," I warned, "and I'll send the Ai'Lee ladies after you."

"Fiery tempered as always. Here's another reason I came to get you." He handed me the local papers. "Read them before you get home." Each of Honolulu's two major newspapers covered local news with their own political slant.

"LOCAL POLITICS?" screamed the bold headlines of the first. In the photo below, the lean bodies of two athletic men in team jerseys and white knickers were twisted together in combat. Blood spurted from the nose of one onto the shirt of a handsome dark-haired combatant who strongly resembled my brother. I quickly read the caption.

"Braxton in a fight? Reginald, I can't believe this," I yelled as he accelerated onto the freeway, leaving the Japanese rice-rockets in the dust. My brother was so conservative he had worn only white-collared shirts to school. He buttered up his teachers with eager answers and toothy smiles and was always surrounded by a bevy of friends, both male and female. He had never been in a fight. In fact, no one ever got angry with him, except me.

"Keep reading." Reginald kept his eyes on the road and changed lanes to avoid an elderly Chinese matron cruising forty miles per hour on the Nimitz.

"Ai'Lee vs. Demming Ties Governor's Memorial Day Game" headed the next paper with a similar color photo above the fold, except Braxton and Demming were tussling on the ground surrounded by their teams in a rousing fist-fight. Demming looked like a solidly built man, about my brother's age, blond, square shouldered, with huge hands and feet. My brother was six feet tall, a rangy, muscular man, well-proportioned and athletic from years of baseball and basketball.

I turned to Reginald, my face cold and drained. "How could this be? You know how Braxton's the conciliator in any argument. He faints at the sight of blood."

He glanced at my shocked expression. "It was an invitation-only picnic given by the governor. You know, payback time for his favorites and their families at the home of one of his biggest financial supporters. There's always a friendly baseball game at these outings. Of course, the factions hand-pick their teams at secret practices so it becomes very political, very contentious," he explained. "Here's the way I heard it. In the bottom of the ninth, bases were loaded 3–0 for the Demming team. Your brother at bat. Braxton's hit soared past the bleachers. Kubo, Blake, and Kealoha ran home. Braxton sprinted for the plate. Braxton claims catcher Chris Demming punched him in the gut when he slid home. Demming claims his eye was on the ball from outfielder Benny Manuel. Everyone ran to the field when Braxton and Chris went down, including the press."

I peered closely at the lurid photos in both papers. The photographer had caught my brother's thick black hair flying back upon impact. Demming's fist was in his eye and his cap was caught mid-fall. Braxton's muscled arm was in the foreground of the photo, his fist jammed against the jaw of platinum-haired Demming.

I put down the paper and took a breath to steady my voice. I asked, "How's Braxton?" His focus was work, so the only time we communicated was when I came home.

"He's sporting a whopping shiner today at work, and proud of it. He strutted around the Capitol buildings like a hero, accepting accolades. He's a master at manipulating the press and getting a good spin. But this has brought back a lot of unpleasant memories. All the lies and deceit between the Ai'Lees and your boyfriend's family have been dredged up again."

I slapped Reginald playfully in the gut with the newspapers. "Alex was a high-school romance. Anyway, I thought he was the last of the Demmings."

"You mean the only Demming not executed or exiled by the Ai'Lees."

I ignored his comment. "I don't know this Chris Demming." I was puzzled. When we were choosing colleges in our senior year, Alex had complained that he, as the last male of his lineage, was expected to take over the Demming ranch. We assumed he had no other relatives.

"Rumor is that one of Alex's grandfather's brothers escaped the Ai'Lee vengeance by hiding on the Big Island of Hawai`i. Married a local girl and named his sons Washington, Adams, and Jefferson, and his daughters Madison and Monroe. He had visions of grandeur. While you were on the mainland, Washington's son Christopher and his cousins became active in politics on the Big Island. Now that we're a state, they've been eyeing Honolulu and D.C." Reginald's face clouded. "And so has your brother."

The airport was ten minutes from town in light traffic. Reginald quickly turned off the freeway at Kalihi. He drove on narrow city streets past sagging wooden bungalows dwarfed by towering bougainvilleas in ten shades of magenta and the Samoan church tucked under the freeway where the congregation was barbecuing lunch. He turned towards the mountains at Palama Settlement where Braxton and I took music lessons from John Kelly Jr. before he became a surfing legend.

My cousin was amused when I waved at the chattering groups of brown-legged children walking home from school and how they waved back, giggling and shy. I remembered how heavy those schoolbooks felt on the long walk home in the sun.

"You still teaching?" Reginald asked. He and I, closest in age among two dozen Ai'Lee cousins, had been childhood confidantes.

"Yes, and still waiting for you to come visit." I was a specialist in myths and symbolism in Asian art. For years I had taught, fought, and published against the constant posturing and politicking of my university colleagues. Last year, I had received the prestigious Crocker Award, awarded to the best young professors in the nation. The accolades were rewarding personally and professionally, but my fellow academics sniped about the attention I received. Even the *Wall Street Journal's* feature on the Crocker awards, after listing my accomplishments, read in part, "Professor Ai'Lee is not your mother's schoolmarm. She strides into her classrooms in fitted suits, her hair in a no-nonsense bun or long swinging ponytail. In a clear, articulate voice, she mesmerizes her students with China's treasures from Shang bronzes to Ming jades. Ai'Lee's combination of sophisticated fashion, long-legged beauty, and captivating intellectual challenge is a winner. Ai'Lee is one of the most popular professors and her classes are consistently packed."

I was embarrassed when my department chair tossed me the article to read. I had seen the balding New York journalist in the back of my classes, shared an occasional cup of coffee with him afterwards in the Commons, and answered his bullet-like questions. I appreciated his praise, but I hadn't set out to charm the grizzled former war correspondent. My colleagues' cold rebuffs conveyed their academic jealousy.

I was restless, ready for something new. Sometimes when I was alone I felt a yearning, an emptiness inside. The fog would roll in, thick and dangerous, cold and lonely. I imagined the brisk winds off San Francisco Bay calling to me. Then I'd hunger for familiar comforts: the voices of my family's stories when we gathered at night around a flickering bonfire on the beach, the ghostly whispers in the wind, and the life-replenishing showers.

I threw back my head and let the tropical sun melt the San Francisco fog from my skin. Reginald's three plumeria leis, petal-soft against my skin, blissfully smothered me with their scent.

My cousin laughed at my expression of utter joy. He turned onto the quiet tree-lined street of my old neighborhood and said expansively, "Welcome home, Miki."

~❀~

At the sound of our footsteps in the driveway, my father straightened on his gardening stool in the front yard and peered up from under his "Ai'Lee for Senator" baseball cap. Kam Ai'Lee had a wiry body, youthfully agile for seventy. Only his thick, wavy hair, once jet-black, belied his age, growing more salt-and-pepper each year. He was tall for a Chinese, about five foot ten. The rest of him was as Chinese as his conservative Confucian beliefs: the fair skin and high cheekbones of the northern Han, and the well-shaped muscular body, black hair, piercing dark almond eyes, and full lips of the southern Pearl River Delta men.

"Miki!" He leapt up and hugged me as if I might disappear. "You're home at last." My father was a soft-spoken gentleman: gracious, elegant, with a handsome, open smile. When I hugged him, his bony shoulders wore his familiar scent of sweat, earth, and sunshine.

Reginald followed behind me, effortlessly carrying both my luggage and the box of roast ducks. "Hi, Uncle Kam. Sorry I can't stay, I've got to get back to the office."

My father greeted him, then turned to me. He pushed back his cap. "Come, Miki, I have your room ready." He gestured me to follow.

My room of white eyelet curtains and bright yellow walls looked the same as the day I left for San Francisco. Rag dolls and schoolbooks, neatly dusted on low white shelves, had waited for my return. I changed to a cotton sundress and joined my father in the front yard.

I picked up a weeder, a lethal-looking pronged bar, and knelt beside him in the grass. Strange as it seemed to others, this had been our ritual since I was a child. Here, among the plants he loved, we felt most comfortable to talk and share our thoughts.

When my father bought this land, our neighborhood was considered outside the city limits. It was so quiet, neighbors swore they could hear the spirits of the dead rise from the three cemeteries on our street. Older residential areas like ours had no sidewalks. Instead, grass sloped down from the house to the paved street. Now, our neighborhood was considered almost downtown Honolulu, and our yard was a congenial stop for neighbors on their way to and from the Liliha-Pu`unui bus.

"Remember when we used to weed when you came home from work?" I asked him. In the garden, we were in our own world, hidden from the street by rows of vanda orchids on stiff green stems. I also remembered the office smell that used to cling to his suits, a mixture of paper, smoke, and air conditioning. In those days, when he came home from work he would change to shorts and a sleeveless white undershirt like those the old men wore in the back alleys of Chinatown.

"Ah, that was so long ago," my father said. He tried to suppress the smile that said he was pleased I remembered. Widowed for eight years, he poured the energy he had once devoted to his children and his wife, Ellie, into his gardens. His soil was fragrant, dark, and rich with fat worms. Twice a day he inspected the foliage of his tropical plants. He plucked the insects he did not like from the full and perfect leaves of the Chinese cabbage and rare herbs. He built wooden braces for the laden branches of the pomelo tree and carefully bagged the mango blossoms to protect them from the birds.

A fat earthworm wiggled free from the roots in my hand. I dug a shallow hole and carefully reburied it. "How's Popo feeling?" I asked, using the Chinese honorific for grandmother.

He squinted at me in the bright sun, generating a sunburst of fine lines around his eyes. "Saw her this morning. Dr. Lee ordered bed rest, but you know how stubborn she is. I told her you were coming in this morning and that you'd be up right after lunch. She's glad you're home." He picked up the pace. We combed through the dirt leaving a rich dark layer of earth, and inched further along on the grass beside the flower beds.

"I'm home just for the summer," I reminded him.

He nodded, anticipating the coming months. "That's enough."

I was reluctant to break his happy mood to ask about Braxton. I knew he had grown up with a generation of hatred against the Demmings. My father was a worrier who kept his feelings to himself. The only way I knew he was upset was when he pounded the arms of his chair with his fists when he thought no one was watching. "Reginald showed me today's papers. I read about the fight. He said Braxton's fine. He's using the incident to gain empathy."

My father blinked angrily. "Damn Demmings! This is the fourth generation of troublemakers they've spawned," he snapped. He pitched his weeder in the dirt with such force it sunk up to its wooden hilt. "They should have been wiped off the earth a generation ago. That cursed Demming hit my son."

"Dad!" The first time Mom heard my brother use profanity, all our neighbors could hear Braxton's flailing screams when she washed his mouth out with soap. "Dad," I reached for my father's arm. "Braxton hit Chris Demming, too."

The sinews of his arms tightened. "Good! Demming should go back to the Big Island where he came from." His voice was taut and angry.

I wiggled his buried weeder from the grip of the dark soil and handed it to him. "It was just a baseball game. The media hyped it up to make it look worse than it was, I'm sure." I patted his arm and coaxed a faint smile.

"When your brother comes for dinner, you'll see. You'll see what Demming did to his eye!" He turned back to the dark cool earth.

Then he stopped. He thumped the ground with his knuckle and smoothed the dirt with his hands around the edges of a large oval. "Look, Miki, one of your pets!" He lifted a gigantic turtle, a foot and a half across. "Every once in a while, I see him sunning himself on the rocks in my planting beds. Sometimes I hear when he dives in the fishpond." My father sat back on the steaming grass, a nostalgic look softening his tanned face.

"Tommy Turtle!" I plucked the heavy critter from his hands. Black shiny eyes stared at me from the turtle's withdrawn head. His feet and tail were firmly tucked in. The last time I saw him he had been only five inches across, a troublemaker from the day we met.

﹏❀﹏

On the first day of our junior year, I found Alex waiting for me at my locker at noon. "Miki! Our schedules have us in different buildings all morning. I have so much to tell you." We couldn't hug, not in school, nor chance a quick kiss. So we grinned like Cheshire cats.

"Alex!" I was excited to see him. My summer was the usual: piano and Chinese brush painting lessons, and weekends at the beach with the Ai'Lees. "Did you do anything interesting this summer?"

"Up every morning before dawn, saddled and riding the fence with Pops," he groaned. "My calluses are thicker than a horse's hoof. But I found you a present."

"You found me a present?" I hurried to keep up with Alex's long strides. We waved to our friends headed, like us, to lunch. Voices were louder on the first day of school: excited greetings and clusters of friends catching up from summer.

He winked. "It's for your menagerie." We had reached the steps of the cafeteria. He raced me up. At the top of the steps he dangled a square box, about ten by ten, vented with air holes and tied with heavy twine. In my eagerness I hadn't noticed it.

"Alex! I do not have a menagerie!" I argued. A dozen parakeets, two bantam chickens, a dozen ducklings, five tanks of tropical fish, and a koi-filled fishpond were not a strange and exotic collection in Hawai`i.

"You have such a fiery temper, Miki Ai'Lee. Just for that, I'm not giving you Tommy until after school." He grabbed my hand and we joined our friends at the corner table where excited greetings and animated back-to-school chatter consumed most of the lunch hour. The mystery box was forgotten until I heard an ominous scraping. I was sitting on Alex's left and he had put the vented box on his right.

I whispered, "Alex, what's in there?" I was worried. Just when I thought I knew Alex, he'd surprise me. For instance, although Alex was gangly and uncoordinated with a known aversion to team sports, he was determined to get on the field hockey team, despite monstrous bruises on the parts of his legs and arms not covered by padding during tryouts. Fortunately for the team, Alex missed the cut. His presents were also unpredictable: a kindergarten photo of himself with missing front teeth, a butterfly cocoon mounted on a twig in a jar, a bag of pink guavas hand-carried from Kaua`i.

Alex shook his head. "You'll find out after school."

Kelly Malone, one of Alex's oldest friends, joined us with her tray of Hawaiian stew. She was wearing a new floral shirtwaist dress, fashionable and flattering. She said matter-of-factly, "It's a scorpion. Lots of those where Alex is from. Giant ones under every rock." Her waist-length blond hair trembled when she visibly shivered.

Kalia Gomes, sitting next to her, said it was a plantation spider, a ten-inch thick and hairy black and yellow arachnid. "My Gramps says they're all over the sugarcane fields. I hope Alex is giving you a glass case for it. They like to crawl around and hide in dark places. Their bites are deadly. Sixty seconds and you're dead." Even experienced cane workers wouldn't get near them.

Cecilia Wong, porcelain-skinned and slender, leaned over and winked. "It's a foot-long centipede. The kind with a thousand legs. They grow fatter than a pig on horse manure, which is plentiful at the Demming ranch."

I recoiled. "No! Alex, you wouldn't." Other friends yelled it's a snake, a feral pig, a mongoose.

"Alex," I implored. "What is it?" The scratching increased. The quaking box had riveted our attention.

Alex stuffed the last of his sandwich in his mouth and mumbled. "All right, Miki. It's feeding time anyway."

Everyone at our table stood up and leaned forward. We stared at the center of the table where Alex had placed the vented box and was slowly untying the heavy twine.

The first thing I saw was a small green head. Then an oval shell five inches across. Beady eyes blinked. Tiny claws attempted to climb the walls of the box as the creature stretched his neck up at all of us peering in.

I gasped, then laughed. "Alex, a turtle!"

Alex had found him crawling along the mountain stream that flowed through the Demming ranch on

Kaua`i. "Turtles aren't native to Kaua`i. Someone's pet must have escaped. I'm glad I found it before one of the dogs did," he said. "I've been feeding him lettuce from my mother's garden. But," he grinned mischievously, "Tommy Turtle prefers chomping on flies." Alex refilled Tommy's water dish and put in a handful of greens. "He'll be happy in your fishpond, Miki."

The novelty of a turtle in the cafeteria didn't escape notice. Shouts echoed across the glass-enclosed room. Classmates rushed to see. Within minutes, the supervising lunch teacher had found the source of the commotion and, because pets were not allowed in school, sent both Alex and me to the principal. Everyone solemnly watched us march down the hall.

I groaned under my breath as we sat on the cold wooden chairs outside Mr. Iams's office. I anticipated my parents' anger—and worse, their disappointment—if I were suspended. They distrusted the Demmings and my friendship with Alex. This would prove them right. We watched the second hand on the school clock tick its ominous countdown until unreadable Mr. Iams returned from lunch.

As punishment, we were given two weeks of detention. Every day after school we sorted boxes of labeled slides for Jerome Bellamy, who had just arrived to teach courses on the history of art. As Alex and I loaded and labeled dozens of slide carousels, Mr. Bellamy ran through his lectures. He projected pairs of slides in contrasting or comparable pairs, from Minoan pottery from Knossos, Greek caryatids, Gothic gargoyles, Michelangelos, Sung Dynasty scrolls from China, wood guardian kings from Japan's Heian period, and linga, the phallic symbol representing Shiva as the Creator.

Our punishment became our passion. We looked forward to Bellamy's explanations of artistic perfection and cultural expression, not only because we were together, but also because art transported us to fascinating worlds. We didn't know that these ideas would one day entice us far from Hawai`i. And when we lost our way, they would guide us home.

─❀─

After lunch with my father, it started to rain, warm and sweet, when I headed for my grandmother's house. I ran up the slopes of the misty Honolulu valley, up the grass walkway edged with coconut trees and a low lava-rock wall to her house at the road's end. Plumerias and white ginger planted on either side suffused the rain that swept my face with their seductive scents. I arched my neck and stuck my tongue out to taste the familiar sweet drops. How I missed these cleansing rains and redolent humidity.

In my childhood, I had recklessly raced my brother up this hill through torrential downpours. Cascades of water rose up to our knees. Above us, sheets of lightning exploded with the wrath of the gods. Braxton, three years older, would tear through the flood screaming like a madman as we dodged each boom of thunder rolling through the valley. These days, my brother scoffed at such childish exploits. He was a rising young politician who rubbed elbows and fists with the power brokers in Hawai`i.

I still loved the feel of grass and mud squishing through my toes. Racing through the rain made me feel as reckless and carefree as I had when I was a child.

"Miki Ai'Lee, at last you come home!" My grandmother, Lailee Ai'Lee, waved from the landing at the top of her red concrete stairs. Her hands were worn by nearly a century of hard labor and wrinkled by the unmerciful sun. "Good thing you come now. Maybe next time I won't be here!"

I bounded up stairs swathed in clouds of yellow ginger planted along the railings. I kicked off my sandals into the row of shoes and slippers outside the door and kissed my grandmother's bony cheeks, creviced with experience and hardship. I hugged the thin woman who, for as long as I could remember, exuded the scent of camphor and incense. I felt the solidity of her unconditional love. But more important was the serenity I felt whenever I was with her. She had taught me patience when my brother enjoyed privileges I was denied, and sacrifice when I cared for my mother the last six months of her life.

Lailee moved gracefully in a blue and white cotton cheong-sam, a form-fitting Chinese dress. She stood five feet four, tall for a Chinese woman born in Kwang Tung's Pearl River Delta in the 1800s. Wrinkles lined her face like a dried riverbed, but they added wisdom and character, proof of a life well lived.

"You never change, Popo. You never look any different. But what did you do to your head?" I peered at the ominous egg-shaped lump that bulged through the strands of her skimpy white bun. She swatted away my hand when I reached out to touch it.

"I am getting old. Ninety-one! Dr. Lee says I need tests to find out why I get dizzy. I told him no need for tests. Soon I'll cross the Heavenly Bridge and join your grandfather." Lailee brushed droplets from my hair. "Why do you always walk in the rain? So unladylike."

"You said when it rains in Hawai`i, the gods are crying tears of happiness," I answered. My wet sundress clung to my skin, but it would dry quickly in the heat. I kissed her fingers, knobbed and curled with arthritis, and caught the familiar whiff of chopped ginger and green onions: the smell of hundreds of meals prepared for dozens of children, grandchildren, and great-grandchildren.

"When are you coming home to stay? That place, Gum Sahn, San-Fran-Cis-Ko, is too far," she scolded. She waved away vast distances with frail fingers. "How many years you've been gone and still you find no Chinese boy to marry."

I shrugged to appease her. "Chinese boys don't like sassy girls. You said so yourself." I shook the last drops of moisture out of my hair. I had always worn it in thick black waves to my waist. In San Francisco, I tied it into a professional bun to appear serious, older, and studiously academic. Now I wanted to unwind, to blend in.

"Ai-ya! Younger generation too picky." Lailee emphasized the last word. "By the time I was your age, I had ten babies." She spread both hands in front of me for emphasis. "Ten!"

"Popo, you were married in the 1890s! Times were different." When Lailee married, Hawai`i was still ruled by the Hawaiian Monarchy. Three governments had come and gone since then.

"Humph!" She dismissed my argument with a decisive flick of her fingers.

I followed her into her living room filled with memories as familiar as her threadbare sofas, ancient koa bowls, and heavy monkeypod rockers. Here, my grandmother told stories of nostalgic times, mystical tales of old Hawai`i, and passed on her words of wisdom. Each hand-tatted doily covering the worn arms and headrests was woven with stories of her ten children: one son lost in the flood during the hurricane, the death of others when they could not afford flu medicine, the raising of children who answered her Chinese questions with English words.

"Ah, Miki, when will you stay home for good? I have no one to help me. Auntie Pua has Parkinson's. Your father has cataracts and arthritis. Your brother Braxton has no time. You read the paper? Ai-ya! I called your brother last night. Told him it is dishonorable to fight like that. He has a good Ai'Lee name." The furrows in her brow deepened. A person's personal honor reflected on the entire family. She leaned forward to confide, "You cannot trust four generations of lies." She waved her hand as if displaying the past.

She honed her sharp eyes on me. "But you, Miki, how long will you be here?"

I poured her tea from the pot on the koa coffee table. "I'm home for the summer." I handed her a teacup with both hands.

Popo Ai'Lee accepted with a nod. "Good. Then you have time to take me to the Kuan Yin Temple. I must pray for your brother's protection."

My grandmother stepped up the marble steps of the Kuan Yin Temple through the procession of black-robed monks. She held her head up as if to smell the air, humid with the scent of vanilla from the golden shower trees that bloomed so profusely they seemed to shimmer solid sunshine.

It had started to rain when Lailee and I arrived. The golden shower trees sparkled with the first raindrops, then bowed to the tropical cloudburst, one of dozens that drifted daily over O`ahu. Without missing a breath in their hypnotic prayer, the ranks of black-robed monks parted like seaweed flowing to a contrary tide to let us through.

When I was a little girl, I walked with Lailee to the Kuan Yin Temple on Vineyard Street where the red tile roof curved above the shower trees. I lugged her shopping bags, almost as large as I was then, stuffed with gilded paper we had folded into ingot-shaped offerings for my great-grandfather Chun Ai'Lee, and my grandfather Gung-Gung Ai'Lee. Twenty-seven generations of Ai'Lees had been recorded in the Ancestral Hall of Siu Yun Village when Chun Ai'Lee sailed to Hawai`i in the 1800s. Old-timers told legends of adventurous Chinese who sailed between Hawai`i and China in the 1700s: some with the whalers, some with the explorers of the Pacific. When I was older, I heard the romantic tale of how Chun Ai'Lee had wooed and married a Hawaiian princess. And how American entrepreneur Arthur Demming, coveting the same woman, had plotted and taken Chun Ai'Lee's lands. The ancient rivalry between

Ai'Lees and Demmings erupted into four generations of mysterious deaths and open animosity.

Here, in the oldest Buddhist temple in Honolulu, I learned to pray as my grandmother instructed: two sticks of heung clasped between tiny palms. In the middle of the temple, a gold statue of Kuan Yin towered to the rafters. According to legend, Kuan Yin was a disciple of Buddha who had achieved Nirvana. But as she ascended to Heaven she heard a human cry, so she returned to earth to help others overcome the pain and suffering she had spent hundreds of lifetimes trying to escape. She became a Bodhisattva, one who has achieved Nirvana but chooses, instead, to help others achieve enlightenment. Women, especially, prayed to the Goddess of Love and Mercy for her compassion.

I bowed three times to Kuan Yin. Then three times on my knees. My forehead tapped the cold polished floor while Popo Ai'Lee burnt her offerings. She chanted ancient prayers and cast her oracle stones, divining the fortune and future of the Ai'Lees. The distant ringing of ceremonial bells echoed through the thick incense haze in the peaked temple. Monks, fop see, knelt in a meditative trance as monks had done for centuries.

Through the clouds of incense I was startled to see Alex Demming turn from where he had been studying the Buddhas and Bodhisattva statues in the back of the temple. His head was bent over a leather notebook marked by dark stains and worn edges.

Alex, a look of surprise on his face, stopped writing when he saw me. He shoved his battered pen into the pocket of his denim shorts and strode towards us.

I felt a sudden jolt, the deja vu nightmare of tumbling from the sky. We had parted with hot-blooded, unresolved wrath. Stinging from my fury on our last date, he had flown away to college while I stayed home at the local university. Our years apart should have tempered my anger, cooled my passion. Within seconds, he was in front of me, searching my face with those eyes I knew so well. They were still the blues and greens of the sea, but a frown steeled his piercing gaze.

Time had not been kind to my old classmate. The Alex I remembered was six feet tall and lanky, not this weathered. His cropped beard couldn't hide the seared look of his skin. His dark brown hair, coursed with white, curled loosely around the edges of his ears and a beard gave him a rough look—so unlike the studious, awkwardly shy classmate I once knew. In those days, we had raced from class to class through sudden rainstorms. I flushed with the memory of evening drives on Round Top Drive through clouds of eucalyptus and ginger, and the taut skin of his cheeks when he dropped me home after school and we kissed good-bye.

"Alex?" I was as startled to see him now as I was when he stormed out of my life.

"Miki, I heard you moved to the mainland," he answered, as surprised as I was. His voice, low and measured, had lost its boyish enthusiasm. Caution had replaced his youthful shyness of long ago.

"I did. I'm home for the summer." I didn't have to ask Alex what he'd been doing for the last twelve years. His life had been mapped out long ago on the lush green slopes of the former Ai'Lee lands on Kaua`i where William

Demming had groomed his only son as his heir. I envisioned him comfortably striding his ranch lands at dawn and riding with their manager Eddie Kekaha during the day. On lonely weekends when I looked out my window in San Francisco at the enveloping fog, I thought of Alex and the paniolos, the Hawaiian cowboys. I imagined them gathered for a Hawaiian-style potluck under the old tree behind the Demming ranch house with their guitars, singing the songs of old Hawai`i until the moon shone like a torch.

"Miki, who are you talking to?" Lailee Ai'Lee walked up behind me and stared at the grizzled stranger standing before us. The cloud of a frown darkened her face. She clasped her hands at her waist and looked up at Alex, then at me.

I put my arm around her. "Popo, do you remember Alexander Demming, my classmate from high school? His parents are William and Celie Demming from Kaua`i." Genealogies were part of introductions in an island society in which we were all linked by history and close family ties. Even high schools, which revealed one's social and cultural connections, were cited.

Alex held out his hands to Lailee. "It's a pleasure to see you again, Popo." In Hawai`i, we considered all elders as our grandparents and addressed them respectfully.

My grandmother nodded and made that judgmental sound that signified a Chinese of that generation has made up her mind. She narrowed her eyes and peered critically at my old classmate. "Humph! You look tired, worn out."

I cringed. Popo was often blunt and direct, a privilege, she felt, of her great age.

Alex rubbed his face ruefully. "I've lived in some unpleasant places, Popo. They've taken their toll, I'm afraid." His eyes, blue-green like the changing moods of the sea, could calm a storm. Now they were guarded, with a flash of stormy cobalt.

"But you used to claim that life on Kaua`i was idyllic," I protested. Alex Demming had inherited a life of security and comfort as the only male heir of the Demming ranch. I was incensed he would take his birthright so lightly, especially since he lived on lands the Ai'Lees claimed as rightfully theirs.

"I never went back to Kaua`i, Miki." His expression was dark, his voice rough. He raised his head and looked out at the golden shower trees bobbing in the trade winds outside. "I just flew in this morning."

"Miki!" Lailee turned to me with a sudden gasp and grabbed for my arm when she collapsed. Alex caught her before her head hit the cement floor.

"Popo," I cried. I felt her pulse and rubbed her hands. She fluttered her hands like a wounded bird.

"I'm parked outside," Alex said softly. He swept my grandmother up in his arms and out the temple before anyone noticed anything amiss. I grabbed her bags and followed.

Fifteen minutes later, Lailee lay in her bed covered by a red and white Hawaiian quilt. She had protested when Alex insisted on carrying her up the stairs and protested even more when he refused to have a cup of tea before he left.

Alex pulled up a chair so he could sit naturally at her eye level. He was concerned about her pallor. "I don't want to tire you, Popo. Miki says you've been suffering from vertigo. Dr. Lee is on his way and you have Miki here to take care of you." He massaged her hands to increase her circulation.

She nodded, placated by his charm.

When he stood up to go, she rasped, "Bring me the phone, Miki."

I placed the black dial phone where she indicated on her bed with an impatiently tapping index finger. "You should get some rest before Dr. Lee gets here," I suggested.

She gave me a look that told me that rest was not her intention, and waved us out of her room.

Alex and I walked to the front door, awkwardly silent. When he turned, his eyes had lost their wary look. "I owe you an explanation, Miki. You're wondering what I was doing at the Kuan Yin Temple. But, as I remember, you don't ask direct questions. You'll wait for me to volunteer an explanation."

I nodded. "You have a good memory." We walked out the door. I sat on the front steps and patted the empty space behind me. He joined me on the steps, leaning casually forward with his arms on his knees, his feet on the step below. Together, we looked over the city of Honolulu, at the tall reflective towers that spiked the skyline and dwarfed the palm trees that had once been so prevalent.

Alex looked down at his clasped hands, broad with strong, square-tipped fingers. He picked his words carefully, slowly. "I never got to Kaua`i. I've been in Southeast Asia. A few years ago, we had some family problems. As a result, my father feels he can't run the ranch any longer and asked me to return. I was at a point where I needed a change. Someday, not now, I'll have the courage to tell you the whole disastrous story."

He searched my face, cautiously watching my expression. "It's been twelve years since I've been back in Honolulu, so I was feeling nostalgic, a little lonely. I stopped by your house. I don't know why I assumed you would be there. Your father told me you didn't live there any more."

I opened my mouth but words failed me. My father hadn't mentioned Alex being there this morning. Maybe Alex looked so different he didn't recognize him. "Did you tell him who you were?" We must have missed each other by hours, both at the airport and at home.

"Yes. He looked at me strangely, but then, I've changed." He ran his fingers through his roughly cut hair and shrugged. "He said you were working on the mainland and asked if I wanted to leave a message. I said no. We're thirty years old. I figured by now you were married with three children clinging to your knees." He picked up my left hand. "I figured wrong, didn't I?"

After twelve years, his touch was rough and awkward.

We picked our way carefully through memories and questions, cautious not to hurt, wary of the past.

Then I asked, "Why did you come looking for me after twelve years, Alex? You could have sent a letter or called."

He stiffened. "We didn't part as friends, Miki. I was arrogant and full of myself in those days. I've been taken down a few notches since then."

I lowered my voice. "Alex, when did you develop an interest in Buddhist temples?"

His blue-green eyes grew light with amusement. "You want to know why I was at your Popo's temple, don't you?

Remember Mr. Bellamy? Art history? I was intrigued when he showed us that art was not a static study, but a living dynamic. Then one of my archaeology professors transformed my interest into a career. When I left your house today, I remembered your stories about how, when you were a little girl, you used to walk to the Kuan Yin Temple, the oldest Chinese temple in the islands, with your grandmother. I wanted to look at the hundreds of Buddhas and Bodhisattvas in the back niches. Some were reputedly brought to Honolulu in the 1800s. You told me you used to walk up those long steps with your grandmother carrying her bags of candles and incense and offerings. I see you haven't changed."

I laughed, a little more comfortable in his presence. While we talked, I could hear Popo Ai'Lee dialing, talking in Chinese to her friends, hanging up and dialing again. Then silence. "No, that hasn't changed, Alex. And yes, someday I'd like to hear what kept you from Kaua`i."

He abruptly turned away. He looked far into the distance where the deep Pacific met the azure sky. When he turned back to face me, I saw such anguish it hurt my eyes to witness his pain. "I'd like that, Miki Ai'Lee," he whispered. Alex kissed me on the cheek, almost out of habit. "I'll call you. Same phone number?"

Then he loped down the steps, two at a time. Once Alex and I had been so close. Now he was a mystery. I wondered what had changed him. I watched him chug away in his '47 Oldsmobile Woody, weathered and worn like its owner.

In the distance, the moisture-laden clouds slid across a brilliantly blue sky and washed the city that stretched before me: from the towering Ko`olaus to the downtown towers of Honolulu and the beaches of Waikiki.

I had returned to Hawai`i to dig into the warmth of the beach and smell the salt spray, to listen to the endless rhythms of the surf off Sunset Beach, and to chase the fishes hiding in the coral reefs at Hanauma Bay as I had when I was a child. I thought that once I returned to my birthplace, my refuge, my restlessness would end. When I was away from this magical place I believed that time stopped. And when I returned, I expected everything to be as I left it.

Now I realized I had been gone too long.

Chapter Two

Like a Moth
to a Flame

 $\mathcal{M}$ y father ran barefoot to meet me when I came up the driveway. "How is your grandmother now?" he asked. Concern shook his voice. He had showered and changed into a cotton Hawaiian print shirt and tan khakis. His hands were wet from cooking.

"When Dr. Lee came, she insisted she was fine," I said. I patted his arm and assured him not to worry. "Auntie Vanda arrived with groceries and her overnight bag. She's taking Popo to the hospital tomorrow for a dozen tests Dr. Lee ordered. When I left, Popo had already called Mrs. Chu and Mrs. Low to come over and play mah jongg." Vanda was Dad's third sister, a perky widow who lived in an air-conditioned condo in Makiki with expansive views of the city. Slender, stylishly coifed and manicured, dark-haired fair-skinned Vanda never considered remarrying after Uncle Mark's heart attack at the Pearl Harbor Shipyard. Since she had no children, she indulged favored nieces and nephews, like Reginald and me.

I didn't tell him I knew Alex had come by that morning. After all, he had honored Alex's request with his silence.

My father shook his head. "Your grandmother will keep Vanda up until midnight," he predicted. By now we had reached the front door and the irresistible aroma of a Chinese banquet was drifting through the screen door.

I patted my growling stomach. "What are you cooking?" I asked. I hadn't smelled such delectable odors for years. My mother was so famous for her artful presentation of Chinese foods that none of us dared to cook when she was alive.

His eyes twinkled. "I use Mother's recipes now. Hurry up and shower. Then you can help me get dinner ready," he ordered before he hurried back to the kitchen.

Braxton arrived with characteristic thunder, gunning his engine so the reverberation could be felt through all the homes in the neighborhood. He had loosened his tie and hung his suit jacket, neatly buttoned, on a hardwood hanger behind his seat. My brother stepped out of the sleekly polished New Yorker, his state-issued car, and ceremoniously opened the door for his wife.

"Welcome home, Miki. How's my little sister doing in San Francisco? Still braving the big world as an 'independent woman'?" Braxton was a head taller than Dad. He had the fair complexion and high cheekbones of Popo Ai'Lee, long-lashed ebony eyes that slanted like happy commas, and Dad's thick black hair. He turned his head so I could appreciate the monstrous black bruise surrounding his left eye.

I winced at its mottled puffiness. "Chris Demming must have an iron fist," I exclaimed.

Braxton winked his good eye. "I dislocated his jaw. He hasn't been able to talk back to me since." He laughed heartily. "You know island politics are hands-on."

"That used to mean candidates walked door-to-door asking for votes and stood on street corners with a sign waving at your constituents."

"It still does! Miki, I'm glad you've returned home where you belong. There's nothing like a daughter to take care of her father." He intoned each word with practiced definition and nodded self-assuredly.

"All right!" I sighed. My brother was overbearing in his expectations for his little sister. But I was happy to see him.

My father grunted and shook his head. "Listen to Braxton talk! He'll make a good senator. He beat that Demming guy yesterday."

"He's supposed to beat him in an election, Dad, not on a baseball field," I reminded him. I turned to my brother. "I like your black eye, Braxton. It adds a racy touch to your conservative image."

My brother spread his arms in an expansive welcome and gave me a crushing hug.

Braxton's long-sleeved white shirt smelled of starch, bringing back memories of Saturday morning ironing. When I was a child, all our sun-dried shirts, pants, and dresses had to be sprinkled with water, then wrapped in a huge plastic bag. By Saturday morning, the contents were a damp smelling mound as tall as I was. It was my duty to press them crisp and creaseless. I had timed myself: five minutes per shirt, six for trousers, and ten for a full-skirted dress.

Sondra Ai'Lee alighted from the car and cooed, "I honestly don't know what I would do so far from family. You must be lonely and homesick. Have you come home to settle down?" she asked breezily. She poised her head so her curls fell away from her perfectly made-up face and curved at the nape of her creamy neck.

"No, but I'm home for the summer, Sandy." I picked up the diaper bags and double stroller as she unloaded them.

She smiled at my brother, who was unhooking the twins from their car seats, and smoothed the wrinkles from her sleeveless linen shift. "*Son*-dra," she corrected me. My sister-in-law hated the familiarity of nicknames. "So plebeian!" she squealed. "Remember the 'o' sound." Her high-heeled sandals, the same bright pink as her dress and toenails, clicked happily on the concrete driveway.

"Thank Sondra for making a list of all the eligible young men," my brother said. He handed one of the twins to his wife. "She's going to keep your calendar busy." Sondra flashed him a glistening smile.

Braxton's smooth tongue and charming ways had endeared him to Sondra's high-society family, who were some of his staunchest supporters. In the early 1900s, when no banks would accept Chinese customers, her grandfathers on both sides founded the first Chinese-owned bank in Hawai`i and subsequently became two of the most influential Chinese in the islands. Although Hawai`i's voters never kept to strict ethnic lines, most Chinese and professional Asians would follow Sondra's family's recommendation and support Braxton Ai'Lee.

Braxton cradled the other twin in his left arm and closed the car door. "Now that you're home," he asserted, "I feel better knowing you're looking after Dad and Popo Ai'Lee every day. After all, you know that's what Mom would have expected of you."

"You're the oldest son," I reminded him. According to the sixth-century Chinese philosopher Confucius, harmony would be maintained if everyone observed their position in a strict hierarchy. Braxton, as my elder and a male, was expected to carry the family responsibility.

"Me? You know, Miki, I wish I could. With my latest promotion I have no free time. Of course, I try to spend as much time as I can with Sondra and the twins." Braxton shrugged importantly. "In the eleven years we've been a state our economy has grown with new business opportunities and federal funding. What a future for our children." He popped the twins in the double stroller.

The twins, Bradley and Bernard, chubby-cheeked clones of my brother down to their crowns of slick black hair, cooed for attention. I knelt down and smelled their sweet baby breath. I contorted my face, eliciting toothless wide-mouthed smiles, and tapped their little noses.

"Will you teach them Chinese?" I asked.

Braxton chortled as if I had made a joke. "No, my sons will be too busy playing baseball and studying to go to Chinese school. I'm raising them to be one hundred percent American."

Braxton's excuse for rushing through dinner was an early meeting with the governor the next morning. "Breakfast in the governor's office with the big man himself. He's considering me for an important appointment. Can't tell you, of course, until it's official. But it will be a great honor for the Ai'Lees."

—❀—

My brother, the master of manipulation, was well-suited to be a politician. When he sulked, my mother ordered me to give in to him, her number-one son. "After all, you're the girl," she reminded me when Braxton wanted his way,

"Braxton carries the family name." The last time she reminded me, I left for good.

One of the traditions in our family was that each girl received a camphor chest from her mother, her hope chest to fill with the heirloom jades, gold jewelry, and silks gifted from the ladies in the family. When Braxton and Sondra got engaged, Braxton promised Sondra a camphor chest as a wedding present. Auntie Lehua had only sons, so she offered Braxton hers, a chest carved in classic, simple lines. It was well made, although weathered after twenty years of sitting in a humid basement. Braxton brushed off the cobwebs and cockroach eggs. He consulted a Chinese cabinet maker and came home with special sanding compounds, fine brushes, and rubbing oils. He laid out newspapers in the atrium and brought the chest to a deep luster.

A week later, my mother came into my room as I lay reading on the hardwood floor, the most comfortable place on a warm day. Mynah birds hopped from branch to branch on the magnolia tree outside my window in a flurry of chirps, wing beating, and rustle of leathery leaves.

My mother's red skirt swirled softly around her legs when she sat next to me. With a resigned glance she surveyed my room, an eclectic collection of gymnastics trophies, books, art posters, dried leis, and handmade dolls.

Where the banks of windows met in a corner, three matching camphor chests sat in a pyramid, one on top of the other. She had given me these chests, which her wealthy family had commissioned especially for her in China when she got engaged. Every Saturday when I cleaned house, I would trace my finger along the folds in the gowns of the willowy ladies and curves of the flowers framing the vignettes of imperial life carved on every surface. I imagined what life must have been like in that ancient time, dreaming a young girl's fantasy that I would live their fairy-tale life of grace.

I closed my book and smiled expectantly when my mother stroked my hair. Her friends often said they hoped I had inherited her beauty and charm. I was just a late bloomer, I told myself.

She reached out her hand to touch mine. "My dearest Miki, your brother Braxton has a problem only you can help him with. I have taught you that as women we must make sacrifices for the happiness of our men." She paused. "A true lady has the ability to withhold her own feelings for the good of the family. I have given you three camphor chests, Miki. Give Braxton one," she suggested with a smile that matched the warmth of her touch.

I didn't understand. "Auntie Lehua gave him hers. I've seen him working on it."

"He's doing a skillful job of restoration," she sighed proudly. "When Braxton sets his mind to something, he is thorough and meticulous."

"Sondra will appreciate his hard work. He works on it every day."

"Well, that's what I want to talk to you about, Miki. Braxton doesn't think it's good enough for Sondra. You know the Ai'Lees are farmers. That chest is plain with simple carvings. Sondra comes from a family of bankers and they have high expectations for their only daughter."

"Sondra should be honored to receive it," I protested. The deep and well-balanced carving of the double dragons on the lid, the plum blossoms for good luck on the front panel and the side carvings of calligraphy for "double happiness" were masterfully sculpted.

My mother glowed. "I knew you'd see it my way. Miki, you have three chests. Give your brother the medium one. In exchange, he'll give you Auntie Lehua's—it's the same size. Fully restored, it looks brand new. To me, you're getting the better part of the trade."

I gestured to the pyramid of intricately carved chests that were once hers. "They're a matching set. If I give him the middle one, my set will be ruined. How can you ask me to do this? You gave them to me."

She sat up and took a deep breath. Her eyes flashed what was in her heart.

I slid my book across the floor and slammed my fist down on the cool, polished floor. "Why does Braxton always get everything he wants? It's not fair."

The look in my mother's eyes told me I wasn't going to win. Braxton, number-one son, bearer of the family name, wanted what I was determined to keep. She rose. When she got to the door, she turned. "For your brother's sake, let him start his marriage with Sondra off on the right foot."

Later that week, my mother and I listened to the evening rains pound heavy tattoos on the roof while we chopped the choy for dinner. Mom said in a quiet, off-handed way, "You know, you hurt Braxton's feelings." She glanced at my quizzical expression and continued. "He says you don't love him enough. He's upset because his only sister is so self-centered."

I turned to her, speechless.

"Don't be so selfish, Miki," she admonished.

"You gave your chests to me."

"With your sharp tongue, it will be a long time before you need them," she huffed, exasperated.

I refused to cry. I wanted to show her that her words didn't hurt me.

"He's your brother," she added, emphasizing the last word.

I threw down the choy with a splash and stormed out of the kitchen. "Give him the chest. I don't care. I don't want it. I don't want any of them. Give him anything he wants that's mine."

I slammed the door and ran barefoot to Popo Ai'Lee's house. I crumpled at her feet, defeated. She rubbed my temples and didn't even move when the phone rang and rang and rang. We knew it was my mother.

When the offer came to go to San Francisco, I left.

—❀—

My father habitually watered his potted plants in the court-yard after dinner. It was during this hour, between sunlight and moonlight, that time seemed to stop in Hawai`i; the skies turned violet-blue, the trade winds picked up, and the sun floated into the Pacific. My father turned off his hose and pulled up a chair next to me where I sat under the lychee tree in the center of the courtyard. I looked deep into his brown eyes, mirrors of Popo Lailee's. "Does this tree still have the sweetest lychees on the island?"

My father looked up at the full spread of branches over-head. "This year wasn't good. I don't know why. The birds ate many blossoms before I could tie them in paper bags. I remember when I couldn't find you, I would close my eyes and listen. If I heard 'tap tap' and saw a shower of little brown shells falling in the courtyard, I knew where you were. Up this tree with a book, eating lychees. If you didn't throw the shells down, I never would have found you."

I was surprised he remembered. "I didn't have any place to put them!" I said.

He chuckled at the memory of my brother chasing me up and down trees like monkeys. He picked up a root-bound orchid and, with his fingers, separated the tangled roots that poked out through the bottom of the pot. But now his voice was troubled. "Popo said when you took her to the temple, Alex Demming was there." He paused. "We did not approve of you seeing him."

"That was a long time ago, Dad." Misunderstandings and anger had stretched into years of silence.

"He came by this morning. After twelve years he returns! He didn't want to leave a message." He added softly, "I don't want you to get hurt." The muscles in his jaw tensed in tight ridges.

"Alex has been out of the country for a long time. He was just feeling nostalgic, Dad." In Alex's husky voice, his was the logical explanation of a homesick expatriate. But now I was confused, sad, and hurt by twelve years of silence.

My father pursed his lips as if thinking, then relaxed. He was not the kind of man who could say something negative about anyone unless it threatened his family's honor.

The only time he expressed any opinion about Alex was when the electricity went out during the hurricane of

'55. The islands were plunged in darkness and all we could hear was the howling wind-swept rain pounding on the roof and assaulting the windows. My mother and I had lit the candles set out on the kitchen counter, the dining room, and the living room. Dad and I walked from room to room with flickering candles clutched in our hands to check the windows for leaks.

When I lifted my candle to the upper bathroom windows, a moth twice the size of my hand swooped down from the darkness. I yelped when its huge gray wings batted the flame that I held. I felt its wings, soft against my face, struggle furiously for the light I shielded with my hand. Our grandmother had warned us that moths were spirits of the dead, not to be harmed. I gently shooed it away. But it spiraled back with quick and deliberate turns, always returning to the heart of the flickering flame. Again. And again. I screamed in frustration. Finally, Dad pushed me out of the bathroom and slammed the door behind us.

I leaned against the closed door. My heart pounded so hard my candle shook. "What was it doing?" I asked him, breathless. I was awed by how brilliantly the moth's wings could glow in the light, yet disappear in the darkness.

"The moth was attracted to your candle. Did you ever hear that saying, that some people are attracted to things 'like a moth to a flame'?"

I shook my head.

My father stroked my long black hair. "No one knows whether they're drawn by the bright light or the heat. But it's a deadly attraction." He turned away and said softly, "Like you and Alex."

I wondered then, which of us was the moth? Who was the candle?

I heard the rustle of the leaves and the sighs of the trade winds through the courtyard, like the voices of the gods that had lured me from San Francisco. A cool trade wind crept under my shirt. My skin tingled. I clasped my arms around me and shifted uneasily in the sudden chill. Chicken skin. The memory of that moth spiraling towards the flame gave me chicken skin.

❧

I was born in 1940, the Year of the Dragon, the fifth sign of the Chinese Lunar calendar, symbol of the Emperor, mighty and powerful. On the day I was born, the willowy Ai'Lee ladies were making gin dui, sweet doughnuts the color of gold, to celebrate the eighth day of the Chinese New Year. The Chinese believe that eight is the luckiest number, so my arrival was auspicious.

Lailee and her three fair-faced daughters, Pua, Lehua, and Vanda, were mixing gin dui in a massive steel bowl. Lailee's daughters-in-law—my mother, Ellie, and Verna, Teddy's wife—rolled the dough into pork-filled balls the size of their palms. Lailee scooped these balls into a wok of bubbling oil with just the right pressure so they puffed up to three times their size. Her youngest daughter rolled the gin dui, which resembled miniature suns, in trays of sesame seeds to symbolize abundance. The women's laughter was as plentiful as the rice flour that flew up in clouds from their slender hands and remained visible as silver rays in the afternoon sun.

Kam and his younger brother Teddy carried in a whole roast pig. With swelling forearms, the broad-chested brothers, as fair and tall as their sisters, landed the massive wooden tray and whole crisp-skinned suckling on the table where the glistening pig sat grinning among stoneware bowls of shiny vegetables, velvet-skinned chickens, crisp roasted ducks, whole steamed fish, and stuffed oysters.

When the Ai'Lee family sat down for this glorious feast, Lailee and her daughters served Kam's wife first. Ellie was pregnant; she carried this baby, her second, neat and tidy, like a ripe melon. The Ai'Lees said Ellie's child would run fast like the chicken, swim like the fish, be sweet like the duck, be content like the pig, and be as delicate as the oysters they heaped on her plate.

My father was a quiet, analytical gentleman who thought with his hands. As the only son, he was responsible for the sole support of his mother after the death of his father, and he had rewired Lailee's house himself after buying it for her. Quick with numbers but reserved with his opinions, the family was astonished when he called home from the hospital crying. "A girl! We have a girl," he sobbed. He marveled how exquisite his little daughter was, fair-skinned and light-haired, with a musical wail that sounded like the birds that woke at dawn.

Kam and Ellie had fervently wished for a girl to follow their first son, Braxton. Except for Lailee's three daughters, the Ai'Lees were known for their abundance of sons. Lailee had given birth to six boys, but only two survived to manhood, Kam and Ted. Her three eldest children, Pua, Kam, and Lehua, had already given her eight grandsons. Dozens of sons were favored in China. But this was

America, where little girls with swinging black braids were cherished as much as boys.

After Kam's announcement, Lailee Ai'Lee rushed to her kitchen altar to bow in thanks to Kuan Yin, the Goddess of Love and Mercy. The Ai'Lee ladies clinked teacups. The Ai'Lee men toasted "Okolemaluna!" with their Scotch. Then all returned to their green and white mah jongg tiles, vying to outdo each other with the jade and gold jewelry they planned to give their one and only niece.

Since I was born on the eighth day of the Chinese New Year, they considered the possibilities auspicious. Eight is feminine, a yin number, the number of prosperity and wealth. Then there are the eight treasures of Confucianism. The Eight Immortals, the Taoist fairies who know the secrets of nature and conquered death, have eight symbols. Like Confucianism and Taoism, China's third great belief, Buddhism, also has its eight emblems, which convey various aspects of learning. And the bagua, which feng shui masters consult to increase one's energy or ch'i, has eight trigrams.

I was born in the Territory of Hawai`i, in a culture part-Hawaiian, part-Chinese, part-American. As you can see, it adds up to a culture richer and greater than the sum of its parts.

I did not know that the spirits of this land conspired to lure me back when I dared to leave, and that I would hear the voices of the Night Whispers speaking my name in the wind wherever I wandered.

Chapter Three

Beach Ghost Stories

*B*ecause of the economic and political pressures in the state, the governor needed my brother seven days a week. But Braxton pledged his evenings at home with Sondra and the twins. So, to my father's dismay, Braxton gave us his coveted tickets to the Honolulu Symphony's summer concert featuring Rachmaninoff.

I didn't feel bad about accepting his front row tickets. Braxton had never been wild about Russian composers; he found them too intense and emotional. He preferred Bach's mathematically precise points and counterpoints. Like Braxton, I started music lessons at age eight. Unlike my violinist brother, I played the piano and could spend hours practicing those rapturous composers he dismissed as wildly temperamental.

Despite my promise that he would enjoy the evening, my father grumbled about getting dressed up to listen to music. He sighed loudly when we stepped through the glass doors of the concert hall so I would know he was doing this to please me. Despite his complaining, my father looked natty in a burgundy Hawaiian-print shirt, gray slacks, and black loafers.

I had slipped on a silky emerald-green blouse and long

skirt and, remembering how cold they kept the air-conditioning, carried a black cashmere sweater.

"We never came here, your mother and I," Kam grumbled. He looked up at the slabs of Baccarat crystal that dangled from the chandeliers in the lobby and shook his head. "Fancy," he muttered.

I tapped his arm lightly. "Smell how sweet the air is, Dad," I said. "You can smell the tuberose and pikake leis the ladies are wearing." The cooled air shimmered with the heady scents of tropical flowers: sweet carnations, lightly spiced gingers, and the intensely fragrant white pikakes and tuberoses.

"Tuberoses were your mother's favorite flowers, Miki," he whispered. His eyes misted in the dim light as he recalled the cherished memory. I squeezed his arm to let him know I remembered. The lobby's thick green carpet muffled our voices to a refined murmur.

For me, this symphony hall was a place of sweet memories. During the months that Alex and his sisters attended school in Honolulu, Alex's mother, Celie Demming, volunteered for numerous boards. As a member of the board of the new Honolulu Symphony, Celie led the campaign to build a symphony hall that would attract performers of international caliber. Instead of an out-of-the-way United States territory, Honolulu was hailed as a center of culture in the Pacific. Her children took her husband's place at her side during the season, which included symphonies, operas, and ballets. By the time Alex reached high school, his sisters had left for mainland colleges and Celie was spending more time in Kaua`i with her husband, William.

So Alex and I made good use of the Demming season tickets, transported by music and dance to other cultures and times. Spruced and dressed, we'd slyly ogle at the jewels and leis on opening nights, and sweep in with the well-heeled crowds to our seats up front. The first opera we saw had minimalist staging and we couldn't understand the Italian lyrics. But for us, the symphonies were lush and the ballets uplifting. We shared a love of the arts, where we found beauty, joy, and mystery.

—❀—

As we stepped into the glow of the dimly lit concert hall, Alex Demming strode through the crowd and stopped, a look of surprise on his face. He was wearing dark slacks and a long-sleeved shirt of fine cream-colored cotton.

"Miki. After twelve years I see you twice in two days." His cheeks were cool when he kissed me. "I should have known you'd be here. Rachmaninoff's Symphony no. 2 in E Minor was your favorite. Romantic and lyrical."

He had remembered my musical preferences after all this time. "Yes, especially the third movement," I said, smiling in anticipation. Its distinctive melodic line brought tears to my eyes each time I heard it. "I'm looking forward to the clarinet solo in the adagio." Legend says that the first time the great conductor Leopold Stokowski heard the piece, he wept, touched by the heartbreaking romanticism of Rachmaninoff's greatest symphony.

My father cleared his throat. He glared at Alex.

"Dad, you remember Alexander Demming, my class-mate. Alex, my father, Kam Ai'Lee."

Alex held out his hand. "It's a pleasure to see you, Mr. Ai'Lee. I have my parents' seats tonight." He nodded towards the front row.

My father looked at Alex's hand as if his skin would blister from the contact. But he was a gentleman and took the proffered hand. "Hello, Alex," he said. "Miki and I were just about to get seated ourselves." Then my father put his arm around my waist, handed the usher our tickets, and steered me away.

❧

Alex and I grew up when the ever-watchful eyes of friends and family ensured our innocence. But they couldn't protect us from the dark side of love: anger, sorrow, and pain.

In the midst of the Cold War, Sergei Pedrovsky, the most celebrated male dancer of the Kirov Ballet, defected in New York. It was the fall of our senior year. Sergei toured the United States to frenzied and unprecedented acclaim. The week before Sergei was to perform to sell-out crowds in Honolulu, the air was sizzling with anticipation. All my girlfriends would attend with their families. I had a little money saved up, enough for a ticket. But my father was working two jobs and money was tight. I asked Alex if we could go dutch. He apologized that he had to fly back to Kaua`i for the weekend.

The Monday after Sergei had performed with the Royal Ballet, Cecilia Wong waved me down in first-period physics. "Too bad you were sick, Miki," she said. "Every time Sergei leapt across the stage, we screamed. You missed seeing him suspended in midair," she sighed rapturously. "Alex told us you were throwing up the night before. Fortunately, Kelly was available. They sat next to us. Front center. I'm glad you're feeling better. We were all worried about you, especially Alex. Miki, are you all right? You look dizzy."

I couldn't breathe. I grabbed the desk in front of me for support. "Sorry, Ceci. I am sick now." I put my head down on the desk. I felt the air sucked out of my lungs, my body weak and spineless.

I struggled through class. Ceci, convinced I was still recuperating, handed me her class notes when I left.

In second period philosophy, Kelly Malone put her arms around my shoulders. "Alex said you caught that horrible flu bug. I told him he should have taken you, not me. I wish you had come with us." She tried to console me. "Cheer up, Miki. I'm sure Sergei will make another appearance here someday."

I wasn't sure if I wanted to see Alex at lunch. He might offer an explanation. If he didn't, I would have to pretend I didn't know he had lied to me. But Alex was waiting at my locker when I got there. I asked how his weekend was.

He answered, "The usual. You know how hard Pops works me."

I tipped my head and searched his eyes to read his mood. "What did you do?"

He shrugged. "We had a new crop of calves to brand. Do you mind if we have lunch by the library today? I have to study for a physics test after lunch." He took my hand.

His touch seared my palms. We headed in the opposite direction of our friends and sat under a tree to study and eat alone.

"Hey, grumpy," Alex complained after a wordless lunch. He nudged me with an elbow. "What's wrong?"

I crumpled my lunch bag and picked up a book. "I was wondering if there is anything you need to tell me."

"No." He frowned, then turned to his texts.

I looked at his physics notebooks, crazy with numbers and drawings, as confusing as the lies churning in my head. "Alex, did it hurt the calves when you branded them? It seems inhumane to sear their hides with a burning iron. Did they cry in pain?"

He looked up with a scowl. "They're animals, Miki. That's the way we identify them." He sighed, exasperated. "Miki, you know how important this test is, especially with Pop's expectations that I get into an Ivy League. Can we discuss this after school?"

I studied the back of his head for a few minutes, watched his fingers run through the pages of formulas and theorems, debating whether I should tell him I knew. I could be sweet and amenable as he obviously expected. But I couldn't live a lie. I felt like I was falling into an abyss with no bottom, no safety. My tears fell, hot and sad.

Alex threw down the pen he was using to mark his notes. "What's wrong with you, Miki? You know I hate it when you cry. If you can't let me study in peace will you leave?"

"Cecilia said you and Kelly sat next to her Saturday night," I said softly. I wanted him to tell me I was wrong. "You told Kelly I had the flu."

He stared blankly. "They told you?" Then the lie spread across his face like a storm cloud.

I recoiled from his outstretched arms. My anger overflowed like an erupting volcano. I swept up my books. "Pick up your goddamn turtle today! I don't want your damn Tommy Turtle swimming with my goldfish. And I won't need a ride home."

Alex was stunned. His jaw dropped and his eyes turned the palest blue. "Miki! You never swear."

"I never had a reason to until now," I shouted. I knew he hated it when I yelled at him. "And I'm going to cry if I damn well please."

I stomped across campus to a quiet spot shaded by a monstrous monkeypod tree. I put my arms around its ageless trunk and leaned my head against its rough bark, heartbroken and betrayed.

"Miki?" Alex had followed and stood so close I could feel the annoying heat of his body.

I kept my eyes closed. I spit out my words. "Aren't you supposed to be studying for your damn test?"

"Miki, are you upset because I took Kelly?" His voice cracked uncertainly.

Now I glared at him. "Kelly's my best friend. I would have understood. I'm mad because you lied to me. Why couldn't you have told me the truth?"

He dropped his books and shuffled awkwardly.

"Go study for your damn test. If you can't be honest, leave me in peace." I threw his words back at him.

"I didn't want to hurt you. Kelly was going on and on about this Sergei. I didn't know who he was. I told her my mother had a couple of tickets. Kelly asked me to take her.

When you said you wanted to go, I was in a fix. So I didn't say anything."

"What did you think I would say when I found out? How did you think I would feel?"

"I didn't think about it."

"You think I'm that stupid?"

He looked honestly confused. "I didn't want to disappoint you or Kelly. And I didn't want to tell you I made a mistake." He looked miserable.

"Alex, I thought you were my friend, someone I could trust, someone who respected me." I shivered with disbelief. "You lied to me! You insulted my intelligence and feelings." I was a betrayed and disappointed seventeen. Honor, the Ai'Lees stressed, was more important than money or material possessions. One's name, one's reputation, one's "face"—was a person's most valuable asset. Lailee Ai'Lee was right about the deceit of the Demmings. I turned away from him and stalked off once again to find a lonely spot.

At five o'clock, I left the gym after gymnastics practice to wait for Kelly, who was running track. I felt gritty in my practice leotard, but exhilarated after a tough workout that exhausted every muscle and all my emotional energy. We were learning a new vault and I had crashed to the mat a dozen times until I got a feel for the right hand placement. Each time, I got up laughing. My teammates and I were so bruised by the end of practice that Kaila, the smallest of our team, offered us all a back massage. At the end of practice, we lay face down on the dusty mats and let Kaila walk lightly across our backs to loosen our muscles.

I stretched out on a bleacher to watch track and field run their final laps. Kelly, leading the sprinters, waved on her way to the locker room and motioned she'd be right out. I closed my eyes and stretched, luxuriating in the late afternoon heat. Then I heard footsteps and the weight of someone sitting next to me on the bench. I opened my eyes.

"Miki?" Alex put his arms around me.

I shoved resolutely away from his embrace. His deceit gnawed at me.

"I'm sorry, Miki." I felt his heartbeat when he pulled me to his chest and promised never to lie to me again. He said it broke his heart to see my tears, to know he had hurt me. He cupped my chin in his hands and dried my face with a corner of his shirt that smelled of sun-dried cotton and the sea.

I was taught to forgive, to give in to my elders and my brother. Lailee had taught me the Buddhist middle way, to free the spirit by letting go of earthly anger. In our Christian Sunday school, I was taught to "love thy enemies as thyself."

He ran his fingers down my cheek and curved my lips into a smile. I looked into his eyes, soft and sad.

It is easy to forgive when you are young. When your heart is tender you want to believe your first love is true. Your first fight leaves you shattered and disillusioned. So when you optimistically and tenderly reconcile, you defy anyone who threatens to come between you and your love.

"This weekend, I'm yours. Anything! What would you like to do?" Alex promised, contrite and sweet.

—❀—

Most Saturdays, the Ai'Lees went crabbing. Sometimes it was the sandy beach past Niu Valley. Other times, it was to the right of the canal that flowed into the sea. It was always a special location Auntie Lehua's husband, Uncle Robert, chose after consultation with his fishing buddies. All day, the Ai'Lee's were on the phone working out the driving assignments and times to coincide with the surf and tide. We wore our crabbing clothes—old sneakers, shorts, and jackets.

My older cousins had brought girlfriends and boyfriends crabbing with the Ai'Lees over the years. Few endured the chilly surf, the pitch-black night, and the Ai'Lee ghost stories told around the bonfire. Only the hardy and adventurous with an open mind and understanding of local mores survived.

I didn't invite Alex to join us. But I told him that's what I would be doing that weekend. If he wanted to join us he had to be at my house by five PM. I loved him enough to give him another chance, but he had deeply hurt me. He would have to brave a hoard of Ai'Lees to prove himself.

My father glowered inhospitably when Alex arrived at our door dressed in faded jeans and an appropriately worn sweatshirt. My mother bristled when she saw him, but— perfect hostess that she was—she smiled efficiently, determined to show that her gracious hospitality exceeded that of the Demmings.

By the time five carloads of Ai'Lees arrived at the beach, including Alex crushed in the backseat of my dad's '52 Plymouth between Braxton and me, we could see Uncle Robert's black hair bobbing over the crab traps.

Bare-chested, with a cotton towel draped around his neck, he knelt over the wire cages tying aku-head bait to the center of the traps with thin nylon twine.

Alex Demming's presence didn't faze the Ai'Lees. Lailee and my aunts and uncles nodded stiffly when I introduced him. Warned by my parents that he might be joining us, I was sure they had spent the whole day deliberating what this meant. My cousins, curious about the Demming who dared to step within the den of the Ai'Lees, saw that he was well-bred in the local style. But they would not be fooled or bamboozled by the easy way he had about him. They liked having the enemy within their grasp.

While we fanned out across the shallow surf to set the crab traps by torchlight, Uncle Ted, Dad's younger brother, started the bonfire with seasoned tree cuttings. I looked back at the beach and saw Uncle Ted crouched low over the fire, aiming sticks into the fire one by one. I wondered if he was thinking of the bombs he dropped over Germany during World War II.

Only after I started dating Alex did Popo Ai'Lee explain that Uncle Ted's dark moods were caused not by the war, but by the Demmings. According to my grandmother, the day after Pearl Harbor was attacked, Ted Ai'Lee and four buddies from the University of Hawai`i enlisted in the U.S. Army. All five returned from the war flush with cash. The friends put together a plan to build affordable housing for returning World War II vets like themselves. Mayor Johnny Wilson, the father of one of the members of the hui, gave his full endorsement. Uncle Ted and his friends, newly married with babies on the way, invested their life savings into the project, the first of many they planned to build.

But once the purchase was made, the hui couldn't get the promised permits. Jefferson Demming, head of the Building Department, said his hands were tied—the land was zoned for agriculture. After years of lawsuits drained their savings, Ted Ai'Lee and his friends sold the land at a loss. When the sale was finalized, the new owners told the press that they held building permits for a luxury five-star hotel and golf course, expensive condominiums, exotic waterfalls, and five swimming pools. On the day of the ground-breaking cere-mony, Uncle Ted, fists flailing, rushed Washington Demming, the banker for the hotel project. Fortunately, Mayor Johnny Wilson was there; he made sure Ted Ai'Lee, after a month at Tripler Army Hospital for battle-stress, received a well-paid job as a civilian engineer at Pearl Harbor, out of reach of the Demmings.

But on these dark nights, Uncle Ted put his disappoint-ments aside. He knew the young Ai'Lees looked forward to his towering bonfires that danced with sinewy fingers. When we returned, chilly and wet from setting the crab traps, we expected the Ai'Lee ghost stories told in chilling, spine-tingling detail. Sparks flew in sudden puffs—ghostly breaths that reminded us to listen carefully.

Alex, soaked from the waist down, was shivering by the time we trudged out of the surf. I grabbed his hand and pulled him closer to the bonfire with Braxton, Reginald, and me. The stories were about to begin.

The hair on our arms and necks rose and we shivered with goosebumps when Dad described the koa rocking chair on their front porch that, without a breath of wind, rocked back and forth when the air was hushed still as death. The breeze quickened around us. Flickering phosphorescence fluttered in humanlike shapes, lighting our faces with a surreal glow. We waited breathlessly for the tale of the ghost who frequented the bedroom that Auntie Lehua, Auntie Vanda, and Auntie Pua used to share. Without warning, a dark-haired girl would appear, wave her arms as if to invite herself into their company, and comb thick tresses that curled down to her lap. She smiled. My aunts screamed.

"We used to walk home from school," Auntie Lehua said, "past one of those neglected graveyards where tombstones stand kapakahi, tipped this way and that. A concrete wall topped by sharp black lava rocks surrounded the cemetery. Mausoleums covered with ivy were gated with wrought iron. Low walls surrounded monuments topped by angels or lambs, some dating from the 1700s. But if we saw a funeral, we walked fast and kept our eyes straight." Auntie Lehua, who still wore her hair marcelled in the style of the forties, had been serious about her responsibility as second-eldest daughter.

She traced a circle in the air with her hands. "One afternoon, we saw fifty men and ladies, all in black, around an open grave. The sky was dark, overcast, and threatening to rain. The wind was blowing so hard the monkeypod trees above swooshed and dipped as if they were going to crash on our heads. We heard the mourners chant in Hawaiian when the wind blew our way. Their wails shivered the air. When they lowered the coffin into the grave with ropes that squeaked and moaned in protest, the mourners bowed their heads."

She threw up her arms, leaning close to Alex's face. "Whoosh, a ball of fire rose from the grave, as big as the moon, glowing yellow and orange and red. The fireball hovered over the mourners and shot straight up in the sky. It exploded and showered sparks that burnt like hot sand."

Alex recoiled, his mouth agape. We cousins had heard the tale before, yet we huddled closer to the bonfire, holding our hands out to the pulsing waves of heat. Our faces were flushed, our bodies facing the fire toasty warm, but our backsides shivered in the blackness. Our eyes were riveted on Lehua. Her eyes shone in the flickering fire like glistening black jewels.

"The next night, some teenagers were necking behind the tombstone topped by a broken column." She paused, building suspense with silence. She slowly curled her fingers into curved talons. "A creature as tall as the sky rose from the grave. Its flaming eyes and hungry mouth lit the night. Its robes flew out, its tiger claws flashed, and the couple was engulfed within its stinking folds. All that was left the next morning were shreds of fabric and flesh in the grass."

Alex grabbed my hands. We shivered in delicious horror, tingling with chicken skin.

"Obake!" the Ai'Lee cousins screamed the name of a hungry Japanese ghost. "More ghost stories," we begged.

Uncle Ted fed the fire with handfuls of twigs that crackled like breaking bones. The night closed in on our backs. By this time, we were too afraid to venture out into the dark waters where, according to Uncle Ted, monsters dripped seaweed and sharks lay in wait for tender children.

This was the moment my father and uncles decided to collect the crab traps.

I turned to Alex and said. "You should help them." I laughed at his horrified expression. He was caught in the spell of our stories when he looked out at the dark waves, yet he braved the surf at my command.

The men dumped their catch into metal buckets and loaded them into our trunk. All the way home we could hear the scratching of hundreds of claws, *scree-scree-scree,* frantic to escape.

At Popo Ai'Lee's house, the aunties boiled pots of water. All of us laid layers of newspaper over the kitchen table. The aunties poured the crabs into the pots, then scooped them, steaming, out on the newspaper. Saturday night ended only when everyone was stuffed with crab-meat, there were no more stories to tell, and nothing was left on the newspaper to roll up but paper napkins and empty crab shells.

But Lailee Ai'Lee watched Alex with piercing eyes. Her memory of the past was vivid and exact. Friendships between the Ai'Lees and the Demmings had been forged before, but they had ended in death and deceit.

Chapter Four

The Demmings

I met Alexander Demming on my first day of high school.

All I remember about that day was how nervous and out of place I felt. During my last class, journalism, Kelly Malone plopped her books next to mine. She tossed her thick sun-streaked hair, blunt cut at the shoulders, and grinned. "I'm Kelly Malone and you're the new girl. Did you know I'm in all your classes?" Kelly had broad shoulders, a wide friendly smile, and a bouncy, confident personality. Her gregarious nature and the numbers of friends that clustered wherever she went intimidated me. She was half a head taller than I and wore a crisp sleeveless white blouse and a short blue skirt. But what struck me were the freckles that covered her arms and legs, and swept across her cheeks and nose like a breath of sunlight.

"I'm Miki Ai'Lee. Sorry, I didn't notice," I admitted, flustered by her friendliness. Most of the students had attended this private school since kindergarten. I was one of the later admits who tested in for the few open slots, so I was left out of the energized back-to-school chatter. I had smiled shyly at my classmates and hoped no one would notice I was lost, or that the dress I wore was homemade.

"Nothing to be sorry about, Miki Ai'Lee." She pulled Alex, tall and gangly like a thoroughbred colt, over to our desks. "Alex, meet Miki. She's new." She added teasingly, "Our parents expect us to get married!" Kelly and Alex had been friends since kindergarten. An alliance of the Malones and the Demmings, both descendants of Americans who came to Hawai`i during the Hawaiian monarchy, would have combined land, old wealth, and power.

Alex grinned and elbowed Kelly. Despite his embarrassed blush, his smile was friendly. Unruly cowlicks stuck at odd angles in defiance of his attempts to comb his dark brown hair. I was struck by his eyes, blue-green like the ever-changing sea.

Suddenly Kelly gasped. Her hands flew to her mouth. "I forgot. Demmings and Ai'Lees have been killing each other for a hundred years."

I didn't know what she was talking about. I didn't want to act stupid on my first day of school, so I didn't ask what she meant.

"Those Ai'Lees couldn't have been as pretty as Miki," Alex blurted. He blushed again.

I looked down, embarrassed. I felt out of place until Kelly crooked her elbow in mine. "Then you'll have to forget she's an Ai'Lee. She's Miki, our friend."

Later, while we worked on layouts for the school paper, Kelly confided that she had known Alex since first grade. "We've practically grown up together! I know everything about Alex!" Her green eyes sparkled mischievously. She sighed, "I love Alex, but like a brother. I'm looking for romance, the love of my life to sweep me off my feet!"

As children, we eagerly anticipated the islandwide celebration of Hawaiian song and dance on May 1. We practiced our songs and hulas at school to share with our classmates and parents at the May Day program: four-part harmonies to Queen Lili`uokalani's favorite songs, the songs of the islands written by Charles K. Davis, the dynamic kane hulas for men and the graceful wahine hulas for women.

At my new high school, the May Day festivities climaxed with the elegant Holoku Ball on campus. The girls wore holokus, long mu`umu`us that flowed like rippling waves, and handmade flower leis from our beaus. Our dates wore formal Hawaiian-print shirts. A King and Queen and their court were chosen from among our classmates. On that night, we exchanged leis and danced barefoot under a moonlit sky.

Two weeks before the dance, I asked my mother for permission to go to the Holoku Ball. It was dinnertime. Exotic Chinese scents oozed from the pots on the stove. My mother held out a dish of fresh fish in black beans. The steam puffed around her like a furious cloud when I told her my date's name. She paused and frowned. "Isn't he William Demming's son?" she asked.

"Yes. Alex is a friend, Mom. A classmate," I answered demurely, hopefully. My heart hammered like a rabbit's and sunk to my toes. While teens on the mainland flaunted authority with cigarettes rolled in the sleeves of their skintight T-shirts, I was burdened with centuries-old Confucian ethics of obedience and filial piety.

My mother straightened. Her voice stiffened. "The Demmings are not our friends."

"Alex has been Kelly Malone's friend forever, and you like the Malones."

"But we do know the Demming family, much too well." She placed the fish on the table. "Do you want to break your father's heart? Do you want to break Popo Ai'Lee's heart?" Her eyes, deep pools of dark brown sugar, simmered a warning. "I'm telling you from my own experience. Your father and I know best." She shook her head and turned towards the kitchen. "I'm sure a nice Chinese boy will ask you," she assured me with a bright smile.

"Just this once," I pleaded. "I promise I won't ask again."

My mother turned quickly to my father, who was holding the evening newspaper up to his face. "Kam, do something. Talk to your daughter!"

My father muttered under his breath, "I told you what would happen if your daughter went to that prep school."

"Mom! Dad! I'm not marrying him! I'm only going to a dance."

"Miki Ai'Lee," My father's voice was low and dangerous.

I had crossed the line, shown disrespect of my place in the hierarchy of family. I stomped off to the kitchen to serve the rest of the dinner with sullen impertinence.

After dinner, I ran to my grandmother's house. Lailee was reading in a koa rocking chair in her living room under the glow of an ornate brass lamp. She looked up from her book when I jerked open her unlocked door and threw myself at her feet. I pouted, feeling unloved and sorry for myself. I pulled myself grudgingly from the floor when she stood up, smoothed the front of her cotton cheong-sam, and went to her kitchen. I slunk in after her.

Lailee Ai'Lee brought a pot of fresh jasmine tea to the kitchen table where I slumped with my head propped in my palms. The tap of light rain, which had started just as I got to her house, grew to a steady downpour. From the back of her cupboard, she chose two porcelain cups finely painted with pink peonies and rimmed with gold. Curls of steam drifted in the trade wind when she filled our cups. She sat down opposite me, folded her hands, and said, "Why the sad face?"

"It isn't fair, Popo. My first date! My mother won't let me go."

"That doesn't sound like Ellie." My grandmother tipped her head, and waited.

"He's just a friend, a classmate." I looked hopefully at her.

"What is his name, and who are his parents?"

I was sunk. Everyone in Hawai`i was connected by threads of family and friends. Our genealogies bloomed behind us like fully inflated parachutes. "Alex," I mumbled. "His parents are Celie and William Demming of Kaua`i."

My grandmother straightened abruptly. She turned away and looked out the window. When she turned back, her frown had smoothed from her forehead but her face was ashen. "Your parents know best, Miki. Terrible things happened long ago."

"Long ago?" I asked. "What difference does it make now?" I watched the steam rise up in a translucent curl when she refilled the teacups before us. "If it's so important, why won't they tell me?"

Lailee patted my hand. "To protect you. They hoped you never needed to know."

"Know what? Whenever I ask, they mutter that the Demmings are cursed. They refuse to say why." I shivered, chilled by a cool wind that swept in through the windows.

My grandmother leaned back and took a deep breath as if gathering strength. "Who knows what is in the hearts of men when they covet what someone else owns? What happens to anger passed from generation to generation?" She inhaled the steam of her tea with a sigh that ached from her heart. "We Chinese have a saying, 'When you drink the water, remember the source.'" She cocked her head as if appraising me. "You are a result of your ancestors and their deeds. We must always remember the sacrifices they made for us and be respectful of our culture and family. That means living honorably and," she narrowed her eyes, "obeying your parents."

I lifted my chin defiantly. "I want to live my own life."

She shook her head patiently. "I will tell you a tale that would never have been told if all men were honorable." My grandmother leaned back. Her voice became dreamy, sliding back to the past, when time was thick with myths and legendary characters; drawing me into an earlier time, before statehood and territorial days, when kings and queens ruled the Hawaiian Islands.

—❁—

Long ago in the early days of the Hawaiian Monarchy, men came to these islands looking for adventure. One was a Celestial and the other was a Barbarian, as the Chinese and Westerners were called by the Hawaiians in Old

Hawai`i. These two men, Chun Ai'Lee and Arthur Demming, desired the same woman. One man would win her heart, the other, her lands.

Chun Ai'Lee was born in a village in the Pearl River Delta. He was tall and lean as the willow, clean-shaven, with a queue down his back as required by the Manchus who had thundered down from the northern plains and conquered China in 1644. Legend says that the Manchus required Chinese men to wear the queues so they could reach down from their horses and chop off Chinese heads. Annual cycles of drought, flood, and famine made life in the villages difficult. With a vow to return to his homeland with honor and riches, Chun Ai'Lee sailed off on one of the sailing ships plying the silk and fur trade routes between China and the Pacific Northwest in the early 1800s. Ai'Lee, enterprising and quick, became a master seaman on an American ship.

Of all the ports he saw, the tropical temperatures and balmy weather of Hawai`i were most similar to southern China. If he had land, he could farm the rice and sugar from his village. He could grow familiar vegetables and, for beauty, the Chinese flowers he missed. Under the old Hawaiian system, the king owned the lands and the people were its stewards. But the Barbarians had pressured for change, especially the missionaries who wanted to build homes, churches, and schools. So Ai'Lee, now knowledgeable in English and American ways, stayed in Honolulu as a master craftsman to the many clippers that sailed into Honolulu Harbor.

In those days, the Celestials were welcomed in Hawai`i. The first Chinese Ball, hosted on November 13, 1856, by the Chinese merchants, businessmen, and leaders, was hailed as the most glittering and brilliant affair the Hawaiian Islands had seen. At this ball to honor the marriage of King Kamehameha IV to Queen Emma, Ai'Lee was as captivated by a young cousin of the king as she was smitten by the well-traveled Ai'Lee. They married within the month. As a wedding present, his wife's family gave the couple an ahupua`a, a large parcel of fertile land that stretched from the mountains to the sea at Anahola on the island of Kaua`i, her family's home. With his experience and knowledge of Western ways and fluency in Chinese, Hawaiian, and English, Ai'Lee became counselor to the king.

Now Ai'Lee had rich lands, a position with the monarchy, and a beautiful Hawaiian princess who gave him three healthy sons. He named his first son Haunani, because as first son he would be the next leader of the Ai'Lee clan. His second son he named Kekailoa, meaning "distant ocean," because he wished his second son to return to China with him when he retired. His third son practically leapt from his mother's womb when he was born, so he was named Ikaika, for he had shown that he was strong and powerful.

Arthur Demming, son of an American missionary from New England, had met the king's pretty cousin from Kaua`i long before she became Ai'Lee's wife. Everyone knew he pinched his pennies to buy her a memorable token of his love. Some say the eleven-carat Burmese ruby, surrounded by diamonds and set in gold, had once been part of a maharajah's hoard stolen by one of the many British officers who frequented Hawai`i's ports. Its fiery red, the color of passion, was the signature brilliance of the Hawaiian goddess Pele.

Stout and beak-nosed, with flame-red hair and a temper to match, Demming had great ambitions. He was a big man, almost seven feet, with a barrel chest and a loud, commanding voice. But Kamehameha IV's anti-American sentiments were no secret; Demming's ruby necklace was immediately returned. Demming seethed with jealousy when the young princess married Ai'Lee. Some say the enraged Demming flung his ruby necklace into the Pacific, never to be seen again.

Even when Demming's shipping business in Honolulu grew, even when he could look with pride at his five strapping sons and plump New England wife living in the upper-class section of Makiki, jealousy contorted his face when he heard of Ai'Lee's success in the courts, his profitable sugarcane fields, and his growing wealth. Demming, now a powerful politician among American businessmen seeking to overthrow the monarchy, allied himself with the Americans and their prosperous businesses. He helped to introduce business taxes levied only against the Chinese, anti-Chinese craftsmen taxes, and the Kingdom's Chinese Exclusion Act in 1886.

Meanwhile, Ai'Lee's prosperity grew so great that he no longer needed to work. Content with the success of his sugarcane fields, Ai'Lee and his princess returned to China, as he had promised, and bought up all the fertile lands around Siu Yun village for his second son, Kekailoa. Ai'Lee retired in palatial splendor to a walled estate in his village with dozens of servants for his Hawaiian wife. He offered an open door to anyone from her family to visit, so she would never get homesick.

Ai'Lee's unmarried third son, Ikaika, had inherited his father's talented craftsmanship and enjoyed working with his hands. So when his parents and brother left for China, he chose to stay on Kaua`i with Haunani, his eldest brother, and use his skills to increase the profitability of the Ai'Lee sugar fields for future generations of Ai'Lees.

By then, Demming's sons, all attorneys, had become friends with Ai'Lee's eldest son, Haunani, who was addicted to gambling and drink. Unlike his hardworking father, Haunani, the spoiled first son, had grown as fat as he was tall. The Demmings, as they fished Haunani's body out of Honolulu Harbor, revealed that they now owned the Ai'Lee lands in repayment of his gambling debts. The Demmings sent the sheriff to evict Chun Ai'Lee's youngest son from his home with only the clothes on his back. All of Ikaika's tools, the means by which he made his living, were claimed by the Demmings.

On the day Haunani Ai'Lee drowned, the Demming's China trade shriveled to the most unprofitable runs. When Arthur Demming received the news from Hong Kong that only the disreputable and unbondable companies would use his ships, his roars exploded from the Demming shipping office that overlooked Honolulu Harbor. Incensed, he ran out to his docks where his once profitable ships had been displayed as a visible testament to his fortune. In his fury, he imagined the local children fishing from his piers were the sons of Ai'Lee. He set upon them with his cane and the whip he used on his horses.

Financially wounded, flame-haired Arthur Demming sailed to Kaua`i. He surveyed Ai'Lee's swaying sugarcane fields and the gentle slope of the mountains touching the clouds. Ai'Lee may have won Demming's woman, but Demming now owned Ai'Lee's land.

Arthur exulted until, just as mysteriously as his shipping firm went bankrupt, Chun Ai'Lee's sugarcane died. All that was left of the once-lush fields were ugly black stalks. Arthur brought in experts from Honolulu and China, but no one could make sugarcane grow again on the land his sons had won.

Penniless and homeless, Ikaika Ai'Lee sailed to Honolulu. He spent long days bent over the earth as he dug and built and labored with his bare hands in the taro fields. He refused Mr. Hart's offer to buy the plots he sweated over. Each night, Ikaika drank a jigger of home-made rice wine from his home-crafted still. Then he would remember the Demmings with bitterness and curse their generations for the dishonor they brought upon the Ai'Lees. Ikaika died young. He was only fifty-six when a flu epidemic swept through Honolulu claiming him along with a daughter and a son.

— ❀ —

"I married your grandfather, Ikaika Ai'Lee, when I was seventeen," my grandmother said. "My parents and I had sailed here just eight years before. Ikaika was already a farmer in Manoa Valley. Broad-shouldered. Dark from working his taro fields. Huge arms and hands. At night he would drink and rant about stolen lands and curse the Demmings. After one jigger of mao tai his bellows were so loud they echoed off the valley walls. Even the air shivered when he was in a black mood.

"But my husband was a skilled craftsman. He knew the secret of distilling and had the knowledge to make a home still. The Chinese and the Hawaiians came for your grandfather's home-brew which was sweet as honey, smooth as spun silk, warm as the morning sun, and more precious than gold. In exchange, they would bring us chickens and slaughtered pigs and fish for our children. These were precious because it would have taken all day on a horse cart for us to go to town, if we had the time, to get food. These friends told me about the Demmings and the Ai'Lees and how their histories intertwined. The Hawaiians believe that the Demmings are cursed."

"It happened so long ago, Popo," I fussed.

"It was not so long ago if you consider we can track the Ai'Lees back twenty-seven generations. The Ai'Lees value honor. The Demmings deceived the Ai'Lees. Remember, Arthur Demming's shipping business went bankrupt and your great-grandfather's cane fields died when Demming took the Ai'Lee lands. The Demmings continue to suffer with each generation."

"Maybe there never was a curse, only bad luck. After all, those were difficult times. For instance, has anything happened between the Demmings and Ai'Lees since then?"

My grandmother stiffened. "Each time Demmings and Ai'Lees meet there is catastrophe." Her voice constricted as if her words were caught in her throat. She looked out

her window and lifted her face to the breeze as if to wash
away the sadness that clung to her. She refilled our teacups
and gently placed the porcelain pot back on the table. The
wrinkles on her forehead deepened to crevices. "You are
your mother's only daughter. She does not wish you to get
hurt." My grandmother patted my hands. "You are so
young. You have many more dances in your future."

But I was as strong willed as the Ai'Lees before me. I
fought her every argument. I could be stubborn, as stubborn as she. I refused to let the past dictate my present.

The night of the Holoku Ball, Alex braved the strained
interrogation of my parents, oblivious to the slammed
doors in the Ai'Lee household for the previous two weeks.
Even the moonlight magic under the canopy of coconut
fronds and sprays of dendrobium orchids, the buoyant
strains of the live band, and the light-hearted conviviality
of our classmates couldn't dispel the uneasiness I felt.

I was torn between familial obedience and first love. I
glowed when Alex smiled at me across campus. My heart
soared when I heard his voice. By then, buoyant Kelly was
wildly in love with blond, blue-eyed Raleigh, whose military family had just transferred from Virginia. She told
Raleigh that kids in Hawai`i always double- and triple-
dated; the more they could stuff in a car, the more fun they
had. From then on, my parents only saw carloads of friends
pick me up on the weekends. As far as they knew, we were
going out as a group.

They needn't have worried. By the end of our senior
year, Alex was leaping with gusto with each college
acceptance, as were all my classmates going off to the
mainland. I avoided the clusters of friends who poured

over college view books and pondered winters knee-deep in snow. The parties grew more raucous as senior fever spread. The guys, cocksure and exuberant, chugged beer outside the homes where our parties were held.

Doomed to a scholarship at the local university, I would stay behind, at home with my parents, while others savored life abroad.

As yearbook editor, Alex planned the final picture to be a spectacular sunset on a deserted beach. This was his artistic statement of the future that beckoned us: the unlimited possibilities open to our youthful exuberance and an embrace of the great unknown. I accompanied the shoot to write the copy. Alex and the photographers spent the afternoon finding the most dramatic stretch of coastline, the right curve of the beach, and the most artistic angles. I listened to their philosophical discussions on photography, traced lace patterns in the waterline, and chased skittering sand crabs. Alex ordered his photographers into position for the "magic hour" of sunset lighting that lasts from a half an hour before sunset to a half an hour after. They intently composed and snapped until the sun crashed into the ocean in fiery purples and reds with a rushing crescendo when that green spark shot up from the center of the sunset like a flying spear.

When the yearbook was unveiled, the final picture was not the sunset that Alex had written into the layout. Instead, he had placed my picture in the final spot: the wind blew through my hair as I sat on the deserted beach gazing wistfully, longingly, out across the flying waves.

I bowed to the centuries-old training for young Chinese girls and bent like the willow. As a child, I had buried my thoughts and feelings to avoid conflict. Sometimes I thought I was invisible. Growing up, however, didn't mean I had outgrown the need to please my family. I listened and watched so when my family did notice me, it was only to praise and congratulate my accomplishments and success. I hid my rebellious dark side.

Chapter Five

Lailee's Secret

Hawai`i, 1970

I walked to Popo's house each morning when the air smelled sweetest, right after the early rains had drifted through Nu`uanu Valley. By the time dawn broke over the Ko`olau mountains, tile roofs and vines were dripping soft patterns in the grass. I rounded the bend of the quiet road and bent my head toward the steep grade. Scents of plumeria and white ginger on both sides of the grass walkway filled my lungs with their seductive fullness. I arched my neck and stuck out my tongue to taste the familiar sweet drops.

Up ahead, Popo Ai'Lee, a slender, shawl-wrapped figure, glided down the stairs. "I have tea and toast all ready," she greeted me. "Aren't you cold, Miki, in just T-shirt and shorts?" I shook my head. She held out her arms and enveloped me in her camphor scent.

"Are you done with your bai-sun, Popo?" I followed her cautious steps back up the stairs. Whenever I arrived at her house before she was done, I could hear her chants, her voice forming round and melodious words like bubbles in the wind. I'd sit on her steps and listen to her words flow like a meandering brook until she rang the brass bell with the tiny matching hammer, signaling to the gods that her prayers for that morning were done. We children had never learned her Hakka dialect because our parents wanted us to grow up without the stigma of a Chinese accent. Now I wish I had so I could understand the heart of her prayers.

"Five o'clock this morning I prayed to the goddess Kuan Yin. I thanked her for bringing you home. I lit extra heung, incense. Maybe she will do something special for me."

"Like what?"

She waved her hands evasively.

We Ai'Lees whispered that Popo had a special relationship with the gods. When my mother threw up fountains of blood in the middle of the night, Lailee promised Kuan Yin a special offering of heung blessed by the high monk in Hong Kong. Ellie recovered within a week. But the following month, doctors and specialists hovered at Ellie's bedside, unable to determine why she was passing blood black as death. I caught the first flight home from San Francisco. I sat by my mother's hospital bed, recounted tales of my studies and life in San Francisco and listened to her hopes for my future. While she slept, I hurried home to cook dinner, then rushed back in the evenings with Dad and Braxton. Dad slept upright in a chair by her side each night. Late at night when no one else was there, he'd cry himself to sleep.

My mother begged the doctors to let her go home and die in her own bed. But no, they promised, they were working on a cure. They drugged her pain and punctured her arms for tests until she cried that she had no blood left. In her sleep, I heard my mother call out to her father who had died thirty-five years ago and speak to old friends long gone. When she clutched my arms and asked, I told her I did not see them as she did. But I was glad they had returned to guide her into the next world.

The day after my mother died, no incense burned at the family altar in Popo's kitchen. The offering bowls were empty, turned upside down.

"Stupid gods," Popo grumbled when she came over to help me lay out my mother's clothes for the funeral. "Every day, all day, I prayed to the gods to cure Ellie. I told them every hour she cries to come home to her husband and children. I promised Kuan Yin a new altar, 'Make-Well Buddha' extra-long prayers, and for all, gold bowls for offerings. They do not listen to me."

"Okay, I said, take my life. I am old already. My daughter-in-law has two children. Humph! They do not listen. So now, I do not listen to them. I burn no heung. No more fresh rice. No whiskey. No sweet chicken. No roast pig. Nothing!" I had never seen her eyes snap the way they bristled now. "The gods can go hungry."

I was afraid to question Popo's break with her gods.

A month later, Popo called me in San Francisco. "Miki! I saw your mother."

"What? What? Popo, are you all right?"

"Of course," she answered. "I was walking back to the house after watering my plants. One hand was already on the doorknob when I hear her voice call, 'Ma!' I turned this way and that. 'Ellie,' I called, 'Ellie.' Then I saw her. She was swimming at the beach. So young and pretty, just like when she was dating your father. She said, 'Ma, how are you?' She waved her hands and yelled, 'Don't worry about me.' I saw her smile, shiny like yours. She laughed and swam away. Her hair was a long brown wave in the water. Oh Miki, she was strong and happy. I told Kuan Yin I'm so sorry I got mad. I apologize." Popo's gleeful laughter filled the distance between San Francisco and Hawai`i. Lailee resumed her morning meditation and prayers. Our link to the gods was reestablished.

I kicked off my sandals at the door before I entered her house. "How are you feeling this morning?" I asked. "Auntie Vanda says Dr. Lee was here."

She flicked her fingers to show how she had dismissed him. "Just old age, I told him. I've been resting. I want to go out." She walked to her bedroom to change.

I followed, shaking my head at her self-diagnosed recovery. "Dr. Lee says you have vertigo. You can't hop on the bus whenever you feel like going to Chinatown or to the temple. You must call someone to take you."

She turned and raised her voice impatiently. "Too humbug. I have always done everything myself. If you were to stay here you could take me anywhere I wanted to go. What do you do in the mainland anyway?"

I am a professor, I explained. My parents had deemed my love of Asian art, myth, and symbolism an impractical profession, not conducive for raising a family. To please them, I abandoned my desire for exciting site research and travel and became a teacher.

"But why San-Fran-Cis-Ko?"

I explained that San Francisco was a city of breathtaking views and a gourmand's delight; I could eat many kinds of foods: Thai, Italian, Caribbean, Chinese, French, Japanese, and more. There were more museums than in all of Hawai`i, all begging to be explored. I met collectors and artists, viewed their private collections and working studios. My students were challenging, my colleagues sometimes helpful, and I had greater opportunities in my career.

She threw up her hands in exasperation. "San-Fran-Cis-Ko! Too far! Too far!" Her eyes widened in disgust. "How can you come home quick if I need you?"

"You have my father, aunties, uncles, and dozens of cousins who snap to your command."

She tapped my chest possessively with her index finger. "I want you."

I knew better than to argue when she had her mind made up. I had three months to get her used to the idea. Her vertigo meant someone had to keep an eye on her. I shuddered to think what would happen if she were alone the next time she fell. At her age, a broken bone or bump on the head could be fatal.

I cajoled her, "Come, Popo, let's make breakfast. Coffee and pancakes."

Her eyes twinkled. "I'll teach you sweet pancakes. My own recipe. With Poha jam." I put my arms around her as we walked to her kitchen.

After a hearty breakfast, I washed our dishes and left them to drain.

My grandmother boiled water for tea. "Your father gave me this Dragonwell tea. Very special. See the leaves how evenly rolled? How fragrant the scent? It is good for your health and increases your body's ch'i." She brought the pot to the table to steep.

While I poured, she watched the steam rise from our cups and spiral up in the morning breeze.

Her voice was strained, confidential. "Miki, I must tell you a family secret. You live so far away. I am afraid for you. Now you've returned and resumed a dangerous friendship."

I turned away. I didn't want to hear the Demming lecture again.

Lailee grabbed my hand. "Miki, I disowned my own child. It has been almost fifty years since we promised never to mention her name. She was my baby, my youngest."

—❂—

In the early 1900s, the Territory of Hawai`i sent all new teachers to the neighboring islands for their first teaching assignment. These women, most in their late teens or early twenties, would have to work many years to earn a position back in O`ahu closer to their families. When Lailee's youngest daughter graduated from teacher's college she was sent to Hilo, Hawai`i, the Big Island. Formed by five volcanoes, the island of Hawai`i has a land mass twice the area of the rest of the Hawaiian Islands, which accounts for its nickname as the Big Island. The towering peaks of Mauna Loa and snow-covered Mauna Kea dominate the lush landscape of tropical forests and waterfalls. Fountains of molten lava from Kilauea's Halema`uma`u crater continue to reshape the growing island. The sleepy town of Hilo was so far from Hawai`i's busy capital of Honolulu, Lailee's daughter had to sail all night across the rough and swift waters of the Pacific before she arrived in picturesque Hilo Bay.

"Your father's youngest sister was engaged to a young Chinese man here, the son of your grandfather's best friend. Her fiancé was studying at the university. A kind and scholarly man, he had a good future and she would not have to work after marriage. But my daughter was headstrong. After she graduated from teacher's college, she wanted to work for a few years." Lailee's voice dropped. "Before the end of her first year of teaching, she wrote that she had married. Her father was shamed, our family dishonored. Her fiancé's family was disgraced. Imagine what a loss of face it was for us, especially for your grandfather. We were poor, but your grandfather was an honorable man with a good name in the community."

"What is her name? Where is she now? Did she have children?" I was astonished. I thought back on all those many days and nights that the Ai'Lees spent together at dinners, crabbing, and family gatherings—had anyone slipped just once? Had they said a forbidden name, a reference to someone or something the younger Ai'Lees didn't understand?

My grandmother shook her hand in front of her face as if to ward me off. "It was my fault, Miki. She was too pretty, too young. I should never have let her go to college. We have not said her name since 1928."

"That was forty-two years ago, Popo!"

Lailee wrung her hands, smoothing out the skin as if she could remove the wrinkles. "Do not judge me, Miki. There is more to this story. The man was a local fisherman and not Chinese. That would have been enough to dishonor our family in those days. But she further disgraced us. I cannot speak of that now. She was never welcomed home again. I do not want you to make the mistake of marrying out of loneliness or a memory of a happier time." She slumped back wearily. "I wish you could stay with me until the end of my days, but you choose this far-away path. I want you to have happiness with the love and support of your family. Do not repeat her mistake."

Chapter Six

Family Ties
and Curses

Sheets of lightning flashed electric white, blanketing the city of Honolulu. We yelled over the crashing thunder when the next clap boomed over our heads. Then all of us, aunties, uncles, and dozens of cousins, vied to talk simultaneously, raising our voices above the loud and brilliant display of our gods.

The aroma of another feast trailed behind the Ai'Lee aunties who burst from Popo Ai'Lee's kitchen carrying platters piled high with pineapple-glazed ribs and overflowing with papayas and mangoes and more. The uncles and cousins, in Hawaiian print shirts and shorts, congregated on Popo Ai'Lee's lanai where Dad smoked his honeyed turkey. At Kam's side, Braxton Ai'Lee, in a white shirt and ironed khakis, was coaxed to retell and embellish the Memorial Day baseball game that had made the front page a week ago.

In the dining room, Auntie Lehua clucked, "Too bad you don't look like your mother, Miki." She handed me the stack of dinner plates for the table I was setting. My aunts and uncles delighted in pointing out our similar traits as if these connected us like a giant web. The sons of Auntie Pua and Auntie Lehua were big men: bronze-skinned, square-shouldered, with generous smiles that framed husky laughs. The rest of us cousins shared features we could track through the generations: thick, wavy black hair, fair oval faces, black almond-shaped eyes, long lanky bodies, and the calm Ai'Lee disposition. This last trait I did not have.

My father overheard our conversation when he left his barbecue duty to get a glass of water. He joined us. "Everyone said Ellie's eyes were like heavenly full moons. Too bad, Miki. None of my kids got her eyes," he teased.

Auntie Vanda shook her finger at Kam. "You were lucky Ellie chose you."

My father smiled proudly. "Her waist was like a bundle of silk. I could touch my fingertips around her. Eighteen inches!" he gestured with his hands in a circle. "Too bad Miki didn't get her mother's figure, either."

Popo Ai'Lee walked in with a teapot and added that it was a shame I didn't have my mother's enchanting personality.

I whirled to face them. "What's wrong with me the way I am?"

Lehua, Vanda, Kam, and Lailee stopped, stunned.

"Lehua meant you look like an Ai'Lee, and I think we're beautiful," Vanda fluttered.

My father looked anxiously at his sisters. "It never bothered her before," he said. "Do you think she's ill?"

They tiptoed out.

I was used to my family comparing me to my mother, to what I was not. When I returned home I was treated—as all my cousins were—like the child I had been. To our aunties and uncles we would always be their little keikis, their children. It used to be comforting to hear their squeals of welcome, the joyous hugs, and the flower leis that accompanied our traditional greeting of abundant kisses. But they still saw me as Kam and Ellie's little Miki, Braxton's baby sister. I had changed.

Alone in Popo Ai'Lee's dining room, I sensed my mother's presence. The awe she inspired in the Ai'Lees gripped my father's family, even in death. I shivered with hurt, or was it the cool breeze that blew through the open sliding glass door? The scent of blooming tuberoses drifted into the room.

Through the flickering lightening, my mother glided into the room and placed her ornately decorated dish among the plain stoneware platters.

When she was alive, Ellie overshadowed everyone with her gold-edged platters of Cantonese-style noodles decorated with radishes, carrots, and cucumbers carved to resemble flowers and dragons. Instead of appreciating her artistry, I was embarrassed by her elegant displays in the midst of the Ai'Lee's simple ironstone platters. "Use a plain plate," I begged her.

"No," she would insist. Her dark eyes shone with concentration as she adjusted each delicate carving around the perimeter of her dish. Shiny brown curls fell from her flawless brow giving her an intent, girlish look. "Presentation is very important. Watch how I do this." Then she'd walk up to the buffet table, shoulders back, accepting the oohs and aahs, pleased with the effect; the creator as stunning as her creation.

Tonight, her eyes met mine and her smile filled the room with a glow.

"Welcome home, dearest," she said. Her voice, so melodious and warm, brought tears to my eyes. I reached out to her. When she wrapped her arms around me, I hugged her tight. I felt that warmth of being her little girl again, safely nestled on her lap, listening to bedtime stories. Her voice was so rich and magical that on Sundays, everyone in church would turn to search out the voice that sang clear and strong.

"My little girl," my mother said longingly. She ran her fingers through my hair. I had kept it long because she said she envied it, thick and heavy, whereas hers was a cascade of fine, dark curls. "So fair," she said, running her fingers along my cheek. Those words, irritating when I had wanted to be tan like my friends, were now dear to me.

"I miss you," I said softly.

"I know," she answered without words.

"I have so much to ask you."

Her face glowed. "My dearest Miki, follow your heart." I felt the touch of her fingers on my chest. "Find me here."

I begged her to stay.

"You know I am always with you, Miki. Always," she whispered. Her voice blended into a wisp of breeze. The scent of tuberoses dispersed in the wind. Then her image shimmered and faded into the night.

❧

Thunder boomed, and with the next brilliant flash of sheet lightning Braxton entered the dining room. "Dad's turkey is ready," he warned. "Ready or not, I think the cousins are headed in for chow." He closed his eyes and sniffed the air as if remembering.

He stared out the glass sliding doors. He said hesitantly, "For a moment, I thought Mom was here." The storm winds, sweet with rain and the scent of flowers, blew gently into the room. He cocked his head to listen. I didn't tell him he was right. We heard the sounds of the patio door opening and closing. Cousins streamed barefoot into the house carrying pupu trays, now empty. His twins, Bradley and Bernard, were asleep in their stroller, dreaming milk-sweet baby dreams.

Braxton eyed the buffet table. He plucked a slice of char siu, juicy barbecued pork. "Mmmm. Auntie Lehua's finest, the perfect balance of sweet and spicy." He chose a tall crisp celery stalk. "Ah, cream cheese with fresh crab!" He moved through the buffet, sampling and commenting.

"You haven't changed!" I scolded him. Mom would have disapproved of him picking through the buffet like a starving peasant.

"I have. I'm a mature, sophisticated, well-connected, hard-working family man." He eyed a tray of sushi and chose a couple from the back so their absence wouldn't be obvious. "When I'm under a lot of stress I'm forgiven a lapse of manners." Braxton's black eye was now a faded purple with yellowed splotches. Definitely not as impressive. I hoped he had eked out all the sympathy from his supporters the first few days of its glory.

"You can't do it all," I warned him. My cousin Reginald had just told me that Braxton had convinced his friends to help out in a mentor program for kids at risk, specifically vulnerable preteens, that he started back when he was single. His baseball clinic for seventh and eighth graders was a big draw. On Friday nights, Braxton had all his buddies teach boys and girls to play a mean, clean game. The gyms were now packed with supportive parents, aunties, uncles, siblings, and grandparents.

"I don't have a choice. You don't know how hard it is to be the eldest son in this family. I'm expected to be perfect in all things Chinese, American, and Hawaiian. I have to be the paragon of Confucian ethics and culture, savvy in American business, and aware of Hawai`i's issues. Men have no room for sensitivity or softness. Dad expects me to be the filial Chinese son, Sondra needs a husband who provides to the level of her family's expectations, the twins need a father, and the governor needs an effective deputy commissioner." Braxton selected a glazed baby-back rib dripping with Korean spices.

I hadn't thought of my brother from that point of view. "You've set high standards for yourself."

"No, society sets the standards. We meet or change them. Simple pleasures like this," he held out the rib, "make it worthwhile. Be glad you're a girl and not expected to carry on the family name. Popo sees all that is distinctively Chinese disappearing: the new world absorbing the old. She's worried that soon we'll all be the same as everyone else, like homogenized milk."

"Harry Matsui used those words when I saw him the other day. Like us…"

"And our Americanized ways. It's sad, but they're right. Ironic," he said with regret, "even the shave ice man worries when he sees his children turning American."

Yesterday I had taken Lailee for a drive along the Diamond Head side of O'ahu and back through rural Waimanalo. On one side of the freeway we passed the Hawaiian homesteads: rough wooden homes where children and dogs played on broad lawns landscaped with plumeria trees and hibiscus bushes. The azure and white ocean where the locals still cast their nets in the old style beckoned from the other side of the road. I pulled off to the quiet back roads of wood frame storefronts and dusty sidewalks. I swung by Matsui's Shave Ice and Grocery. "Shave ice?" I asked.

"Yes. Rainbow with ice cream," Lailee answered. "I have not been to Matsui's in a long time." She sat up and stretched her arms in front of her.

Harry Matsui, a smile permanently creased in his skinny face, waved from his customary seat on the weather-beaten bench in front of his storefront. Here, he talked story to anyone who passed by. He looked just as dark and wrinkled as when we were little Ai'Lees, thirsty and hot after a day at the beach. His hair, thick and black when I was a child, was now a wispy fringe across the top of his head. He wore a white T-shirt, rubber zoris, and swim trunks that had seen a thousand sunny days.

"Hi, Miki. Two rainbow with ice cream?" Harry Matsui asked with a quick, knowing nod. He jumped up and tugged a large block of ice out of the freezer. He centered the ice in a vise and flipped a switch that whirled it around a scraper. Within minutes, he had fashioned two cones of finely shaved ice with his hands and twirled three bottles of colored flavorings across the top of each to create a rainbow of red, yellow, and blue. "Okay, Miki. One dollar, please."

"Arrigato, Matsui-san," I thanked him. I placed a dollar on the wooden counter. I nodded to Mrs. Matsui, who leisurely dusted and wiped the shelves of canned goods and toiletries. Through the back door, wooden stairs led upstairs to where the Matsuis had raised their seven children.

"Long time no see you, Miki. You on vacation?" asked Harry. His smile was wide and white in the cool shade of his shop.

"Uh huh," I answered. I picked up the cones of shave ice from the wooden holders that held them upright on the counter.

He wiped his hands on a drip-stained apron. "When you come home for good, Miki?"

I shrugged. "I don't know. It's hard to leave here."

"Then mo' bettah you move back Hawai`i." He chuckled. "Kids," he laughed to his wife, "always want to be someplace else." Mrs. Matsui nodded from the waist and covered her laugh politely with her hands.

Harry Matsui walked me out and waved to Lailee waiting in the car. "You just like my kids, Miki. Seven I raise all the way through college. Now they live on the mainland. They send Christmas cards and come home in the summer with their children. My grandchildren speak such good English, they cannot understand when I talk. They don't know Japanese ways. Don't know what fun times we had when we were growing up in Hawai`i. Pretty soon, everyone will be same-same, like homogenized milk."

"Harry, that's what I tell Miki. She does not listen to me," my grandmother agreed.

—✿—

Towards midnight, the Ai'Lees hugged their farewells and clattered noisily down the front steps.

"Tonight we were all together—like old times," my grandmother sighed as we watched the taillights disappear down the hill.

"Don't you get together when I'm gone?" I asked in surprise. I didn't tell her that my mother had been with us, too.

"No, only us old folks. Everyone is too busy with children and jobs."

"No crabbing?" I asked. "No ghost stories on the beach? No afternoon swims while the teriyaki barbecues on the hibachi?" Popo Ai'Lee sighed and shook her head after each question.

I always imagined my family would continue the traditions of my childhood, of a territorial Hawai`i of the forties and fifties, a time of traditional values and community ties. Eleven years ago when Hawai`i became the fiftieth state, the younger generation embraced American culture with wholehearted enthusiasm. The sixties had brought the sexual revolution, the British cultural invasion, and television. But we were Ai'Lees, bound to our customs and traditions.

Lailee stepped wearily into the living room and motioned me to join her on the sofa. "When your mother was alive, she had the next weekend planned before anyone left. Ellie remembered who brought what foods and who made what best. Now you can organize it. You're like your mother."

"I'm not at all like my mother," I answered quickly.

"Aah," my grandmother sighed softly to herself. She looked down at her hands. Each wrinkle told a tale of meals prepared over open fires and gas stoves, of babies loved and disciplined, of passions lost long ago. She blinked back her fears and said, "I have been thinking how your friend, Alex, helped me when I fell. Tell me about him."

I leaned back and told Lailee how Alex had grown up in Kaua`i on the green slopes called Anahola, rode horses barebacked with his four sisters, and learned to run the vast Demming ranch under the watchful eyes of his father, William, and their indispensable manager, Eddie Kekaha. Demming wealth and power encompassed all aspects of industry and commerce now. I told her how Alex and I had raced through the rain at school and how we keenly competed in class. Alex's closest buddies carried the names of the old-time Hawai`i kama`aina families of Dillingham, Alexander, Baldwin, Montague, and Malone. Although the Ai'Lees and Demmings were separated by generations of anger and hate, Alex and I had become friends.

I didn't tell her about one hot afternoon in early fall when I had bounded barefoot out of gymnastics practice, headed for the track where Kelly Malone was running sprints. I usually stretched out in my blue practice leotard to study and pursue a tan while I waited for her to give me a ride home. I passed Alex in the deserted hall. He balanced an armload of books and a bag of photo canisters on one arm, and struggled with the key to a door with his free hand. He was casually dressed in a faded Hawaiian print shirt, khakis, and loafers, no socks.

"Hey," he called, "you're Kelly's new friend, aren't you?" I mumbled a yes. "Could you help me?" he asked. I slung my books and gym bag to one shoulder.

"What are you doing?" I asked when he piled his load of books in my arms.

"Developing pictures. Come on," he said, finally unlocking the door of the photo lab. "I'll show you how it's done." I remembered my mother's warnings and declined. Alex retrieved his books from my arms. "But you can't go barefoot in here," he warned, ushering me into the lab. He ignored my reluctance and fished my sandals out of my gym bag. I slipped them on.

Alex gathered chemicals from the refrigerator and poured them into assorted pans. He flipped on the air-conditioning and the developing lights. He showed me how to take the film out of the canisters and dip them in the developing trays in a timed and precise order.

The process fascinated me. "Why do you do this?" I asked. It was easy to talk to him when there wasn't anyone else around. He looked approachable in the red developing light. He was a skinny, broad-shouldered guy, a foot taller than I. His tousled brown hair, plagued by cowlicks, hopelessly flopped in his eyes.

"I like mysteries. A single image tells an entire story," he said. Alex wasn't athletic like his buddies and didn't play any competitive sports. But he loved finding stories in pictures.

"You see Kalia Gomes on this wave?" He held out a picture he had just developed. "He's got the wave under control, slightly ahead of the center, the break of the wave above him. This photo tells the whole story of Kalia's control, mastery, and," Alex chuckled, "luck! Here's ol' Trotter Dillingham. Slightly off-balance on his surfboard. He's lost it! A split second later, he'll wipe out!" He showed me more. I saw that my classmates—haole, Japanese, Chinese, Hawaiian, or hapa—all shared the same human foibles. We flirted, fell asleep in class, and made mistakes.

I shivered. The air conditioner was on high.

"You can't come in here with only a leotard," Alex scowled. He whipped off his shirt and threw it at me. When I put it on, I was wrapped in his scent, of hot afternoons on a sun-swept beach.

Alex's life opened up in black and white before me. He showed me close-ups of coral bricks from campus buildings and how the chisel marks meant they were hand-hewn. He pointed out the differences between lava rock construction and brick, and what it meant to the people who built these older buildings. His enthusiasm was infectious. He brought out his favorites and showed me which had balanced compositions and which were printable.

When we emerged from the darkroom, the sun had gone down. Kelly would have assumed I found another ride home and left if she didn't see me. It was past dinnertime.

Alex sensed my panic and offered me a ride in his old Woody. He cut his engine and coasted up to the front door so my parents wouldn't hear us. I remembered to give him back his shirt when I got out of his car. It was then that I noticed his eyes had turned deep azure blue, the most romantic color of the sea.

~✿~

Lailee's brow wrinkled. "You asked me if the Demming curse was real. I must warn you." She leaned forward and shook my arm. "I must tell you what happened while you were in San-Fran-Cis-Ko." It was the Demming curse, my grandmother said, that killed Alex's mother.

I had heard the legend of the mournful lament that rose from the land when the sugar planters and businessmen imprisoned Queen Lili`uokalani in her own palace and seized control of the islands. It was described as an eerie wail that reverberated from the mountains to the sea, from island to island. Five years later, in 1898, the United States annexed the Hawaiian Islands for its "protection." By that time the precontact native Hawaiian population of a million had dropped to 40,000. Less than one percent of the Hawaiians owned the lands of their ancestors. Now, some Hawaiians thought Hawai`i should separate into an independent, internationally recognized Hawaiian nation. Some advocated the nation-within-a-nation status with federal recognition as a Native American nation. Others desired to maintain the political status quo while pressing for redress, reparations, and full control of Hawaiian trust assets by Hawaiians.

Lailee said that one of the more militant groups demanded that all non-Hawaiians return their lands to the native people because, before European contact, the land was for all to use and share as their birthright. The militants targeted William Demming, one of the largest non-Hawaiian landowners. They gathered a hundred people to march in protest. No violence, they claimed: create enough attention to get in the news.

William Demming shook his red hair and howled with fury. He had rightfully inherited the land from his father, the fifth son of Arthur Demming. The land was an ancient ahupua'a, a pie-shaped territory encompassing all the land from the mountain to the sea. In the days of Hawaiian kings, the people living within each ahupua'a shared the bounty of the forest, taro and sweet potato areas, and fishing grounds.

When screaming agitators smashed through the front gate of his ranch and threatened his home, William ran out with a loaded gun. The marchers hesitated. Demming, a towering, bulky man, had lived his entire life on Kaua`i, except for four years of college on the East Coast. He was known as a fair man. But when provoked, he had a violent temper—as if all the anger and jealousy and suspicion of his ancestors were balled up in his heart.

His wife, Celie, was a patient woman with bewitching blue-green eyes that shimmered dark to light with her moods. She chided her husband to put away the gun. In a floral mu`umu`u, long and loose to protect her pale skin from the sun, she rushed out and held out her arms, pleading with the protesters to leave. But before his ranch manager, Eddie Kekaha, could stop him, William, his red hair flaring like a torch, advanced toward the unruly group. He angrily waved his gun and threatened to shoot. A protester rushed William and pushed the gruff rancher backwards.

Celie ran towards her husband to protect him. In the struggle, the gun went off.

My grandmother shook her head. "Celie died in William's arms. Luckily, he had four daughters and Eddie Kekaha to nurse him back from shock. Alex was not here. Later, local folks say Alex's girlfriend was killed about the same time as his mother. You know how people talk. Two deaths. Same time. They say it's the Demming curse. Remember what happened to their business and sugarcane after they took the land from the Ai'Lees. True or not, this is Hawai`i. One never takes such things lightly."

She ruminated on Arthur Demming's rivalry with Chun Ai'Lee over a century ago, the horrible deaths of Demming's sons, and Haunani Ai'Lee's mysterious drowning. Each generation had suffered devastating losses. The Demmings blamed the Ai'Lees for placing the curse. The Ai'Lees accused the Demmings of stealing their birthright.

This was the first time I had heard of Mrs. Demming's death. I had been on the mainland when she was shot, and Hawai`i news rarely made the San Francisco papers. We sat in silence, my grandmother and I, until the rain stopped.

Then I stepped out into the night and walked home alone, wrapped in the smells and tastes of the Ai'Lee party: Popo's bai-sun incense and Auntie Pua's fresh macadamia nut cookies. My ears throbbed with the quiet after the cacophony of happy Ai'Lee voices. I didn't realize how starved I had been for boisterous Ai'Lee laughter and carefree banter. In Hawai`i, our family lived contentedly with the contradictions in their life and culture—a family that had struggled, adapted, and endured for over a hundred years in Hawai`i and twenty-seven generations in China. Outwardly, they appeared to have assimilated. But in reality, they clung to their traditions, followed two-thousand-year-old Confucian ethics, and embraced ancient beliefs.

The Demmings had tried to change, too. William and Celie Demming had allowed local people to fish in their streams and along their beaches. They built wood cottages for their paniolos, some who had been with the Demmings for three generations. Yet the curse of an ancient rivalry hovered over them. Maybe this was another reason Alex had stayed away so long.

I missed this blend of reality and spirituality that I had grown up with in Hawai`i. I had become too logical and practical on the mainland. I craved the ghosts and spirits that crowded my dreams.

I opened my arms to the stars. "Are you there?" I called. The black night stretched before me. Whispers hung in the trade winds rushing down the valley. Voices murmured in the heavy rustling of the coconut trees. The late-night winds shifted, but I did not know if they spoke to me.

Then I heard the heavy ritual drumbeats in the distance. They were coming, the royal ghostly procession, across the valley floor. "O'io. Clear the path. Do not look upon us." The sacred chant of the ghostly kahunas announced the approach of the royal spirits. To avoid death, I should hide my eyes and fling myself to the side of the road. Instead, I stood defiantly against the wind. Ghost torches carried by invisible chiefs flickered high above the procession of shuffling feet.

I shivered and hugged my bare arms. Then I took a deep breath and dove down to the earth on my knees, fearing at the last minute to be one of the living dead. The wind swirled and howled with ancient voices. Chills, like the touch of lingering fingers, swept across my back. But this was not the touch of death. It was the touch of knowing. I gripped the grass until the pahu drums and ancient chants faded into the wind.

Reunion
with the Past

*M*y old friend Kelly Malone used to call me a dreamer, an optimist looking for rainbows in far-away places. She said she could look in my eyes and see my thoughts soaring over rivers and valleys unknown. She'd watched me turn over thoughts and ideas, picking them over like rocks in a river. It startled me when she'd lean over and tell me what I was thinking about, as if my face was an open book. It had been so long since I heard her voice that I was speechless when I answered the phone and heard Kelly's infectious laugh.

"Miki! You're home!" she screamed. "Ceci Wong said she thought she saw you at the symphony the other night!" Kelly was home for the summer and was gathering our old group together.

"Did you call Alex?" I asked.

"My buddy Alex!" she squealed. "Call him for me."

"I think he'd rather hear from you," I muttered ruefully.

"He's become a recluse. That man hasn't written or called since we graduated from college. He'll come if you ask. Do it for me," she pleaded—she had a dozen more calls to make.

I acquiesced. After all, it had been twelve years since I slapped and swore at him. Twelve years to mellow since that explosive evening. Upon his return, he had braved my father's ire to find me.

Alex and I drove to the Malone estate on the beach at Mokule`ia via the long route: through working-class Kalihi and Moanalua Gardens, past Pearl Harbor, known in our grandparents' days for its bountiful harvests of dazzling pearls and succulent shrimp, and through the plains between the Ko`olau Mountains and the Wai`anae Range where perfect rows of pineapples and sugarcane marched endlessly in the red volcanic dirt.

When we reached the ocean near the old plantation town of Waialua, we followed the two-lane road to the grass driveway of the Malone estate shielded by ironwood trees. Wide lanais surrounded the rambling wooden house. Bougainvillea vines in vivid purples twined around the covered porch. Behind the house was a fine-sand beach known to the locals for uniform waves ideal for body surfing. Beyond the rolling lawns and ironwood trees on the left were the horse stables. To the right were the tennis courts and volleyball nets. As teenagers, we had gathered here on the weekends when the Malones were home, whiling away tropical afternoons in the surf.

We returned today as adults with careers. Two dozen friends and their families were already scattered on the courts. We talked of where we had been and what we had done, the schools we had attended and left. We bemoaned careers attempted and readjusted. After five optimistic rounds of volleyball, we learned that the years had left us just enough energy to lay prone on the beach. We sighed with relief when lunch was served on the front lanai. When the heat rose in the afternoon, we stripped to

Tahitian print swimsuits. Those with young children laid them down for a nap while others scattered to body surf or sleep on the beach.

Kelly Malone and I headed for the serenity of the living room. We had been a contrasting pair of best friends in school. She radiated the honey-tanned look of the beach, that casual blonde look of shoulder-length hair kissed by salt air and sun. In contrast, my fair Ai'Lee skin never tanned and looked pale against my black waist-length hair. But Kelly and I had much in common. We could launch into abstract topics such as the value of personal fulfillment versus social expectations as easily as we discussed our current infatuations. Kelly had run track and I was a gymnast, so we had little time for after-school socializing.

Kelly had followed three generations of Malones to Cornell. Her parents flew to the East for her breaks and she spent her summers in Europe. Then Kelly married a classmate and her life centered around Hadley's family in Connecticut. Large extended families took precedence over friends while we were building careers and cramming family visits into two-week vacations. This was the first time in a decade that we had the leisure for more than a hurried chat.

Kelly leaned back in a rattan chair cradling her infant, Merilyn. I curled up on the couch next to her. The full, soulful sounds of Hawaiian slack key, ki ho`alu, wafted in from the back lanai. In the 1830s when Spanish cowboys came to Hawai`i with the guitar, Hawaiian cowboys called paniolo loosened the guitar strings to create a sound more suitable to Hawaiian songs. They played the bass with their thumb while picking the melody and improvisation with their other fingers. This technique, called Hawaiian slack key, created a melodious sound of unique tunings learned only by ear, from master to student.

Against the backdrop of rhythmic strumming and deft retuning with each song, Kelly and I chatted as freely as we had done in high school—a little gossip mixed with personal insights. Kelly was interested in my career and personal life in San Francisco.

I gave her the brief outline of my work, then confided, "I had a dream about Alex. Maybe it was the impetus that brought me home."

"Actually, I always thought you were going to get together with Alex, until he took off for the far corners of the earth," she said.

"Not likely. The last time I saw you," I reminded her, "you and Alex were cheek-to-cheek, flying to the mainland." Although Kelly was headed for Ithaca, New York, and Alex for Boston, they had arranged to fly together to San Francisco to catch their connecting flights. When I waved good-bye to them in the crush of classmates, family, and friends at the old Honolulu Airport, I knew I was waving good-bye for good. Even though Alex said he'd miss me, six thousand miles and four years were insurmountable obstacles when we were seventeen.

Merilyn stirred. Kelly loosened her bikini top. Beads of milk dripped from the nipples of her tanned breasts. "A cry at the right time and my milk drops," she said. "Just look at these hands."

Merilyn clutched Kelly's breasts with hands as fragile as tiny shells. Her rosebud mouth sucked desperately. Kelly laughed. "Nothing's so satisfying, Miki. This is love."

Kelly caught my eye. She felt something deeper than we had ever imagined as teenagers. Her voice was warm and content. "In these breasts are my life, Hadley's life, and Merilyn's life. I never thought about my body this way before." We laughed over our high school obsession to be thin and tan. "Miki..." Kelly hesitated, then shook her head.

"What is it? You never kept secrets from me before." I smiled, remembering our girlish dreams.

Kelly asked in a tentative voice, "Did you know that Alex used to be engaged?"

My heart sank. "Engaged? What happened?"

"A year after graduation, Hadley's folks had a dinner party. One of their guests, a Harvard professor, heard I was from Hawai`i. He asked if I knew one of his students named Alexander Demming. Alex and his fiancée were grad students on an archaeology research expedition. Their campsite was machine-gunned at Angkor." Kelly took a deep breath and continued. "I was sick when I heard about it. I couldn't imagine ... didn't want to think that Alex could be dead. Later I found out that Alex was the only survivor."

A prominent archaeologist, Dr. Xi, had chosen his most promising grad students to accompany him on this program with the Angkor Conservancy, financed by the Royal Cambodian government of Prince Sihanouk and France, under Bernard Philippe Groslier. It was rumored that the Khmer guerrillas and the Cambodian government both pillaged from the ancient temple sites and sold the exquisite statues, heads, and friezes on the international market.

I stared at her in stunned silence. My grandmother said Alex's girlfriend had died around the same time as his mother, but I had no idea they had been engaged, nor how horrific her death had been. We sat listening to the familiar voices of our friends: the chatter, the low tones, the nostalgic songs of our youth.

"Miki?"

"Hmm?" My thoughts were lost in the steamy jungles of Angkor.

"You didn't think he'd wait for you, did you?"

I snapped out of my reverie. "Of course not."

A half-smile escaped. "You hear him singing 'Ipo Lei Manu' with Trotter right now?" The voices of the men were gruff. We could see their heads thrown back in song, their fingers intently picking melodies. Forgotten words and forgotten chords exposed how long it had been. There was no mistaking the poignant love song written by Queen Kapi`olani. Legend told how she rushed down to the beach to await the return of her husband, King David Kalakaua, from his trip to San Francisco. When his boat came into view, draped somberly in black, she knew her king was dead. She fled to their summer home in Nu`uanu where she wrote this love song comparing her husband to the magnificent i`iwi bird, whose brilliant feathers adorned his magnificent royal capes.

Kelly's voice dropped. "You were Alex's first love."

She eased Merilyn to her shoulder and coaxed a burp. "You saw Ceci Wong? She only appears to be living the life of the wealthy married matron. In reality, she's living a role to please her parents. She's miserable. Don't live your parents' dreams. We all knew Alex was carrying a torch for you. He even put it in print—think of that picture in the yearbook. Everyone knew."

"Except me." I got up and paced restlessly.

Kelly shook her head. "Quit fooling yourself. You never gave Alex a chance. You lived your parents' expectations. Remember how we used to talk about what we were going to be when we grew up? Are you sure teaching is your one true passion? Is your brother Braxton still bossing you around? My last piece of advice is: loosen up, Miki. I don't want you to let life pass you by."

An angry tear shot down my cheek.

Kelly threw me a diaper that smelled of dried milk. "You okay?"

"No," I growled.

"Good." Kelly tossed her honey-gold hair back and challenged me, "What do you really want out of life, Miki? What's your one true passion?"

One true passion. We had spent hours discussing, dissecting, and philosophizing this concept. I rose to her bait and when we were done, we had inspected universal truths, honest commitments, and empowerment.

Kelly nodded off in the afternoon warmth. She roused herself after a while and left to lay down for a nap in a back bedroom with Merilyn.

I sat alone, enveloped in the smell of rattan and lauhala mixed with the drift of sea spray. In the old living room, polished wooden spears and well-thumbed books lined the mahogany walls. A kahili, probably used during the monarchy, stood half-naked in a corner, its feathers fallen from their mountings. In another corner, dried maile leis whispered of fog-kissed mountaintops.

I started from my daydream when I heard Alex's voice, deep and warm as the afternoon heat.

"How about a swim? The waves are too flat for body surfing right now and my fingers need to unkink." He plopped cross-legged at my feet and stretched his fingers back in a stiff arch. He smiled roguishly. When we were younger, we used to race out to the reef when the sun was sweaty-hot. We made a game of dodging the waves that crashed over our heads like frothy crowns.

I leaned my head back on the couch and nudged him with my toes. "In a while," I answered. "Kelly and Merilyn left to take a nap, and I was too lazy to move."

His hard edge from the other night had disappeared. In the languorous gaze of late afternoon, he looked as if his life had been anything but romantic. White strands coursed through his hair. The texture of his skin had hardened to the rough tan of a restless man challenged by ocean sprays and foreign winds. Creases in the corners of his eyes and the depth of his frown added gravity and intensity. While others laughed and joked, Alex's eyes had pulled back as if he were trying to remember if he had ever been young with this group of friends. Melancholy clouded his face. Then the darkness was gone, skillfully cloaked.

Alex reached over to an intricately carved and feath-ered spear and held it up to the light. "These ancient spears—Kelly's great-grandfather received those from King Kamehameha III. And that kahili," he gestured with a nod toward the royal standard, "one of the last from `Iolani Palace, was once covered with brilliant yellow o`o feath-ers. Too bad the black o`o only sported a single shock of yellow feathers. Four thousand birds died for that." He replaced the spear. "Ornithologists have returned to the Alakai Swamp near Mount Wai`ale`ale during mating season for the past ten years to count the endangered o`o. Four years ago they recorded the unanswered mating call of a single male in the rainforest of `ohi`a trees. Each year they returned to the same spot, never to hear him again."

I winced. The extinction of the o`o bird signified another way an old lifestyle, part of an ancient culture, had been destroyed. I felt pain for that last, lonely survivor.

Alex grabbed my hands so hard they hurt. "Ah, that upsets you, doesn't it? You get really quiet when things bother you or aren't perfect, don't you, Miki?"

His words opened a wound I thought had healed. "I thought you were my friend, Alex," I retorted.

"Always have been. Still am. But you've always been easy to read." The expression on his face made my heart lurch. He was right. My mother taught me to put on a seamless front; a well-bred woman hid all negative thoughts. Ellie paddled me for my rage when Braxton teased me to tears. She spanked me for slugging him on the head with a brick when he threw my dolls in the mud. She scolded that a proper girl doesn't climb walls and dare the neighborhood boys to see who could jump the farthest. To make matters worse, I could never lie; I revealed the truth in my face. So when I was worried or upset, I withdrew, holding my anger and fears within. But I could never hide my feelings from Alex.

His gaze shifted to the display of dried maile and pikake leis worn for traditional Hawaiian weddings. "I bet there's one here for every Malone wedding," he said. I felt the increased pressure of his hands around mine. Scented like crushed vanilla, the vines of dark green maile leaves symbolized fertility. Hawaiians intertwined them with pikakes, the flower of love.

In my head, I could hear my mother's admonishment, "Forget him." I heard Popo's words even louder: "He is trouble. I must warn you—the Demmings are cursed!"

Alex joined me on the rattan couch. He'd lost contact with all of us when he left for college. The rest of us had been so engrossed in having fun that he hadn't wanted to ask too many questions, or have to answer them.

I told him that Kelly flourished as a wife and mother in Connecticut. Her parents had been concerned about her marriage to a mainlander, but when the Malones met his family, they discovered they shared a passion for polo. The New England–Hawai`i marriage was blessed.

But Kalia Gomes and Peggy Maughan were gone. The Maughans had disapproved of their daughter living with Kalia on the North Shore. They demanded she move back to town and join the family's land-development conglomerate. Instead, she lived contentedly in an ocean-front cottage while Kalia, champion of the perfect deadly waves and shallow killer reefs off Banzai Pipeline, surfed the big ones at Sunset, Waimea, and notorious locales in California and Australia. Kalia's picture on the cover of *Surfing* magazine wasn't the Maughans' image of success, either. Even though Peggy profitably marketed Kalia's designs for surfing jams and shirts to a mainland firm, the Maughans ignored Peggy's invitations and personal pleas to come to their wedding. Then she was diagnosed with breast cancer. She died six months later.

Surfing legends from throughout the world paddled alongside Kalia when he carried Peggy's ashes out to sea and scattered them in the waters they loved. It made the front page of both local papers, the *Honolulu Star-Bulletin* and the *Honolulu Advertiser*. But Kalia never heard a word of sympathy from the Maughans.

Some said he couldn't go on without Peggy when he disappeared in that crushing wave the following December off Waimea Bay. High surf warnings had been up for twenty-four hours. No one could stop him from diving in with his longest and heaviest board. Some said the wave that took him was a rogue, over sixty feet tall, that glowed with an unearthly silver sheen.

Alex whistled softly. "Kalia was always happiest in the sea. Didn't the Maughans realize that most of us surfed? That didn't mean we were beach bums. Kalia was more talented than the rest of us. Remember when he won the Duke Kahanamoku Surfing Championships? We were only juniors then. He was our golden boy."

"At least Peggy was happy, if only for a few years," I ruminated.

"What's with Ceci? She cried when I asked about her family. Did I say something wrong?" Alex asked.

"You know she always planned to snag a Chinese doctor and live on Tantalus, like her parents?" I answered tentatively.

"She said so often enough. Her father called her Little Princess, and reminded her to find someone who could take care of her the way he did."

Ceci's parents didn't know that half the time their daughter's husband was called on emergencies he ended up in the arms of the mistress he kept in a Kahala condo. Ceci resolutely drove her children to school in her Mercedes and pretended that her life was perfect, but even her weekly facials couldn't erase the sadness that lingered on her perfectly made-up face. Ceci, once soft and gentle, found she was a tiger in the financial investment world. That was a game she excelled in.

Alex ran his fingers along my cheek. His sonorous voice was low. "We all make our choices. Ceci knew exactly what she wanted a long time ago. So did Kalia and Peggy." He cupped my face in his hands. "And you, Miki, how about your happy story?"

"According to Kelly, I haven't figured it out yet." She had been too perceptive, as usual.

He pulled me close against his body. "Don't pull back, Miki," he asked so gently I felt his voice tremble.

"No, Alex," I gasped. I pushed my hands against his bare chest. *Trouble*, Popo Ai'Lee called him.

He kissed me slowly. So slowly that time stopped, suspended between the steady beats of his heart. "Listen to me, Miki," he whispered. When I struggled, he held me tighter.

I felt his heat, the tautness of his muscles, and the tenderness of his kisses. All the emotions I had ever felt for Alex flooded back. His callused hands, his arms wrapped around my body, spoke to me. What we had tried to say with our eyes we now said with our hearts.

Together, we floated out the back door of the house to the beach, hands and hearts intertwined. After all these years, he was my friend. Always had been. Still was.

I gazed at the sea, my endless sea, the giver of life. I saw Peggy Maughan and Kalia Gomes skipping gaily along the tops of the waves. Peggy's tawny sun-bleached hair flew back from her buoyant spirit. She flung her arms back in joyous abandon. Kalia threw us a shaka sign, a local wave of love and aloha. His wide grin glowed against nut-brown skin. The last rays of sunset shimmered through their bodies. I reached out for them, but they were already waving good-bye. Hand in hand, they flung their arms towards us, engulfing us in their happiness like a warm wave.

Alex stopped. He had seen them too. Slowly, like the flush of the rising tide upon the sand, I wrapped my arms around him and inhaled his salty warmth, the heated smell of sun-kissed hairs on his bare chest. He buried his fingers in my hair.

Arms entwined, we wandered along the curling edge of the surf until the sun disappeared in dramatic sweeps of purple and orange.

Chapter Eight

The Cycle of
Past and Future

*T*he next morning, Auntie Vanda arrived at Lailee Ai'Lee's after my grandmother had finished her prayers. We heard the hum of her black Cadillac on the street and the click of her high-heeled sandals up Lailee's red stairs.

"Hui," she called, a Hawaiian "hello" that trilled the air like a dove's morning song. I opened the unlocked door before she got to the landing. We kissed and hugged our greetings. "Popo and I were just sharing tea and a thick slice of Portuguese sweet bread for breakfast. Want some?" I asked. Auntie Vanda was wearing lavender shorts and a matching T-shirt of soft suede cotton.

"Morning, Miki, you're up early. You'd think at 7:30 I could have found parking in Chinatown. Here's your grandmother's roast pork and soft rice noodles." Auntie Vanda handed me the four bags she carried in her hands and continued her chatter without taking a breath. "Take these in, sweetie, while I slip off my sandals. Everyone was already double-parked around O`ahu Fishmarket. Hi, Mom." A cloud of Chanel No. 5 followed Vanda to the kitchen. She untied the net bonnet wrapped around her lacquered curls and started unpacking her shopping bags.

"How much do you think I eat?" Lailee grumbled. She unwrapped the packages wrapped in pink butcher paper and red string, sniffing the fish, fruits, and vegetables for freshness.

"I'm cooking for two, you and me. That's why I wore these shorts instead of a dress. Whew, it's hot. Good thing this outfit is sleeveless. Poor Miki is spending her vacation listening to you complain all day. So I'm staying with you." Auntie Vanda looked around the kitchen with narrowed eyes. "And I'm cleaning house." She opened her purse and pulled out a pair of heavy rubber gloves. "I had a manicure and pedicure yesterday," she explained.

"I don't like the way you clean. I can't find anything afterward," my grandmother threw her daughter a defiant look. "You move my stuff here and there," she gestured with an emphatic sweep of both hands. "I like my things my way, where I put them," she complained.

Auntie Vanda smiled at me, a generous wide-eyed look of joy. "Listen to her! She's feeling better, don't you think? You take off now, Miki. You're young. Enjoy yourself while you're home."

"Humph! She's seeing Alexander Demming today," my grandmother muttered.

"Oh!" Auntie Vanda tilted her head and stared at me, wondering. "You mean the Demmings from Kaua`i? They had an old house in Kailua, where Celie lived with the children while they were going to school in Honolulu. The Outdoor Circle had a home tour there a dozen years ago." She turned to Lailee who was headed into the living room with her cup of tea. "Of course, I didn't go, Mom, but my friends told me about it."

⚬

No one had been in the Kailua house since Celie
Demming's death. When Alex returned to Honolulu, a
layer of dust seven years thick covered the floors and beds.
Unable to face the ghosts that lingered there, his first reaction was to slam the door and leave. Fortunately, his sisters
on the mainland remembered the name of their mother's
cleaning lady. It took Mrs. Morgado and her husband a
week to clean up the house and grounds. Alex had asked
me to help him get the house organized so he could stay
there when he was on O`ahu.

First, we went to Chinatown for fresh fruits and vegetables. We wove through the narrow sidewalks elbow to
elbow with locals carrying canvas and straw bags. A hundred years ago, Chinese men outnumbered Westerners in
the Islands. At the turn of the century, only Chinese and
Hawaiians frequented this area bordered by Nu`uanu
Stream and Honolulu Harbor. Now we could hear many
languages, including Tagalog, Korean, Vietnamese,
Japanese, and dozens of Chinese dialects, as well as English.
Buckets of tall heliconias and gingers in sun-bright colors
lined the sidewalks. Fresh tuna, whole mullets, trays of live
crab, fresh squid, and shrimp packed in ice scented the narrow aisles of O`ahu Fishmarket at the corner of King and
Kekaulike Streets. Mountains of leafy Asian vegetables,
Hilo-grown papayas, and Lanai pineapples enticed our
senses.

Alex, who had spent most of the past dozen years in
Southeast Asia, blended into the crowd with ease. He

plucked fruit under the scrutiny of steel-eyed Chinese grocers and sniffed the mangoes to determine their variety. After two hours, our fingers were numb with the weight of a dozen shopping bags.

We drove to the Demming house via the Nu`uanu Pali highway, through the Ko`olau Mountains separating the windward side of O`ahu from the leeward, Honolulu side. Alex detoured off the freeway and followed the ancient footpath up the steep cliff called Nu`uanu Pali. I turned to him, amazed. "You remembered my favorite drive." More than a dozen years ago, he would drive me home from school this way so we could breathe the intense jungle scents of the Old Pali Road. Wild waterfalls dropped from steep precipices of the Ko`olaus to the jungle floor. Occasionally, we paused at a break in the jungle where a driveway disappeared behind lava rock walls overgrown with the giant monsteria ferns, and fantasized what lay beyond. These were the estates of the old and moneyed families. A hundred years ago, you could see Honolulu Harbor from here, but that was before homes sprawled up the slope of the valley.

Nu`uanu Valley had once been the home of the Menehunes, the mythical native inhabitants. As the city moved deeper into the sacred lands of the Menehunes, modern builders moved multi-ton boulders to make way for new roads. The boulders would reappear in their original location the next morning. Menehunes, the locals whispered. Only the Kahunas who knew the proper prayers and offerings could appease them. Whatever work was done during the day was undone by the Menehunes at night. When I was little, I had heard stories about intricately engineered bridges that appeared overnight over mountain streams. *Menehunes*, the locals whispered, when they saw the tiny footprints in the mud. Ancient Hawaiian temples, heiaus, constructed of perfectly fitted stones, stood as testimony to their nocturnal engineering. Honolulu grew. The Menehunes retreated further into the valleys. All that remained were their bridges, fishponds, temples, and the stories of their heroic deeds that the locals told to their children.

We stopped at the Pali, the high cliff from which, legend says, the armies of O`ahu chose to leap to their death rather than be taken alive by Kamehameha in his quest to unite the Hawaiian Islands. Before us, green valleys spotted with homes stretched out to the curve of Kane`ohe Bay and whiteness of Kailua Beach. We saw that twelve years of building and development had chopped the landscape into sheared mountains. By now, we had fallen into a comfortable pattern of remembrances as if we were driving back into the past.

Alex turned off on a quiet Kailua street. At the end of the street, he pulled into a driveway lined by palm trees. Last week, the yard was littered with fronds and leaves, as expected, because this was the windward side of O`ahu, the first to get the storms and the prevailing winds unless the winds blew from the south. Today, it was pristine.

The gleam of the freshly polished koa dining table, chairs, and hardwood floors greeted us when we opened the front door. In the kitchen, cabinets and appliances had been scrubbed, the linoleum waxed, and the counters cleaned. We flung open the bedroom windows to the sound of mynah birds arguing on the front lawn, then made the beds with the recently washed linens Mrs. Morgado had stacked on the freshly-sunned beds. Finally, Alex slid open the dining room and living room doors that faced the pool and the beach.

From the outside, this single-story home, which was angled for vistas of the sea, blended humbly into its tropical setting. But the inside of the house reflected old Hawai`i. Family photos of the Demmings lined the halls: his sisters dancing the ancient hula kahiko, the family on horseback dressed in the sturdy palaka shirts of the Hawaiian cowboy, and Celie and William Demming smiling into the future from a sepia-toned wedding photo.

"Hungry?" Alex slipped his arms around me just as I paused in front of a photo of him on horseback. "I could ride before I could run, I've been told," he said.

"Ah, an adventurous man," I teased.

He bent down. His lips met mine. It was as if time had turned back a dozen years, to the days of warm afternoons and stolen kisses. He ran his hands down my arms. "I can't wait to show you how adventurous I can be. Come," he said, "sustenance first."

Alex opened the box of steamed Chinese pork buns we had picked up from Chinatown. Our stomachs growled in immediate response to their juicy aroma.

"Do I need to put this manapua on a plate?" Alex asked.

"No, we'll eat out of the box," I suggested. I was trimming a pineapple. Holding it in my left hand, I sliced out the eyes in a diagonal pattern, then halved the fruit on the chopping board before cutting slices a quarter inch thick.

"My kind of woman," he exclaimed. He walked out with the buns, a handful of napkins and a carton of milk. He came back for glasses and a couple of beach towels, which he took out to the patio where padded chairs and a glass-topped table faced the ocean.

Over a barefoot lunch on the patio, Alex reminisced about the days following high school. An East Coast college far from home would be his last fling before spending the rest of his life in rural Kaua`i. But his life took a turn one chilly day when he wandered into the Peabody Museum. The exploration of ancient civilizations and cultures captured his imagination. It was the same thrill of discovery he felt playing hide-and-seek with his sisters along the wild Kaua`i coast. He told of sliding down the side of a cliff as a child and landing at the foot of a forgotten heiau. The air was still and cool. No birds sang in the tall white trees. Tracing the rugged petroglyphs with his fingers, he heard the spirits of the ancients calling to him.

I heard the tension in Alex's voice when he described neighboring lands where the perfectly fitted lava-rock walls of the ritual heiaus were gone, buried under the dazzling splendor of a luxury resort hotel. Sculpted golf courses swept over ancient Hawaiian home sites. Tourists scampered in the sacred bathing pools of Hawaiian royalty. His voice bristled. Anger glinted through his reserved demeanor. Then the hard edge disappeared like a blade beneath the waters of a reflective lake. I wondered how much he had changed, this shy friend of Kelly Malone.

He heard that cousins he had never met, successful in business and government, had ambitious plans now that Hawai`i was a state. This meant a lot to his father, who had turned to politics after his mother died. William, who loathed leaving the safety of Kaua`i, had asked Alex to stay in Honolulu and help them. Alex shook his head, "I have no interest in politics."

He leaned forward. "Ready for a swim?" When he slipped off his T-shirt, I saw scars that had not been there before, tanned as if they had spent years in the jungle heat.

"No suit," I apologized. I stood up and cleaned off the table.

"I'll find one for you," he answered quickly. "My sisters left some clothes in their closets." He picked up our lunch dishes and slipped back into the house.

The pool, newly cleaned, reflected a tranquil turquoise sky. How many afternoons Celie Demming had returned from shopping and found a gang of us studying by the pool. She'd walk out with trays of guava juice to where we lay working on our tans, textbooks open. She chatted with Kelly Malone, smiled at the rest of us, and left us to our books. Our minds were always somewhere else, of course.

I heard the phone ring and Alex's voice. He would be awhile. So I grabbed a beach towel and headed for the pool. I took off my blouse and shorts and lay down under one of the palm trees. The waves were steady on this sunny day, warm and rhythmic.

I woke to Alex's cold shadow standing over me. "Don't get up, Miki," he said. "I found one of Casey's smallest bikinis and a bottle of baby oil. It reminded me of how we used to oil up every time we went swimming."

"I could never tan," I mused.

Alex straddled my back and poured the oil in his palms to warm it up. "Am I too rough?" he asked. His hands were callused and hard, but he hadn't lost his touch. No, I shook my head. His hands were moving in slow concentric circles from my back to my legs. Alex was talking but I was floating away. "That was my father on the phone. My father's calling in all his favors from his business associates to guarantee that a Demming will be the governor's next deputy commissioner. He gave me a list of calls to make for him," he groaned.

"Turn over," he said. I rolled on my back. Alex slipped off my bra and poured more oil on his hands.

Only then did I realize the implications of what he was saying. I grabbed his wrists to get his attention. "You mean Chris Demming?"

"Yes. I don't even know him. He grew up on the Big Island, a graduate of Kamuela." Alex's hands were on my breasts, circling them gently, then moving down my abdomen in an erotic rhythm. "Forget him." He slipped off the rest of my clothes and lowered his body onto mine. The slip of his skin against mine was as sensuous as his probing kisses.

"Stop." I held him back with both hands on his chest. "You and your father are pulling strings for Chris Demming?"

He slid his legs between mine. His voice was honey hot and low, a deep growl that pulled at my thighs. "I'm pulling your strings now." His hands skimmed down my back and lifted my hips seductively against his.

"Take me home, Alex," I gasped. Slick with oil, I slipped from under him and grabbed my clothes.

"What is it, Miki? What did I say?" He scrambled to his feet and grabbed for my arms as I streaked to the patio. He was obviously aroused, but I was too mad to stop.

"My brother Braxton is favored for that appointment." I was so angry I shook as I dressed. "He doesn't have anyone pulling strings for him. All he has his name, his reputation. He's doing it on his own merit. I know politics in Hawai`i have always been crooked, but my brother deserves a fair chance. No one is going to take that from him." I threw Alex his T-shirt and grabbed his car keys on the way to the door.

"Damn it, Miki," Alex yelled. He thundered out the front door behind me, his scowl as foul as his temper.

Chapter Nine

The Ai'Lee Ladies

$\mathcal{P}$opo, my aunties, and I cruised the freeway that bypassed the glistening towers and crowded streets of downtown Honolulu. I frowned at the sterile Makiki high-rises that obliterated once pristine views of the sea. Auntie Vanda pointed out where she used to live in Mo`ili`ili. Their once-colorful neighborhood of curved roof bungalows and hibiscus hedges had been razed for a new state highway. The new freeway was now flanked by unimaginative apartment squares with flat rectangular balconies.

"Here! Turn off here!" Auntie Vanda pointed to the Koko Head exit. I swung off the freeway and shifted the Plymouth into low gear. It chugged slowly up the precipitous grade and hairpin turns of Kaimuki Heights. Popo Ai'Lee gripped her seat as we climbed higher, higher, higher. She loudly exhaled when we pulled into Auntie Pua and Uncle Roland's garage.

The Ai'Lee ladies, dressed in bright cotton blouses and shorts, leapt out of the car as soon as I turned off the engine. I unlocked the trunk, lugged out the two bags of food, and followed them into the house. Auntie Pua stood at her open door, accepting our kisses as we walked in.

Like conquering Amazons, my aunties bustled through the house dusting, vacuuming, and cooking. And while they worked, they inquired about each other's health, talked about nieces and nephews and grandchildren, and argued about recipes and, of course, the planting of flowers, their unifying passion.

My grandmother had named all her daughters after Hawaiian flowers. Pua is the Hawaiian word for "flower" and thus, the name of her eldest daughter. Since red is the Chinese good-luck color, she named her second daughter for the brilliant red Lehua blossom. Her third daughter had such a terrible temper as a baby she'd hold her breath until she turned purple, so she was named for the exquisite purple orchid called Vanda.

I tied my hair back in a ponytail and headed upstairs to the library. I oiled the rosewood nesting tables my mother had sent to Pua and Roland when she visited her grandaunt in Hong Kong. I purged years of dust from each Chinese antiquity crammed on the shelves. Reginald was right: the house hadn't changed in years. His favorite carving of the old man with a fishing pole tending the water buffalo was on the piano where it had sat for thirty years. Impulsively, I placed it on the coffee table. I rearranged the glazed statues of the Eight Immortals from their rigid row into a more aesthetic stance, arranged the Chinese platters by chromatic shade, and regrouped the jade carvings so sunlight would dance off their surfaces with a translucent glow.

My cousin Reginald arrived at lunchtime with a white pastry box tucked under a husky arm. I leaned from the library balcony above the entry. "It must be Aloha Friday.

That shirt looks great with your tan," I greeted him. He wore a Hawaiian-print shirt, a pattern of green ferns against a muted blue background, tucked into his slacks.

"Hey, Miki. Howzit! It's a break from the starched shirt and tie I have to wear everyday," he agreed as he kicked off his shoes and socks at the door. Aloha Friday had begun as an idea to boost the flagging Hawaiian apparel industry and encourage local people to wear the Hawaiian-print shirts and mu`umu`us that tourists loved. Businesspeople welcomed the change. Every Friday, downtown Honolulu blossomed in Hawaiian prints of sophisticated designs and business conversations lightened. The industry of designer mu`umu`us and Aloha shirts flourished.

"Come up, Reginald," I called. "I want your opinion."

My cousin bounded barefoot up the steps. He shouted, "Hey, this room looks a lot better, Miki. You've always been good at organizing and arranging."

"Thanks. Does your mother know the real reason her sisters and Popo come?" I asked in a hushed voice.

"Of course. Her Parkinson's is getting worse but she'd never ask for help. This way, she gets to have company. And it gives the Ai'Lee ladies an excuse to get together." Reginald surveyed the room slowly. "Wow, so that's what was under all that grit!" He picked up a fat laughing Buddha with a dozen children clamoring on its shoulders and tossed the large porcelain statue in his hands. "Yep, old Buddha looks a lot happier!"

"Have respect!" I commanded. "Popo would have spanked you for that remark." I tossed my head so my ponytail whipped past his face as I headed downstairs.

Reginald stopped me. "I'm just kidding, Miki."

I playfully aimed a kick at his shin but he leapt aside.

"To let you know how observant I am," Reginald said smugly. "I happen to know you've been seen around town with a certain rancher."

I stopped, then turned away, shaking my head. I had forgotten how sharp Hawaiian eyes are and how quickly the grapevine worked.

"Who is he, Miki?" my cousin asked, grinning.

I continued down the stairs. "An old classmate."

"What does your dad say about you dating Alex Demming?" Reginald teased.

"Nothing. I'm not seeing him anymore." I had settled into a comfortable rhythm; I saw my grandmother every morning, spent afternoons with cousins at the beach, and spent evenings with my father and aunts.

"You know Honolulu. Nothing you do goes unnoticed. I don't know Alex personally, but I see his uncles and cousins at the capitol all the time." Reginald put his arms around me. "Poor Miki. You've had more rules for growing up than anyone else I know."

He thought that strict parental guidelines, like my mother's, worked for the older generation, not for us. My parents focused on my faults as a way of teaching me the right way so that I would always strive to do better. Instead, I felt I could never please them. "Look at you. You work long hours to establish yourself in your career in a city far away from home. You're independent. Now you have a boyfriend who's exactly the person your parents would disapprove of: a Demming who lives on the land that was taken from the Ai'Lees under suspicious circumstances. And this Demming has two deaths already staining his past. Miki, you're as defiant as your mother."

I flushed. "I am not defiant."

"Auntie Ellie blew the top off her very proper family when she decided to marry Uncle Kam. Can you imagine? Popo Ai'Lee told me that for our parents' generation, marrying someone who spoke a different dialect of Chinese was considered a mixed marriage. Your mother must have been a feisty one."

"She was not feisty," I defended hotly.

"Whoa, Miki, it's okay. But I have to warn you about the Demmings."

I turned to him, eyes snapping. "Popo already has, a dozen times. I know everything comes down to money and land. Four generations of death and deceit." I huffed with exasperation. "Do you really think there's a Demming curse?" I wanted the local version, our generation's version, of the old legend. Reginald, the most Hawaiian-looking of my cousins, had an easygoing manner that loosened tongues and stimulated long-forgotten memories.

He crossed his muscled arms over his chest and lowered his head in thought. Then he looked up at me, his brown eyes soft and sad. "You should have seen the public support for the Demmings after Celie was killed. To this day, William finds ti leaf baskets of fresh fish, live lobster, bananas, and mango bread on his porch every day. Alex's fiancée was killed the same summer, within a month of his mother's death. A coincidence?" Reginald frowned. "Or a consequence? This is Hawai`i. Yes, people believe in the Demming curse. Be careful," he warned. He put his arms around me and I leaned my head on his wide, comforting shoulders.

"I checked on this Chris Demming. His grandfather is Arthur Demming's fourth son, one of the five that took our Ai'Lee land, or, in their version, legally won the entire ahupua`a in repayment of a gambling debt. Haunani Ai'Lee conveniently drowned in Honolulu Harbor so he could not dispute their claim. Dr. Harrison Ai'Lee, son of our grand-uncle Kekailoa Ai'Lee in China, had gone to the Big Island when there was an outbreak of leprosy. He diagnosed Chris's grandfather and exiled him to the leper colony of Kalaupapa on Moloka`i. Kalaupapa was a living hell in those days; the lepers were left to forage for themselves in a valley bordered by sheer rock cliffs and the shark-filled Moloka`i Channel. But Father Damien had begun a mission at Kalaupapa. Some say Demming became a devout Christian who prayed that his sons and daughters would be spared the misfortune of his ancestors."

"Were they?" I asked.

"Not if you believe the gossip. But Chris Demming and his cousins plunged into politics after college. Politically, they practically own the Big Island. Of course, locals remember their history."

Local knowledge was impossible to outrun. When Arthur Demming's eldest son tried to revive their shipping company, he thought he could turn a handsome profit by running arms to rebels who were determined to overthrow the Manchus who had ruled China since 1644. His ship, loaded with guns, was captained by Demming's second son. Everyone knew it was an Ai'Lee son of Chun Ai'Lee's second son who prospered in China, who seized the Demmings' ships hiding behind the rocky shores of Silver Mine Bay on Lantau Island.

Ai'Lee unceremoniously severed the heads of the two eldest Demming brothers and left them to rot on pikes in Hong Kong's Victoria Harbor as a warning. Demming's third son caught the bubonic plague in 1900 just before the city's health officials set the fire that destroyed all thirty-eight acres of Honolulu's Chinatown. Demming's fourth son was banished by Dr. Harrison Ai'Lee to the leper colony of Moloka`i. Frightened by the horrific deaths of his first four sons, Arthur Demming ordered his youngest, Alex Demming's grandfather, to never step off the Demming lands of Kaua`i.

We sat quietly on the sunny landing listening to the Ai'Lee women chatter in the kitchen. They spoke English in a musical lilt, with the hint of the many languages that influenced our speech. They mixed in occasional words in Chinese—for there are emotions and words in Chinese that cannot be expressed in English. The clatter of plates signaled that lunch was on the table.

By the time we got downstairs, Popo Ai'Lee had laid out papaya salads with sliced shitake mushrooms and mango. Auntie Vanda brought out tea for Popo Ai'Lee and guava juice for us.

"All right," Auntie Lehua demanded, peeking into the pastry box. "Who dared to bring these malasadas?" The odor of the buttery Portuguese doughnuts wafted through the kitchen—a rich scent reminiscent of moonlight stops at the bakery on the way home from picnics in Kapi'olani Park. Their light dusting of sugar sparkled sinfully.

"I did, Auntie," confessed Reginald. "I visited the parents of one of my clients on the way over. They made this fresh batch before I left their bakery. Seems their son enjoys surfing with me instead of hanging out on the wall with his old gang at Ala Moana Beach."

"How am I going to keep my figure if you keep tempting me?" Auntie Lehua scolded.

We laughed at the thought. The Ai'Lee women were tall, willowy, and small-bosomed. This last fact had disappointed my well-endowed mother when it was obvious I took after the Ai'Lees.

When we sat down for lunch, my aunts and grandmother fluttered around Reginald. It was typical of the nurturing women in my family to hover around our men, the focus of our lives.

After lunch, my cousin leaned back from his empty plate. He observed, "Looks like you're feeling better, Mom."

"Much better. I take my time," Auntie Pua answered. She picked slowly at her papaya salad. "When your Dad gets back from tennis, we'll go for our evening walk in the new park along the waterfront."

"Where the kids slide down the grass slopes with cardboard?" asked Auntie Lehua. Auntie Pua nodded.

"Sounds like ti leaf sliding," Auntie Vanda exclaimed.

Reginald and I stared in surprise. As kids, we used to sneak off to the steepest slopes after a good rainfall when the mud was slippery slick. Nothing could compare to the death-defying thrill of speeding down steep muddy slopes. We couldn't imagine the Ai'Lee ladies whipping down the steep forest trails of Nu`uanu and Manoa on a handful of ti leaves. A ridiculous thought!

Auntie Vanda tossed her head. "We had so much fun hiking up in the mud. A whole gang of us—ten to twenty—would go together. Kam was always the first one down—the daredevil—to find the quickest run. Pua was too cautious. She would stick out her feet to stop when she came to a tree. No one wanted to follow her. Too slow. But Lehua, we were pretty wild, weren't we?" My aunts cast a sly look at Popo Ai'Lee. Poor reflexes led to broken backs, arms, and legs. Consequently, we never told our parents when we took off to the Hawaiian forests. From Popo's wide-eyed stare, she had never been consulted, either.

Auntie Lehua and I cleared the dishes while Auntie Vanda brought the malasadas box to the table with the coffeepot and six rough-sided mugs.

"Reginald, Mrs. Hayashi who lives in front of me has Parkinson's," Auntie Lehua said, deftly pouring his coffee. "She's much worse than your Mom."

"You mean the Mrs. Hayashi who used to bring us boxes of mochi?" I asked. I remember the wrapped Japanese desserts shaped like exquisite flowers and fishes made from pounded rice flour.

"Same one. Mr. Hayashi has been dead a long time now. Her daughter and son-in-law live with her. Her daughter confided that her mother is afraid of going into her own room. Her mother screams, 'Reiko! Why are all these people here? Tell them go away.'"

Popo Ai'Lee leaned back and asked, "What does her daughter say?"

"She tells her mother no one is there. Her mother insists they are, all in ancient kimonos. They fill her room, she says. No place for her to stand. And her dog barks and barks."

Auntie Pua lowered her voice. "Well, you know some people can sense things. Some people have 'the eyes.'" My aunts and grandmother nodded knowingly.

"Any of you have 'the eyes' to see the latest from the Capitol?" Reginald held out the open box of malasadas. The aunties sighed as if in protest, but each plucked one from the box. "I just came from there, and I'll have you know that my cousin, our shining star of Hawai`i politics, has made us all proud."

"Reginald, get on with it. What?" Auntie Pua gestured impatiently at him with her free hand.

"Braxton was confirmed as the governor's new deputy commissioner. He will have a big budget and a big office. The official swearing-in is Friday afternoon."

The Ai'Lee ladies clapped and talked at the same time. Braxton Ai'Lee had succeeded! I was ecstatic that I could share this moment of victory with them. Family always came first, my mother said. I couldn't help wishing my mother was here, too. But maybe she was.

"In the governor's announcement to the legislature today, he said he owed it to the State of Hawai`i to make this appointment based upon 'meritorious qualifications.'" Reginald explained that the local buzz was that the governor's supporters had pressured him to appoint Christopher Demming instead.

My aunties nodded, pleased.

"Well, the Demmings should have known better than to upstage an Ai'Lee," said Auntie Pua.

Reginald shook his head. "Mom, that rivalry is over a hundred years old, from the days of the monarchy. Our generation feels it's time we moved on. Hawai`i is a state now, and we have bigger issues facing us."

"Humph!" my grandmother exclaimed. The Ai'Lee ladies glanced quickly at her. "It is not over yet." She wagged her finger at him. "The Demmings are the cause of their own downfall. And each generation of Ai'Lees is linked to them."

Auntie Pua, Auntie Lehua, Auntie Vanda, and Auntie Verna stared out the window, at their hands, anywhere to avoid meeting Lailee's glare.

"Never rejoice when your enemy falters, or their curse becomes your own," Lailee warned.

My aunts sat still, unusually silent.

Auntie Pua held out the box of malasadas. "Another, anyone?"

I felt a collective breath being held.

Reginald plucked one from the box and stood up. "I can see you ladies have much to discuss. I think it's safer at work."

At that, the Ai'Lee ladies stood up and protested loudly. I wished I could have left with him when they teased him out the door.

"How about you, Miki? When are you going to get married?" asked Auntie Pua. We regrouped at the kitchen table for more tea. "We'd like to plan your wedding."

Auntie Vanda leaned forward, eyes lit with visions of white lace. "Your mother dreamed of a big family wedding with a thousand guests."

Auntie Lehua got up to boil more water. She glanced mischievously over her shoulder from where she stood at the sink to fill the tea kettle. "Not only are we waiting to plan your wedding, but your father is anxious for you to give him grandkids." She laughed when I choked on my tea.

In answer to their question, "How's your Dad?" I grumbled that he treated me like a little girl. He wouldn't let me drive when we went anywhere. When he did give me the car, he watched until I was out of sight. When Braxton was around, he deferred to my older brother on every decision. My aunts laughed and said, "That's the Chinese way," as if I was doomed to kowtow forever to my father's wishes and my eldest brother's whims.

Auntie Pua shook her head. "You misunderstand, Miki. When we lived in Manoa Valley, Kam had a friend, Don Hing, five years older, who looked after us like big brother. Don started his family right out of high school. All three of his children became doctors, including his only daughter. But your father didn't get married until he was thirty-five."

"He had family responsibilities," Lehua explained. "When our father died, Kam quit school and went to work."

"A good job at O`ahu Railway," Popo Ai'Lee added proudly. "A clerk."

Auntie Pua continued. "He made sure our younger brother and sisters finished school."

"And bought me my house," Popo affirmed.

"He knew his duty and responsibility to his family," Auntie Vanda agreed. "Only after he fulfilled his obligation did he think about his own future."

Auntie Pua leaned back, her coffee cup poised in mid-air. "In school," she said, "you were filled with dreams of going away to college like your classmates. Ellie said you studied hard all the time. Won scholarships. Ellie and Kam were so proud. But Don Hing warned your father that for girls, a profession was a waste of time. He told your father, 'Don't let Miki be a doctor or attorney. No Chinese boy will marry her. My daughter finished medical school ten years ago. Still not married. Gives me no grandchildren. Puts her career first. I wasted rice on her.'"

Auntie Lehua turned to me and lowered her voice. "In those days, you were peculiar if you didn't marry."

I thought that after a hundred and twenty years in Hawai`i, the Ai'Lees would have assimilated into the fabric of Western society, blended in to Hawai`i's famed melting pot. But I still felt bound in servitude to the old Confucian ethics dating to the sixth century.

Auntie Pua said gently, "Kam wants you happily married. A professional career would be in the way. What Chinese man would want you?"

My grandmother reached over and patted my shoulder. "He always has your interest at heart, Miki. Family has always come first for the Ai'Lees."

The Ai'Lee ladies watched me hopefully, nodding in unison. I had always thought I would have a life like theirs: tightly entwined in the family rituals of weekly visits, births, weddings, and funerals. They knew what was expected in their lives. I thought I knew, too. But their pattern didn't work for me.

Chapter Ten

The State Capitol

*B*raxton took the afternoon off on the day of his swearing-in to give us a private tour of the new state capitol building, which had been completed in 1969. He and Sondra picked us up an hour before the grand event. Dad wore a tropical-weight suit. In Braxton's honor, I wore a sunny yellow cheong-sam. Sondra was wearing an ivory Oleg Cassini silk shantung with matching shoes and handbag. Her parents would join us later with the twins at our celebratory dinner a few blocks away, at Wo Fat restaurant in the heart of Chinatown.

My brother zoomed his newly waxed New Yorker into a coned-off space near the new building. "How about this privilege, Dad? They gave me a parking space just steps from my office." He nodded at the architectural edifice in front of us, leapt out, and rushed to open the car doors for his father and wife.

I stepped out on my own after taking a minute to adjust the strappy three-inch heels I had picked up yesterday at pricey Liberty House. Then I stared at the freshly-painted block letters under my feet. "Braxton, your name is painted in this parking space," I exclaimed. "Look, Dad. It says, 'Ai'Lee, Deputy Commissioner.'" I pointed them out for my father.

My father slapped Braxton on the back for the tenth time today.

Sondra beamed at her husband with an adoring sigh. Her hair was newly styled in a pouf, which flipped up in curls at her chin. She looked elegantly perky.

"All right, famous brother, give us that tour of this twenty-five million dollar edifice," I ordered.

He slipped on his suit coat and tucked my arm into his. Sondra and my father followed, arm in arm.

The five-story Hawai`i State Capitol, open-roofed at its center, was designed to evoke symbols of Hawai`i. My brother pointed out how the two volcano-shaped legislative chambers housing the Senate and the House of Representatives flanked the open courtyards. Their two-story cone shapes symbolized Hawai`i's volcanic and oceanic origins. Flaring sixty-foot pillars represented our royal palm trees. The reflecting pool, a glassy sky blue, mirrored the Pacific Ocean that surrounded our islands.

When he opened the door to the Senate chambers, now vacant during the break, I could smell the scent of wood mingled with the aroma of flowers in the air-conditioned chambers. Braxton explained that the interior of the chambers were lined with indigenous Acacia koa wood from the Big Island of Hawai`i. The rich color of the wood gave the massive rooms a uniquely Hawaiian ambiance.

The state capitol had two entrances. One faced mauka, toward the mountain, and the other faced makai, towards the sea. Over each entrance hung castings of the Seal of the State of Hawai`i, which weighed four tons apiece. I noticed our state seal was an edited version of the original

Royal Hawaiian Coat of Arms, and included our local flora and an image of King Kamehameha I.

Over the capitol flew both the American flag and the Hawaiian flag. Braxton said that most people were surprised by the Union Jack in the field of red, white, and blue stripes in Hawai`i's flag. Designed for King Kamehameha I in 1816, our flag reflected both the British and American influences on the Hawaiian kingdom. My father quipped that perhaps wily King Kamehameha wanted to discourage pirates from attacking his Hawaiian ships by making them look like both the American and British ships.

After Braxton's tour, he led us upstairs to the governor's office. *E komo mai*, "Please Come In," were the welcoming words on the oversized doors. We entered to a roar of applause. Reginald had brought Lailee Ai'Lee and seated her near the podium so she could easily see and hear. We greeted them all.

Governor Burns, a patrician, white-haired statesman, presented a polished speech praising Braxton Ai'Lee. My brother accepted his appointment with dignity and a few jokes. After the ceremony, the governor discreetly withdrew and turned his sumptuous office over to the festivities.

The polished wood doors were thrown back and the musicians set up. It only took a ukulele, a guitar, and a bass to bring the party to life. Braxton's fellow staffers brought out orchid-decked trays of pupus: sushi, rumaki, fried won tons, Spam musubi, and sliced pineapples.

Braxton, buoyantly receiving leis from every single friend, coworker, and Ai'Lee there, could barely see over the flowers around his shoulders. He savored every second of his moment and was in no hurry to leave.

Since my father was engaged in a discussion with a young Japanese staffer about the state's budget problems, and Popo Ai'Lee was being congratulated by friends and family, I had time to sneak out for another look at the capitol building. I wanted to study each element the architects had designed in this building. It was truly distinctive, a modern contrast to the flanking buildings: a royal palace and a queen's mansion.

On the makai side facing the sea, I saw `Iolani Palace, the only royal palace on American soil. King Kalakaua built the palace 1882 in the American Florentine style. In one of the ornate tower rooms, our last ruling monarch, Queen Lili`uokalani, had been imprisoned by the Americans who overthrew her government. For nine sad months she prayed for her people and stitched a poignant quilt reflecting her love and hopes for her Hawaiian people.

On the mauka side facing the mountain, stood elegant Washington Place, former home of Queen Lili`uokalani and now the official residence of the governor of Hawai`i. After her regime was overthrown, the queen returned to this graceful 1846 Greek Revival mansion where she had lived prior to assuming her reign. Washington Place, surrounded by lush tropical gardens, continued as the center for royal gatherings through the three governments that followed.

I wondered what the royal ghosts would say about the twentieth-century architecture standing in their midst. Art by local artists was displayed in the capitol's halls, offices, and chambers. But on the side of the building facing the mountain, I was perplexed by a square bronze sculpture. The seemingly grotesque figure wore a round-rimmed hat and a long cloak. He held a cane but his hand was deformed and missing digits. The face of the figure, with prominent bulging eyes, seemed unnaturally misshapen. I was struck by my first reaction to the sculpture, by the emotions of pain and of intense inner suffering it evoked.

"Leprosy is shockingly hideous," remarked a slow, low voice behind me.

I turned, startled by the intrusion. I recognized the squarish face and platinum blond hair, now parted and combed neatly to the side, from the pictures Reginald had shown me the first day I returned to Hawai`i. The man, about thirty, five-foot-ten, barrel-chested, and solidly built, wore his Hawaiian shirt tucked into his trousers and his khakis belted. "Aren't you Christopher Demming?" I asked.

He bowed his head in acknowledgment. "And you are...?" he enunciated gingerly.

"Miki Ai'Lee." I held out my hand. His huge square hand was white and soft.

Chris attempted a smile, but the wires around his jaw limited his lip movements. He lifted his eyebrows in recognition. "Ah! Braxton's sister. You have quite a family gathering upstairs. I congratulated your brother earlier today." We shook hands amicably. He peered at me with gray eyes that sparked with shrewd intelligence. "I saw you studying one of my favorite sculptures." He waved at the statute in front of us. "Meet Father Damien Joseph de Veuster, the Belgian priest who lived and died among the lepers on the Island of Moloka`i. It caused quite a controversy when it was unveiled last year. The artist, Marisol Escobar, based it on an actual photo taken of the formerly handsome priest a few weeks before he died. The artist wanted to show the pain and anguish leprosy inflicts upon its victims. Some were offended by the resulting ugliness. This man is important to my family. Do you know why?"

I shook my head.

"Your ancestor, Dr. Harrison Ai'Lee, condemned my grandfather to the leper colony of Kalaupapa. When I look at Father Damien's face and body, I imagine how horrible it must have been for my grandfather to die of leprosy, alone and abandoned among others like him. How painful to see your fingers and toes and nose rot off your body. How repulsive to feel your body literally eaten alive. How frustratingly helpless to be condemned to a living death." His voice was sad, yet resolved. His slate-gray eyes never left the statue's face.

He turned to me with a frown. His skin was the kind of pale that doesn't like the sun. He wiped beads of sweat from his forehead with a cotton handkerchief, refolded it so the soiled side was hidden, and replaced it in his shirt pocket. "Your classmate, Alexander, came to see me a couple weeks ago. Can you imagine, this was the first time I've met my cousin. The Kaua`i Demmings never come to the Big Island of Hawai`i." He shrugged, amazed at the truth of the statement. "And we Big Island Demmings used to pretty much stay on our own island."

"Except now that Hawai`i's a state, you're here."

Chris nodded thoughtfully. "Our family has dominated politics on the Big Island to protect our interests. Now the opportunity is here at the state level. After Aunt Celie's death on Kaua`i, William Demming contacted me here in Honolulu. He wanted to take action against the activists that caused his wife's death. That unpleasant situation made him understand why the rest of us were so active in politics, about the need to safeguard our families, businesses, and interests. He offered his help.

"I was elated when Alex visited me in my office. If he were to join my campaign, the combined strength of the Kaua`i and Hawai`i Demmings would make me unbeatable. Then he told me not to count on his or William's influence to sway my appointment or any other issues. He believes that we all should be judged on our personal qualifications and accomplishments. I told him he didn't understand local politics, especially here in Hawai`i."

"And what did Alex say to that?" I asked. I didn't think Alex took to criticism, especially if he believed he was right.

"Alex got up and walked straight to the governor's office." Chris shook his head, astounded at Alex's direct approach. "I wish I could have heard what they talked about. Uncle William has so much pull. He must have called the governor to make sure he would see Alex. Damn!" Chris's hands curled into fists. Then he caught himself, crossed his arms over his chest, and glowered at the sculpture of Father Damien.

I was speechless. Alex had done this for me, for Braxton.

I said good-bye and left Christopher Demming alone with his thoughts. He was fresh-scrubbed and earnest. He exuded ambition. But he gave me the feeling that he wanted Braxton's job for its power, not its merit.

I walked back to the Ai'Lee party feeling remorseful. I had wronged Alex. Once again, my fiery temper had gotten me into trouble. I had been rude. He had been noble.

I owed him an apology. I paused at the reflecting pool. I prayed to the gods of the sky and the sea. Would he forgive me again?

Chapter Eleven

Flying through Water

*M*aku, maitre d' at the Canoe Club, waved his hands in surprise. "Alex! Welcome home. When did you get back? None of your cousins or uncles ever know where you are. Always somewhere exotic—Cambodia, Burma, India, Nepal—can't keep track. How long now, over ten years?" Maku's broad smile gleamed in the elegant glow of the foyer.

"And you, Maku. What are you still doing here?" Alex grabbed Maku around his broad shoulders. The men hugged, hearty and strong.

"Ahh, Chrissy and I have number five coming up. So I work dinnertime here, daytime at the telephone company. Foreman of fiber-optic installations." He straightened his six-foot-six frame and puffed his muscled chest. He was an impressively powerful Chinese-Portuguese-Hawaiian dressed in formal Hawaiian whites, a cobalt blue sash around his waist, thick black hair pulled back in a stylish ponytail.

"Five kids!"

"Each one special. Gifts from the gods." Maku smiled proudly. "Is this little Miki from high school time?"

"Hi, Maku! Howzit?" I held out my hand.

Maku buried me in one of his bear hugs. "Forget the handshake. I want a hug. Long time no see. Not since this guy and I used to go boogie boarding in school. Where you been?"

"San Francisco."

"Mainland girl now, huh?" He grabbed my hands and checked for rings, "You guys married yet?"

I shook my head.

Alex shrugged gallantly. "As you said, no one knew where I was."

"Well!" Maku slapped Alex on the back. "Now that you're home, maybe you'll catch up. Five kids." His eyes twinkled mischievously. He picked up two leather menus and motioned toward the dining room. "I have a special table for you—beachside. Come!"

We followed the regal Maku past elegant tables where the familiar faces of Hawai`i's powerfully connected reached for Alex, demanded his acknowledgment. And Alex, relaxed in this familiar enclave of power, waved his apologies.

The open-air dining room of the private Canoe Club nestled on the Waikiki side of Honolulu. On Friday evening, members could sip through the petals of orchid-crested drinks and watch the yacht races. When the sun was still high in the late afternoon, dozens of sleek sailboats beat across the ocean front toward Diamond Head, rounded the buoy off Diamond Head lighthouse, then made a spinnaker run towards Ala Moana Beach.

Towering arrangements of proteas cascaded from marble pillars within the club, framing our final view of the sun diving into the ocean with a brilliant green flash. As night fell and sunbathers abandoned the darkening sands, the bright lights of the catamaran cruises from Kewalo Basin sparkled across the vanished horizon to Diamond Head.

When the waiter had disappeared with our orders, I reached across the celadon tablecloth for Alex's hands. They were callused. Once-smooth hands toughened by searing heat. "Thank you for the lei, Alex," I said.

Five strands of uniform white pikake blossoms, like luminous giant pearls warmed by the heat of my bare shoulders, surrounded me with its seductive sweetness. When the Chinese jasmine was introduced to the islands, young Princess Ka`iulani called them her "peacock flowers," after the brilliantly feathered peacocks that roamed her family's estate. Pikakes became the favorite flowers of the princess who never lived to rule over her beloved islands.

Alex's eyes glistened a dark blue-green. "I always think of you when I smell pikakes. That was the first lei I gave you. Remember the Holoku Ball?"

I flushed, remembering that night.

Alex's grip seemed to sear my skin with his heat. "Miki, I'm sorry I upset you. It was gracious of you to call. I told my father he was blinded by his emotions, which overruled his judgment. Don't look so shocked. I told him these aren't the days of the monarchy when power was bought. We need a powerful state government led by the best and brightest of Hawai`i."

I tipped my head, pleased by his candor. "I'm impressed."

Alex leaned forward and smiled. "I also told him I'm romancing one of Hawai`i's best and brightest."

Startled, I looked down at our clasped hands, then back into his eyes. "I'm flattered, Alex. But I owe you an apology. I lashed out at you for something that wasn't your fault. You couldn't have known that Braxton was hoping for the appointment your cousin wanted. When he received the appointment my family rejoiced, but they also said some nasty things about your family that saddened me. I wanted to defend you, Alex; you were a true friend. Then I met your cousin Chris. He told me about the tongue-lashing you gave him and your meeting with the governor. I had to apologize to you in person and let you know how I felt."

I blushed ruefully. "Forgive me, Alex, for getting angry at you. I'm sorry I was so rude. I apologize for hurting you." I blushed. "I especially want to apologize for interrupting what could have been a lovely afternoon."

"You always had a quick temper." Alex laughed. Then he leaned across the table and kissed my fingers. "I'll accept your apology if you promise we can continue sometime."

I flushed deeper. I remembered the greeting Alex received an hour earlier. I had run to the front door as quickly as I could in a long strapless mu`umu`u when I heard the doorbell ring. My father, in an Aloha shirt and shorts, got there first. Auntie Lehua and Uncle Robert had walked in, dressed in T-shirts, shorts, and sneakers, for a visit on their way home from their evening hike to Liliha Library and back via Nu`uanu Avenue. Despite Auntie Lehua's graciousness when Alex arrived for our date, I knew she was sizing him up. She would notice that the shirt he wore was the distinctively subtle Polynesian pattern from the Ala Moana shop patronized by the men of style and power. She would notice how casually he slipped his shoes off, local style, before he stepped into the house, and how his kiss tenderly lingered on my lips when he placed the strands of pikake around my neck. But my father's visage darkened when Alex appeared at his door. His response was inhospitably crisp. The Ai'Lees would sit around his living room tonight and ponder about my former classmate Alex Demming, the great-grandson of Chun Ai'Lee's adversary. To them, even a dinner date was a prelude, a threat, of what might happen.

~❀~

During dinner, Alex and I discussed our adventures after college. Mine couldn't compare to his archaeological expeditions in Cambodia, India, Burma, and Indonesia. "And all this time you never came home?" I asked.

"I flew back for my orals and a couple of family meetings." His voice caught. "And my mother's funeral." He nodded as if dismissing the pain, but it clearly still upset him. "You know my father. Strong as a bull. Ranching is in his blood and keeps him going. And he has Eddie Kekaha, his right-hand man. But," Alex looked out to where the moonlight was a silvery path beyond the reef, "this time I've come home at my dad's request. I've spent the past few weeks assessing what needs to be done." He frowned. "His only contact with the outside world is via a single phone line. I'm not willing to isolate myself like that. If our plans are to work, I have to set up better communications."

"Running a ranch seems a lifetime away from archaeology," I mused. I thought about the tedious research Alex must have been doing in those steamy tropical climates. My colleagues told horror stories of insects with voracious appetites for fresh blood and invisible biters that left their venom in itchy patches. Thickly twining vines in tropical jungles resisted the persistent hacks of the sharpest trail-blazing machetes. One had to be on guard against strange tropical diseases, the ones that could eat your flesh from the inside out and torment your brain with soaring fevers.

"Ranching is what Eddie Kekaha and Dad trained me for," Alex answered. He described the smell of the crushed grass, the thrill of Demming land stretching from the mountains to the sea, and the thunder of Hawaiian cowboys, paniolos, riding the herds. "You remember my plans to take the ranch into the twenty-first century?"

I remembered his dreams.

"They're part of me. And," Alex's voice lowered, "I couldn't stay out there anymore." Dark shadows hardened his face.

I drew back as if it was the ocean breeze that caused me to shudder. I wanted to ask why, but it didn't feel right. All these years I thought he had continued on his original plan.

Alex leaned forward and held out his hands: the sturdy hands of a rancher, the perceptive hands of an archaeologist. His eyes focused on our clasped fingers as he explained where he had been.

With Picassos and Van Goghs selling for millions of dollars, international art dealers and collectors scrambled to find new treasures and unwary targets: ancient temples filled with exquisite carvings. Until the 1950s, most were left unharmed. But as the price of art rose, idol runners plundered the easy targets. The local people didn't know the monetary value of the gods and goddesses they worshiped. Temple windows and doors were open for the convenience of the worshipers. More than a hundred sculptures were pilfered from the Khajuraho temples, the Chandigarah Museum was robbed at gunpoint, and a seventh-century bronze of tremendous historical importance was stripped from the temple in Himachal Pradesh.

While he was in graduate school, he had been invited to intern with the Angkor Conservancy that took charge of the Angkor monuments in 1908. Alex would work under the direction of Bernard Philippe Groslier, the archaeologist in charge. A number of Angkor's artistically important works had already been removed and were in some of the world's great museums. Through the 1950s the conservancy removed important works when thievery was rising and guarding such a vast expanse became impossible.

Alex stayed in Angkor after he received his PhD. He joined international teams documenting the Khmer heads and sculptures pilfered from Angkor Wat, the provincial museums, and the Depot de la Conservation d'Angkor. Thousands of sculptures had disappeared. The entire Angkor ceramics collection had vanished.

At Angkor Wat, entire bas reliefs were missing. The undulating rhythms of ancient Khmer dancers would never be seen again. Beheaded, the exquisite smiles of the dancers would never again be part of the story expressed by their swaying postures and delicate hands. Perhaps they were lost en route to the Thai border or Vietnam, or smuggled out by diplomats and sold by unsuspecting dealers. Alex's mission was exhilarating. But he was discouraged by the futility of trying to stem the tide of art thefts valued at almost two billion dollars a year. Just before he returned, the Khmer Rouge began a campaign of terror and power. Alex visited other sites in Indonesia where the rate of thefts were increasing because of political instability, poverty, and unscrupulous collectors.

Meanwhile, his father barricaded himself on his lands after his wife's death and refused to leave Kaua`i, even for business meetings. His daughters implored their father to retire and spend the rest of his years enjoying his grandchildren on the mainland. William, no longer the robust rancher who rode out with his men at dawn and returned after twilight, wanted to turn the land over to Alex while he was still alive.

Alex signaled the waiter that we were done. He took my hand and we walked out to the beach. We kicked off our shoes as we stepped onto the sand. We strolled along the water's edge to the lap of waves and heavy rustling of languorous palm fronds.

Alex's voice grew rough with disgust when he talked about the brazen looting he had seen. With his mentor, Alex visited sites and museums throughout Southeast Asia. "When Dr. Xi asked me to photograph and document the conditions at Angkor, I jumped at the opportunity. We were at the Ta Prombh temple at Angkor. I was on my knees clearing the undergrowth away from a squatting male deity. I thought I was used to high humidity, but the jungle heat was stifling." He took a deep breath as if steeling his memory. He said he had dropped to the ground when he heard the machine-gun fire. Sandstone sprayed. Gun powder, blood, and death engulfed the air. He gripped the dirt, waiting for a gun barrel to press into the base of his neck. When the shouts disappeared in the distance, he looked up. All he could see and smell was blood: on the temple walls, on the statues they had been photographing—everywhere the blood of Dr. Xi and his associates. Five guides were shot beyond recognition.

"I was caked with blood and mosquitoes." Alex laughed sardonically. "Maybe that male deity I uncovered saved my life."

"But who would—?" I struggled.

"The statues at Ta Prombh are exquisite. Someone didn't want us to document what was there and what was missing. That day, fifteen full-body statues disappeared at the price of twenty lives."

I wanted to hold him, to take the edge off his pain.

But Alex stopped me, his eyes intense with passion. "There's more. I have to be honest with you," he warned gruffly. "I was engaged, Miki, and Beth was with me in Angkor. She could dig through the most putrid slime and didn't mind dirt in her fingernails. She was a farmer's daughter from the San Joaquin Valley." His face softened with her memory. "She'd tie her curls back so all you'd see were her gray eyes looking out from a brown halo. What a tough woman. A compact fireball. It was a romantic idea—our first dig together: hiking through tropical jungles, sleeping under the stars."

He slowly continued. "She had developed a tropical fever by the time we arrived at Angkor but she refused to be left behind. None of the antibiotics we carried could stop her rising temperature. I wanted to drive her back to Phnom Penh. She begged to stay. Even though she was too weak to go on, she insisted that all she needed was sleep. So I set up a lean-to in a clearing. When I ran back after the massacre at Ta Prombh she was still alive, but barely. The attackers had carved her open from neck to belly."

Alex stood quietly for a long time before he continued. "She couldn't last long. I wanted to go for help, but I was afraid to let her die alone. The trucks were gone. I'd have to go by myself on foot. Her eyes said 'stay.' I didn't know what to do. I yelled for help. The temple was deserted. My colleagues were dead. I was so alone, Miki."

He had wrapped her up in a blanket and held her in his arms, praying all the while for someone to come and find them. He spent the night listening to the crocodiles, bats, and mosquitoes reclaiming their haunts. In the morning she was cold. Both of them were soaked with blood. "She was only twenty-one. I stayed in Southeast Asia. I knew that as long as I was there, I would run into her murderers again."

An icy grimace, an expression I had never seen before, flashed across his face. "I wanted revenge. I thought I could stop them—those killers." He lowered his voice. "And I felt guilty. I kept thinking, should I have gone for help? Was she dead because of me? I was stupid to let her come. I told myself I wanted to avenge the deaths of my friends. I realize now I was a fool." He said the Cambodian government accused the Khmer Rouge of the attack, yet the pattern was repeated throughout Southeast Asia. "We heard that both the Khmer Rouge and the government were selling looted art from Angkor for money to buy arms.

Statues were mutilated or smashed to remove their heads. Shrines blasted. Bas reliefs machine-gunned." His voice steeled.

His anger was spent, he said, sapped by years of frustration and depression. He realized it was impossible to stop the international art rings. He had crossed paths with them many times, but they were elusive shadows in the darkness: well funded, well equipped, and often aided by local governments. They were as professionally run as the most organized drug cartels, and as profitable.

There was no way to protect Borobudur, the Javanese temple built twelve hundred years ago as a model of the Mahayana Buddhist cosmos. Alex was awed by Borobudur's spiritual mystery, but angered by the destruction to this monument of two thousand carved panels and seventy-two stupas. "Can you imagine headless Buddhas meditating peace and enlightenment?" he fumed. He saw the same in Pagan, the ancient capital of Burma. Sculptures had been chiseled off thousands of ancient buildings dating from the eleventh century.

His eyes gleamed when he talked of those ancient places and their secrets, as if he were talking about a women he desired, yearned for. I saw his fingers caressing the sinuous sculptures as if to protect them, to hold them in rapture. They were his mistresses.

I cocked my head and thought. "Is that what you were doing at the Kuan Yin Temple that first day I came home?"

He nodded. "You know, some of those statues are valuable, Miki, brought from China over a hundred years ago. Yet that temple stands unlocked and unguarded day and night." He shook his head in frustration. "Do you realize how vulnerable they are?"

If the Buddha and Bodhisattva statues from Lailee's Kuan Yin Temple were stolen, the loss of such cultural treasures would devastate those who knew their meaning and power. I shuddered to imagine all those shelves bare, barren, violated. Thousands of plundered prayers would go unanswered forever.

The waves lapped at our bare feet in the sand. Alex took my hand and continued our walk along the water's edge. He talked about a new beginning. "I never forgot you, Miki. I used to think I could do anything, be anyone I wanted to when I was with you. But whenever I thought I was reaching you, you closed up like a clam. It hurt when you pulled away. In the past few years when the night sky was blackest, I'd look up and call your name to the stars. Did you hear me?" He shook his head. "Of course not."

I turned to him. By moonlight, his eyes were deep in shadow, unreadable. "You thought about me? I thought you despised me. The last time I saw you, you told me to stay a peasant the rest of my life." My heart sunk. I had hurt him.

"After all we've meant to each other, that's the one memory you kept of me? Oh, Miki! As you remember, I didn't fit into your parents' plans. Are you still fulfilling your role as the filial daughter?"

I shrank from the bitterness in his voice.

Yet his arms were forgiving when he pulled me to his chest. "Let's go for a swim tonight. You can't imagine how warm the ocean's been. I've swum out to the reef and back every night since I've been home."

My breath caught and I pushed away. I remembered the wild churning at twilight around the reefs, the suspiciously fishy smell of death, and the greedy cries of sea birds hovering above the tight circles of frenzied feeding. To me, the night seas teemed with dark secrets.

—❀—

My fears began when I was six. After a family dinner on the beach, Braxton and I paddled through the shallow waters between the reef and shore. With a bloodcurdling shriek, Braxton thrashed wildly in the water and yelled "Shark!" He sank under the surface and popped up again, his black hair plastered to his forehead. Braxton gasped, eyes rolling backwards, and sank again.

I panicked when I heard his cries. Shark! Braxton! My arms froze. The waters closed over my head. I bobbed up gasping for air. I screamed for help. I imagined dorsal fins slicing straight through my kicking legs. My nose filled with water. My eyes burned. I breathed in ocean. I could almost see razor-sharp teeth ripping at my thrashing limbs.

I sank.

Braxton swam to shore, laughing. He waved to everyone that I was only playing shark attack.

When I came to, my father was steadily pumping my chest. I clung to him and wouldn't let go. My throat stung. I couldn't talk. Dad could barely hear me over Braxton's squalling; Mom was paddling his bare bottom.

I never again went swimming after dark.

━❀━

"You're still afraid of the mano, sharks, feeding at night?" Alex asked. His voice was husky with concern.

I felt that tight fear of dark, unfathomable waters. Cold terror shivered through me. "Let's go for a swim," I whispered.

We drove along Diamond Head Road, past towering mansions that clung to the face of the extinct volcano. We fell silent when we passed the blind turns along the curved road where white crosses used to stand when we were children. In those days, each white cross marked where an accident had occurred, where someone had met an untimely death and was doomed to linger as an unsettled spirit to lure the unwary to take its place in the ghost world.

We talked of how comforted we felt in this land we shared with the powerful Hawaiian spirits and gods who watched over us. We drew our strength from this ocean, our freedom from the trade winds, and our power from the rich land of our islands.

The driveway to the Demming home ducked under curved palms half-hidden behind an old lava rock wall. Before he built the house, William Demming had searched out the kahunas of the sacred heiau to pray to the spirits of each tree and boulder on this land. He gave the traditional offerings and asked for permission to build a modest family home on the beach. When his fellow parishioners at church heard about the "heathen ceremony," they were aghast. But William Demming held firm. He said he was guardian of this land during his lifetime. He had to respect the ancient spirits that lived there. Alex would be the next guardian of the land.

With only the moonlight to guide our way, Alex and I walked through the living room, our bare feet noiseless on the hardwood floor. He opened the French doors to the terrace and we stepped out to the swimming pool edged with sanded lava rock. The coconut trees rustled loudly with sudden gusts as if the spirits were aroused by our presence.

Alex guided me to a stone bench. He lifted the pikake lei over my head and laid it gently next to me. Our eyes looked back in time to the years we had lost: our pains, our mistakes, our reckless trials.

It would be different this time. He caressed my bare shoulders. I melted into his lingering touch and inhaled the salty taste of his neck. I kissed away the melancholy of the ancient cities clinging to his sadness and prayed the spirits to kindle the passion in his heart. One by one, I undid the coconut buttons of his shirt to reach the heat of his bare chest. Alex did the rest.

"Come," he whispered, rising naked before me. The moonlight gleamed over his body, highlighting the arc of his back as he stepped to the pool and dove in.

Coconut fronds stirred restlessly overhead. "Come," they echoed in their many voices.

I didn't hesitate this time. I unwrapped the single tie on my mu`umu`u and stepped to the water's edge. Now I, too, was one with the night. The ripples danced across the pool when Alex rose from the water. He reached out for me. I lifted my arms and arched backward, enjoying the winds that licked my body. I closed my eyes and inhaled the lusty Hawaiian spirits that whispered to us this night. Alex waited for me, watching my every move. I dove over his outstretched arms into the dark water beyond. I joyfully surrendered when he wrapped me in his arms and claimed me as his own. All I could think of was Alex. All I could feel was Alex.

We rode the night, the two of us, naked on a bed of white gardenia petals. We wrapped around each other, entwined like jungle vines deep in the Ko`olau Valley. We listened to the cry of the wild peacocks at dawn, their breasts overflowing with life and love.

When the morning rains fell, we rinsed ourselves in their tears of happiness, a gift from the gods. We held out our tongues to drink its pure sweetness. And when the rains stopped, we slowly licked the nectar from each other's body.

"Yes," sighed the Night Whispers, the gods and spirits in the wind. "You are ours. You belong to us."

At dawn, we dove naked into the ocean and met the incoming surf. This was the first time I had swum in the ocean when the sun was not high in the sky. It took Alex to teach me I had the power to fly through water.

Chapter Twelve

The Lu`au

I woke to the staccato of water splashing on the stiff leaves and flowers of the Birds of Paradise. My father was watering the yard before the heat of the day. I had heard the creak of his bed when I returned at dawn and the soft pad of his footsteps when he went to the bathroom. He wanted me to know he knew. Since today was an important day, he would avoid the issue, like an old-world gentleman, until later.

Forty years ago when he built this house my mother had encircled it with an explosion of tropical flowers—Birds of Paradise, red and yellow hibiscus, and a plumeria tree covered with cascades of yellow blossoms. Our house, built in the Chinese style around an open courtyard, had been painted white to reflect the heat as were most of the houses in the tropics. But the eaves, window trim, and walkways were painted a distinctive Chinese red for good luck. To this day, red trim is an indication that the homeowners are Chinese.

By the time he swept off the front steps, I had showered, dressed, and started breakfast. From the sound of the foot traffic and excited voices headed for the church, others were eager, like him, to help with lu`au preparations for today.

Yesterday, the imu pit had been lined with kiawe wood and pohaku, special lava river rocks. When the pohaku steamed white-hot, the men uncovered the imu, lined it with banana leaves, and hoisted a dozen scraped and scalded quarter-ton pigs into the smoking pit. More mats and banana leaves covered the pigs, along with sweet potatoes wrapped in ti leaf packages.

Opening the imu was a spectacle that attracted the entire congregation. Our men, clad only in T-shirts and shorts, removed one steamy layer at a time: the kapolena canvas that covered the entire imu, then the soaking-wet burlap bags we called `eke huluhulu, and finally the banana stalks and leaves that added moisture and fragrance to the baking pigs. Bathed in the smoke and steam of the smoking pit, the rest of us visited with friends and extended family, many who flew in from the outer islands and the mainland for this once-a-year event. We oohed over newborn babies, exclaimed how the little ones had grown to gangly or graceful teens, and insisted on meeting new boyfriends and girlfriends.

"They'll start opening the imu in an hour. You coming?" asked Dad.

"Wouldn't miss it. Myra Ching asked me to work on her crew." I was as eager as he. I placed the papayas, steamed rice, and Portuguese sausage on the table for the traditional meal that started my father's day.

"It's good you see your old friends again. You used to set up and serve every year before you went away." He smiled to himself at the memory.

After breakfast, Marjorie Chu, a 65-year-old widow and longtime friend of the family, knocked on our front door. Dad threw on a yellow polo shirt and, in shorts and old tennis shoes, jauntily accompanied Marjorie to MacKenzie Hall where the seniors would shred the meat of the kalua pigs by hand when the pit was opened. A year after my mother died, the single ladies at the Chinese Congregational Church down the street appeared on my father's doorstep each Sunday. In colorful cotton dresses, they brought my father fruit from their trees or fresh-baked coconut cakes before they walked with him to morning service. After all these years, none had won his affection.

I would be along after I did the breakfast dishes. I swirled the iridescent suds, warm and slippery, with my fingers. Last night felt like a dream, a tantalizing reverie. I missed the feel of Alex's flesh against mine, the beat of his heart when I pressed my lips to his chest. I had tasted his passion. My body hungered for more. Was it his voice I heard calling my name so many times in the winds off San Francisco Bay? Had he reached across time and place and pulled me back?

I closed my eyes and listened. The red torch gingers in the courtyard rustled. "Mom?" I called. Was she here? The stiff stalks bent as if she were running her hands through them. "Mom?" I called again.

I quickly rinsed my hands and stepped into the courtyard. She was there, just as I saw her once when I came home from school. In a chair pulled up to one of the giant fish tanks, she sat mesmerized by the exquisite serenity of our private reefs. Sunlight sparkled off her thick curls like a bronze halo. Her face glowed and her eyes, large dark eyes that snapped with fire and life, softened in entranced relaxation. She turned to me when I entered the courtyard and caught the surprised look on my face.

"How often do you see me sit down?" she laughed when I walked out to join her. She pulled me close and pointed to the shaded tank. A white sleeveless blouse set off the golden tan of her arms. Her gathered skirt, patterned with brilliant red hibiscus on a yellow background, revealed shapely calves and dainty bare feet. "Look, Miki!" she pointed with graceful fingers. "Another world. So peaceful and calm!" Black and yellow angelfish swept past oblivious silver gouramis. Schools of neon tetras darted in and out of lava rock caves. A green turtle the size of my palm stretched out on a floating raft and arched his neck to the sun.

I settled cross-legged at her feet as I had done as a child and leaned my head on her lap, inhaling the just-ironed smell of her cotton skirt.

"I did the best I could, dear," she said from her heart. "My only daughter, I tried to teach you as I was taught." She stroked my arms, her touch as warm as the tear that rolled down my cheek.

I wanted her advice. As she spoke, her words were the words in my heart. They lay where she had carefully planted them over the years. She had nurtured these teachings so carefully, I was unaware that they had blossomed. I realized I was more like her than I had ever acknowledged to myself.

"In the end, you will choose the path that makes you happy," she whispered.

I reached up and touched her cheeks, warm and soft in the morning light. Then her image shimmered into the trade wind that bobbed the leaves of the gingers.

—❀—

The old kitchen in MacKenzie Hall echoed with the convivial chatter on the kalua pig assembly line. Men and women expertly wielded the shoulder bones from the carcasses to strip slabs of meat off the steaming pigs hauled in from the imu pit, one by one. Smoky meat juice splattered across heavy canvas aprons covering T-shirts and mu`umu`us. Jaunty paper hats barely protected salt-and-pepper hair. Three thousand guests were expected this evening—one of the best showings yet. Both seatings had completely sold out. Only take-out orders, sold at the front steps of the church, could be purchased today.

The lu`au began as a fund-raiser for new pews more than thirty-five years ago. In the 1930s, twenty Chinese families led by the Reverend MacKenzie had bought the old McInerny mansion, a three-story filigreed wood Victorian with Corinthian columns and an imposing porte-cochere. Services were held in the living room where the morning light streamed in through multipaned glass walls and glowed on the old pews: termite-eaten hand-me-downs. Church socials, teen athletics, and a dynamic minister attracted an active and growing multigeneration congregation. A large chapel of sturdy cinder block was added. Now, French doors opened out on both sides to welcome the trade winds during services. Passers-by could hear the sermons, given in both English and Chinese, and the familiar hymns rising on the booming swell of the new organ.

To raise money for pews crafted by local woodworkers, the congregation thought of presenting a Hawaiian feast called a lu`au. Someone knew how to prepare the traditional Hawaiian foods. Another knew hula dancers and singers who would contribute entertainment. The lu`au became an annual event. The number of seatings doubled when the Hawai`i Visitors Bureau recommended the two-day event to tourists, starting with the preparation of the labor-intensive traditional preparation of the imu pit.

—❀—

"Is there room for me?" I asked, raising my voice above the cacophony of clanking pans and happy voices in the church kitchen. I wiggled in beside my father.

"Oh Kam, your daughter is so tall now," one of the ladies called out. She waved a gloved hand dripping with pig juice.

Familiar faces, crinkled in smiles from my childhood, welcomed me. Voices from long ago jogged memories of starched cotton dresses and patent leather shoes. A familiar voice crackled, "I remember when you were only so high, Miki. You were in my third grade Sunday school class."

"Miki, you remember Mrs. Tang, your kindergarten teacher, and Betty Foo—she taught the older kids. And Millie," my father gestured with the shoulder bone he was using, "led the youth choir. Say hi to Auntie Grace, Herbie, Auntie Susan, Dr. Fong, Auntie Mabel ... and you know Marjorie, Mrs. Chu," he continued with the introductions. I nodded and smiled to each. We kids had grown up under their watchful eyes. I wondered if I should be flattered that they thought I looked exactly the same as when I was a child, or distressed that my maturity didn't show. They pinned a paper hat over my hair. I pulled on rubber gloves and joined them around the heavy steel pans.

Four hefty men, their forearms bulging as they hauled in the next massive tray, charged through the back door of the kitchen. "Hey! No slow down! Plenty more coming," they grunted through gritted teeth. They were dark and tanned, exuding the husky smoke of banana leaves and hot lava rocks. Their T-shirts dripped with sweat. They landed the pig with a resounding thunk that filled the room with the pungent steam of the opened pit.

"Billie, Milton, Eric, Layton!" I called to these faces from my childhood.

"Hey, lookit, the squirt is back," they teased. "Is this little Miki?" I couldn't escape their slippery hugs.

Eric shook his head. "No tan. She looks like a mainland girl."

"Such white skin and rosy cheeks," giggled Mrs. Tang. I shifted uncomfortably under their scrutiny.

Dad stayed with the seniors while I joined the ladies decorating the stage and tables. We arranged immense banana leaves as a backdrop. Clusters of flowers—crimson, yellow, and white—were tied in lush arrangements. We washed hundreds of ti leaves in clean water, wiped them down with soft cotton towels, and stapled them to long tables radiating out from the stage.

When Dad and I returned an hour later, after showering and changing into Aloha shirt and mu`umu`u, we joined the serving teams laying out the sliced pineapples and coconut cake.

Before the first guests were allowed in, Dad escorted Lailee Ai'Lee to the tables Myra and I were hosting. A stately couple glided behind them; Pearl Wu, in a formal fitted holoku and a jade flower lei of blossoms curved like crab claws, held the escorting arm of a bald Chinese man in a white tropical suit. My father ceremoniously seated his old friends in the chairs he had reserved for family and friends. Greetings were kissed and hugged.

I held out a seat with a clear view of the stage for Popo Ai'Lee. "Pretty mu`umu`u," I commented, catching the crisp, freshly-ironed smell of the green and white cotton that fell in gentle folds to her toes.

She smiled and lowered herself into the seat I had saved for her. The lump on her head, although tender, was imperceptible now, and perfectly hidden by her sleek white bun.

I had paused to chat with Dr. and Madame Wu when Braxton and Sondra hurried towards us. "I told them at the door we were all together," Braxton nodded towards the Wus. "So they let us cut in line." He grasped Dr. Wu's hand with zealous greetings. "Uncle C.C. was one of the governor's friends who suggested me for my new position, Miki," he acknowledged. "I have him to thank." Braxton, in a bold Hawaiian shirt, seated Sondra and himself next to the Wus.

My brother had on his impenetrable public face of cheerful confidence: his eyes were wide and smiling, without a frown shadowing his forehead.

Dr. Wu accepted Braxton's praises graciously. He insisted Braxton's own merits had made it easy for him to forward his career. He clasped my brother on the shoulder, then turned to my father. "Braxton's a credit to you, Kam," he boomed.

My father modestly agreed.

Dr. Wu leaned back and patted his rotund tummy, the round belly that my mother dubbed the "Chinese sign of prosperity." In a crisp linen suit, Dr. Wu exuded abundance. He continued, "My own sons are successfully launched in their own careers. You know Alfred—his pediatric practice is booming. The other two are in business, doing fine."

"These men!" Madame Wu turned to me and lowered her voice. "Of all my children, Gwendolyn's the smartest one. So organized." She raised her left eyebrow and caught my eye. "These men can't see it." My classmate, Gwendolyn, was a mother of three and CFO of a local bank.

The musicians on stage launched into their first set to the accompaniment of guitars, ukulele, and bass. The front gates opened and the crowds streamed in. Hosts and hostesses filled the tables we had carefully set that morning, starting with those closest to the stage. It was a crowd of familiar faces and jubilant greetings called across crowded aisles.

Popo Ai`Lee tugged at my arm. "Miki, who is this seat for?" She pointed to the empty chair next to her. A friend, I told her. She raised an eyebrow and sat back.

When Alex arrived, I introduced him to my family and guests. I hoped no one would notice how I flushed when he was near.

Braxton welcomed Alex, but cast me a questioning glance. However, when C.C. and Pearl Wu struck up a discussion with Alex about the size and productivity of the

Demming family ranch, Braxton and Sondra politely joined the conversation.

My father walked over from where he and others set up the food serving trays, visiting with friends along the way, to check on his guests. A disapproving frown creased his brow when he saw Alex.

Myra and I maneuvered through the rows of guests to serve the poi, kalua pig, lomi-lomi salmon, and haupia. We swayed our trays to the beat of the music and sang the songs we knew. Between seatings, we picked the butcher paper linings off the tables and rolled everything up—the ti leaf decorations, paper plates, and bowls—to reveal another table setting completely laid out. Eric and Layton hustled over whenever they could to help us carry the heavy pitchers of punch and newly filled trays. In typical Hawaiian style, the evening was filled with buoyant greet-ings, abundant kisses, and affectionate hugs.

My brother and his wife had been noticeably impressed when Dr. Wu whipped out a small jade fondling piece from his suit pocket. "You will appreciate this, Miki," C.C. enthused. "Spring-Autumn period, 800 BCE." He dropped the white jade carving of a dancing man into my hands. "One of only two in the world," he puffed proudly. "This little man has flown around the world, feasted at palaces in India, and swum the China Sea in my pocket. He's my tal-isman, my lucky charm."

I ran my fingers over the mutton-fat sheen of the jade figure and marveled how it warmed to my touch. I was filled with questions about how and where he obtained such a rarity, but one never asks direct questions of an elder. The zeal of collectors like C.C. Wu amazed me.

Sondra gushed, her eyes wide. "And you walk around with it in your pocket, Dr. Wu! But it's priceless." She clasped her hands to her neck and gaped wide-eyed at him.

Dr. Wu smiled broadly at Sondra and turned back to me. "Impressive, isn't it, Miki?" He chuckled when I agreed. "Everyone needs a simple, small indulgence. My little jade man soothes all the dissatisfactions and irritations of daily life. A bit of magic created by an ancient craftsman."

"Pleasure and power, Uncle C.C.?" I suggested. I handed the dancing jade man to Alex. Confucius had identified jade with purity, intelligence, justice, music, loyalty, sincerity, heaven, earth, and truth. What else could a scholar wish for?

"Exactly, Miki—you understand!" Dr. Wu enthused.

I went back to work with Myra while Alex engaged C.C. in an intense conversation about his collections.

Lailee's eyes danced when Alex leaned towards her during dinner. He and my grandmother exchanged quiet words and understanding nods. She gestured with her hands. Alex tipped his head in encouragement. I had always admired Alex's easy way with people. When we were in school, I had seen him banter with society mavens one minute and in the next, with the locals.

One of these occurred at Matsumoto's Shave Ice stand in Haleiwa. A bevy of ladies with Alex's mother, all in stylish white linen, had alighted from a Cadillac at Matsumoto's at the same time we pulled in. They were returning from the Sunday polo matches at Mokule'ia. Alex and I, barefoot, in swimsuits and T-shirts, had been watching Kalia Gomes compete at Sunset Beach.

"Alex, dear," Celie Demming had called, "come introduce your friend." I watched with amusement at how perfectly Alex handled our introductions without mentioning I was an Ai'Lee, then expertly engaged his mother's friends in light conversation. The minute they were gone, he began speaking pidgin to the cane workers who had come in for cold beers. We sat cross-legged on a wooden bench for the next hour, eating shave ice and talking story. I imagined that Alex, for all his fine breeding, could comfortably squat in the dirt with the natives of Cambodia or India and speak the stories that came from his heart.

His tall frame settled comfortably in the metal folding chair. I thought back to those warm afternoons under the monkeypod tree outside Bishop Hall when we were in high school and how I took his friendship for granted. I was shy and naïve in those days. Overshadowed at home by my mother and Braxton, I had already learned to keep silent. Alex was a special ally and friend. We had spirited discussions during study hall about Kierkegaard and Sartre. We compared our interpretations of William Carlos Williams and the meanings of *Ulysses*. We tallied our As and competed in each class we had together. When I was on the gymnastics team, I saw him sneak into the gym during our practices, sacrificing the time that he, as editor, should have spent putting together the yearbook.

"You can be friends, that's all," my mother had conceded. Her honey-gold eyes darkened with protective fear. "I don't want you to get hurt." She put her arms around me and ran her fingers down my cheek. She was truly sorry.

When I turned my back and walked away from Hawai`i, I never thanked Alex for being my friend. I never told him that when he smiled at me, I felt a glow, a special feeling that no one else kindled.

My grandmother, I observed, had noticed that special quality in Alex. Her face lit up when he slid into the pidgin of the local folks to talk to her. She caught my glance. "Aah, my dear Miki, this was so ono, delicious," she sighed. The guests were leaving. She looked around for Braxton, but he and Sondra were halfway out the churchyard with the Wus.

Alex leaned towards her. "Popo Ai`Lee, may I take you home?" he offered gallantly.

"Thank you, Alex," my grandmother replied with a nod. As I helped her up, she whispered loudly, "He has fine manners."

I brushed off the food clinging to my mu`umu`u, evidence of the difficult time Myra and I had maneuvering between the crowded tables. Dad and I had to clean up after the lu`au, so I would join them later.

❦

After a hot shower, I popped in on my father. In comfortable blue pajamas, he had settled in his favorite stuffed armchair with a cup of tea, his weary legs propped up on an ottoman. The brass lamp at his side cast shadows across his closed eyes. His freshly washed hair was neatly parted and combed. A frown creased his forehead. I sat cross-legged at his feet, nursing a cup of jasmine tea.

My father smelled of the locally made soap, spicy and sweet like a tropical bloom. "Your friend got along well with Popo," he said.

"Yes, Alex has always been kind," I assured him. I wondered if he had chosen this moment to lecture me about my night with Alex.

My father placed his hands on my shoulder with a faraway look in his eyes. "When I was a young man," he began with a deep sigh of remembrance, "I went to Maui with two other fellas. It took thirteen hours by cattle boat. Up and down that boat went. Up and down in the waves. Side to side. And it stunk! When we got to the coast of Maui, the cattle swam through the surf to the beach."

"How did you get to shore?"

My father chuckled. "My friends rowed a dinky row boat. I told them to throw me overboard every time we hit a wave. I was so seasick! Took me a whole day to recover."

"Why did you go?" I asked. Of all of us Ai'Lees who got air-sick, car-sick, and seasick, my father was the worst. It had to be an extraordinarily compelling reason to get him in a boat. "Were you on vacation?"

His eyes crinkled. "No! I had a girlfriend there. Before your mother, of course."

"Dad!" I perked up. She must have really been something for him to risk the open seas.

"Oh, she was a beauty. Part-Hawaiian, part-Chinese, part-haole. When she danced the hula, the birds fell out of the trees." He grinned. "And her parents liked me."

"What happened?" I pressed. I couldn't imagine my father as a lovesick young man.

"Oh, your Popo threw a fit when she found out. She said, 'Whatsa matter you? No more Chinese girls?'" His voice caught as if he still remembered the pain. "I was the number-one son. I had responsibilities. I couldn't marry right away. My father had just died. Who would support my mother and my younger brother and sisters? My girlfriend got tired of waiting for me. I made your grandmother happy when I married your mother. Ah, Ellie was a gorgeous woman." Our eyes met, mirrors of each other. "What do you think about that, Miki?"

"It must have hurt for you to give her up," I said. "Your girlfriend in Maui, I mean."

My father smiled a faraway look. "But your mother captured my heart. And I didn't have to get seasick to see her."

"I hear you two were pretty racy. Wasn't it considered a mixed marriage, Hakka marrying Bhunti?" The two major groups of Chinese in Hawai`i were the Hakka, the mountain dwellers, and the Bhunti, the farmers. Each group spoke different dialects and, in China, each considered themselves superior to the other. Their prejudices followed them to Hawai`i.

"Oh, those were the old days. Our parents were so old-fashioned. So conscious of class and clans. Ellie's grandparents said we Ai'Lee farmers were not good enough. But Ellie and I were the younger generation—born and raised in America. We married for love," he said.

"Dad, if you could marry for love, why couldn't your youngest sister? Popo Ai'Lee told me that she was disowned."

My father sat up. He picked up his tea and sipped slowly. His eyes drilled me with piercing sharpness. "I was the eldest living son, bound to honor my mother's wishes when she cut her ties to Ginger. My sister was eighteen when she made her choice."

"You never saw her again?"

My father sighed. "When I got married in 1935 she came alone to my wedding. She caught a cattle boat from the Big Island."

"Do you have her address?"

My father shook his head. "You know your grandmother. She never spoke of Ginger again and no one dares to mention her name. But when your mother passed away, a huge heart-shaped bouquet of blood-red anthuriums was delivered to her graveside. The ribbon said it was from Ginger and Jeremiah. When I called the florist for an address so I could write a thank you card, Mrs. Ikeda said it was called in from a Hilo florist and paid in cash."

With a single glance he knew what I was thinking. "Leave the past alone, Miki. It's too dangerous." His voice was barely a whisper.

I kissed him good night and headed up the hill to Lailee Ai'Lee's house, up the dark mountain path lit by the iridescent sliver of moon. The sweet winds rushing through the valley breathed their haunting secrets. I yielded to the wildness of the night. I stopped by a low lava wall and slipped off my sandals. The wet grass, sensuous and soft, squished between my toes. I laughed to myself. A strange warmth tingled my body. I held out my arms and tipped my head back to breathe in the quiet darkness.

What spirits roaming the lands called to me? What was it about the whispers I heard in the trade winds, the calm sighs of the surf, and the wise silences of Popo Ai'Lee? I whispered my secrets to them, thinking of the lives I had here and elsewhere. I filled my lungs with the power that comes only from this ancient land. All around me, I felt the presence of the unseen and heard the Night Whispers in the rustle of the leaves repeat their chant, "You are ours. We belong to you."

I reached out for the ancient ones dancing in the sway of the trees and felt them caress my fingertips.

Chapter Thirteen

Ga Na Gnew, The Hawaiian

*T*he familiar scent of Chinese sandalwood wafted from Lailee's house when I opened her unlocked door. Low conspiratorial voices floated from the living room.

My grandmother sat in the golden glow of a yellowed fringed lamp with a photo album on her lap. "Aah, you come, Miki," she beamed.

Alex jumped up from my grandmother's side on the tropical print sofa. "Popo is showing me her family." He greeted me with a hug. "You know how old photographs intrigue me."

"Oh, Popo," I moaned, "when we were kids?" I knew her entire collection by heart but I had never seen this black, deckle-edged album. Its edges were frayed and its cardboard cover splotched with white and brown cockroach droppings.

Despite her age, my grandmother's memory was exact and picture-perfect. Once, when I had driven her through the maze of steel skyscrapers and concrete slab buildings butted side-by-side in Ala Moana, she remembered what the going price was for the swampland offered for sale in the twenties—pennies per acre. On the spot, she calculated the profit she would have made if she could have bought the acreage then.

"Not your family, my family. Gung-Gung Ai'Lee and our children. See?" Lailee replied. She motioned Alex back to his seat next to her. I knelt at her side and peered at the photo.

An imperious, heavyset man, thick cigar firmly clamped between the second and third fingers of his right hand, leaned forward from his seat. He held his elbows away from his broad shoulders and rested his thick hands on muscular thighs. Popo Ai'Lee, in younger days when her black hair was pulled back from a smooth, unlined face, sat on his left. She clutched her hands awkwardly on her lap. Their children—four willowy young girls in long cotton cheong-sams; Kam and Ted, the lanky young sons in white mandarin gowns and skull caps—stood solemnly behind them with faraway looks in their eyes.

"That year, my husband, your Gung-Gung, insisted we take a family picture. All in Chinese dress, cheong-sam. See? The photographer took the picture in our front yard against the hedge. Aah! Makes us look like country folk."

"No, Popo, it looks wonderful—like old Hawai`i," I disagreed. I stared at the faces in the sepia photo. "I've never seen this picture before. In fact, I've never seen a picture of Gung-Gung Ai'Lee until now." He was a powerful man, judging from his firmly set jaw, used to giving absolute commands and being quickly obeyed. His brows were low in a frown, as if he were threatening the photographer. "Look at his heavy build." I pointed out to Alex. "The thick features, full lips, wide nose, skin the color of kukui nut. Looks full-blooded Hawaiian, doesn't he?" Exactly like Auntie Pua's and Auntie Lehua's boys. My cousin Reginald was the spitting image of Gung-Gung Ai'Lee.

And the little girl with the crooked smile and giant bow on her head must be Ginger Ai'Lee.

"He spoke Hawaiian," I told Alex. He understood the way of the older generation, their pride in being pure Chinese, whereas today, most people boasted of their ethnic mixture. "He was called 'Ga Na Gnew, The Hawaiian,' by the Chinese and the Hawaiians." I did not mention that in his darkest moods, my grandfather's curses against the Demmings echoed off the valley walls.

"Too bad he didn't pass the Hawaiian language on to his children and grandchildren," Alex mused. "Too few of us speak the native language."

"Humph! Baba and I spoke Hawaiian when we didn't want the children to understand what we said. They already knew Chinese and English."

As Lailee turned to each photo, she wove nostalgic tales of a long-ago Hawai`i. I learned that my grandfather leased acres of land in Manoa Valley, where he hired Japanese women to stand knee-deep from sunup to sundown in the flooded taro terraces. Their few neighbors were farmers, like themselves, who lived hours away by foot across numerous streams. His true talent was in his hands and brawn. He built my grandmother a house surrounded by a huge porch and a penned yard with coops for her chickens. Here, Lailee delivered all ten of their children herself. Each time, Ga Na Gnew left for the banana or taro fields and by the time he returned at sundown, Lailee had delivered her baby, slaughtered a chicken, and picked the vegetables for dinner. Of the ten, six survived to adulthood.

Their first son slipped in the fields when the flood waters rose in Manoa Valley during a hurricane. Ga Na

Gnew went hoarse screaming for his son through the wind and rain. The next day, they found their son's twisted body in one of the numerous streams, wedged against a mountain apple tree. Eight years later, when the flu killed thousands of people, there weren't enough coffins to bury everyone, including another son and daughter.

Lailee said that she heard her little ones cry in the winds that swept through Manoa at night. The Japanese workers told her that their spirits were in good company; at night, Hawaiian spirits walked the valley paths as they had in the days before the Americans came. Lailee recalled harrowing tales of hurricanes that swept roofs off sturdy wooden homes, of tidal waves that washed away whole villages, and how everyone had run out to their porches that Sunday morning, December 7, to watch Pearl Harbor explode in flames.

Lailee leaned back. "Miki, you see it is better you live in Hawai`i. Here you have history all around you." She circled her hands expansively.

"My job is in the mainland, Popo." I bowed my head when I saw how her eyes bored into me, trying to hold me close once again.

"Humph, I know why you left home, Miki Ai'Lee." She wagged her finger at me. "Too bad you're so smart. When you were a little girl, we said, 'Ah, too bad Miki isn't a boy. Smart boys can get ahead, not smart girls.' But times are different."

I turned away from her and defiantly stepped out of the circle of light framing Popo and Alex. I sought the darkness of the picture window overlooking the city and the gloom of the night shadows.

Popo's voice softened. "My Miki, how I miss your sharp tongue and sassy ways. Braxton and Kam grow soft without you to prod them and make them think."

I blinked back the tears, but the old hurts surged forward and tore me apart.

My grandmother leaned back, clutching the photo album to her chest. The golden glow of the lamp could not hide the pain in her eyes. For the first time, I saw her as a vulnerable woman, not the strong, all-knowing matriarch of our family. But instead of comforting her, I stubbornly stayed in the shadows and crossed my arms against my chest. I asked roughly, "Why didn't you stand up for me? Why didn't you tell my parents to treat me the same as Braxton?"

"It was not for me for say. Your mother knew how do things right, Chinese-style. She taught you to be a proper Chinese lady. You love what is Chinese and understand Confucian ways. You understand Chinese ways as well as Western ways and respect both. What more can we wish for?"

Alex stepped to my side in the shadows. I was so incensed by the inequities churned up by these long-buried memories that I didn't see him. I whirled angrily when he touched my shoulder. His expression stopped me cold. Alex cupped my chin firmly in his hands. "Shh, Miki, it's the past."

I wished I had his self-contained confidence. But I didn't. I was carrying too much around in my heart and head: anger and old rules that weren't important any more. It was quiet, so quiet I couldn't hear the wind or the crickets. I took a deep breath. Useless anger burned away until nothing was left but ashes billowing away in the trade winds.

Lailee looked up at Alex and said, "How many times Miki's mother cried, 'What am I going to do with Miki? Miki makes Braxton cry. Miki talks back. She always needs to have the last word. Miki is so stubborn! What Chinese boy will want a girl who rushes through housework so she can climb a tree to read? Who will marry her?'

"Your fault, I told Ellie. All the time you tell her 'Study, study, study.' What did you expect?

"Ellie said, 'Whatever Braxton does, Miki must do also. Then she beats him at it. She'd rather pull weeds with Kam than dust the house. When I send her out to hang clothes, she flings the clothespins at Braxton. What am I going to do with her?'" Lailee chuckled so hard her shoulders pumped up and down. "'So?' I said to Ellie, 'maybe Miki will grow up to be like me!'"

Alex was smiling, trying not to laugh out loud.

I turned away from my grandmother and looked him in the eyes.

"You're right, Popo Ai'Lee," he said. "Miki's smart, just like you."

And there, in front of my grandmother, I ran my fingers tenderly along his rugged beard. We wrapped our arms around each other and recognized in each other's eyes a long-ago innocence, a time before pain, of love rekindled.

Chapter Fourteen

Taiko Drum Beats

*O*n hot, humid evenings during Obon Festival time, the air sizzles with the smell of teriyaki on charcoal hibachis. From July through August, sedate Japanese Buddhist temples sprout chains of white paper lanterns, like hundreds of new moons, strung gaily from the trees and fence posts. Mama-sans and papa-sans in summer kimonos or cotton yukatas—short, wide-sleeved garments suitable for hot evenings—flock through the decorated Tori gates. They join the Bon Dancers snaking around the koto players and singers on the bandstand. Their lilting songs draw crowds of celebrants. Some dance, some watch, some stroll the decorated booths of food, handicrafts, and bonsai.

According to a Japanese legend, the custom of dancing in honor of the dead is part of the annual Obon Festival, the Festival of Flowers, which began twenty-five-hundred years ago. Mogallana, one of Buddha's disciples, had dreamt that his mother suffered in a hell of hungry ghosts. Buddha advised him to honor his mother by selflessly giving on her behalf. At the end of the rainy season, Mogallana distributed clothing and food at an outdoor gathering under starry skies. As he did so, he had a vision of his mother enjoying the peaceful tranquillity of

Nirvana. He danced for joy. Obon season became the traditional time of joyously remembering the dead.

Tonight promised to be warm and balmy. A bevy of Chinese ladies in gaily flowered mu`umu`us had whisked Dad off right after dinner for Tai chi class at the church. Would I join them? they asked. I watched as the colorful group of seniors paraded down the street and hoped I would be as carefree at that age as they were.

Alex and I joined the local throng at the Obon Festival at Hongwanji Mission. When we arrived, dancers were already swaying around the bandstand like long-stemmed flowers. Lured by the enticing aromas, we watched men and women in blue-bordered hapi coats grill chicken and beef teriyaki sticks on open air barbecues. The coals, pulsing red and dusted with white ash, simmered and spat like the fires of hell, exuding a thick aroma of onions, garlic, and soy sauce. Mama-sans and papa-sans twirled pots of crinkly saimin and fat udon noodles flecked with red slices of fishcake and diced green onion. Finally, we chose bento boxes of grilled eel musubi, maki sushi, and beef teriyaki sticks.

Alex balanced our boxes of food with one hand and squeezed my shoulder with the other. "I haven't seen a Bon Dance since high school. And I remember the teriyaki beef is the best at Hongwanji," he said. At six feet, he towered over the kimono-clad crowd. The relaxed smile on his face, his casual T-shirt and shorts, reminded me of younger days when we haunted every festival and carnival.

I followed Alex to a clear spot amidst the other picnickers sitting on the grassy knoll overlooking the grounds of the spired Buddhist temple. As we ate, we watched a kaleidoscope of swaying lanterns, waving fans, and flowing kimonos. The familiar polyglot of the Islands and the musical tones of Hawaiian pidgin surrounded us.

Then the music stopped and a rhythmic primal beat began. On the bandstand, Taiko drums, one of the central elements of Hawai`i's Bon Odori since 1910, reverberated with the intensity of the drummers' spruce and oak beaters. The voice of the Taiko is often associated with the gods. Its name means "fat drum," although most of the instruments were smaller than the nine-foot, barrel-shaped monster mounted in the center of the stage. A Japanese man, stripped to the waist, his head wrapped with a red, black, and white headband, powered the thunderous rhythms with clean, even strokes. A high-pitched drum called the shime-daiko wove in and out of the solo beats with a sensuous rhythm. Four large black drums mounted on natural wood stands added propulsive riffs that moved the music with textured complexity. The metallic ring of the tetsu-zutsu, a bell-like instrument, wove through the music like a ribbon.

Alex dumped our empty bento boxes in the metal garbage can nearby. When he returned, I put my left hand on his shoulder and with the other, marked out the music. "Listen! You hear the jazzy rhythm?"

He cocked his head to follow the beats. "I remember when a solo Taiko drum was used mainly in temples and kendo, judo, and karate dojos. What's this sound?" he asked.

"The ensemble style was created by Daihachi Oguchi, a jazz drummer. Sukeroku Daiko started this performing style, emphasizing speed, fluidity, and power. Notice the choreography and flashy solos?" The beat caught my body in its sway.

Mesmerized, we watched the drummers, the intricate rotation from one drum to another, from side to front. The dancers, along with the rest of the crowd, cheered and clapped when an intricate riff was completed. We were all on our feet, hearts beating to the rhythms of an ancient/contemporary music on this warm summer evening. Alex wrapped his arms around my waist and we moved as one.

An hour later, the drums echoed into silence. The singers returned to the stage and the dancers returned to their circles around the bandstand, fans aloft.

Alex held me so we were face to face in the moonlight. He caressed my cheeks. "What have I missed, Miki? What have I let slip between my fingers?" He closed his eyes and we kissed, oblivious to the voices around us, to the pentatonic Japanese folk songs from the stage, the dance of lanterns in the trees, the sway of kimonos, and the enticing scents of exotic foods. "Stay with me. Teach me to see as you see. I want to learn all that I've missed." His voice was seductively low with his longing.

"I will. I'll be here through August."

"No, forever." He laughed. "I've spent twelve years in hell. With you I feel at peace, complete. Come live with me on Kaua`i." His eyes danced with the glow of the lanterns. "The sun is sweet, the sky's so blue, and the wind smells of the sea. And the night sky is so black the stars are rivers of glitter just beyond our fingertips." As he spoke, he threw his arms back to encompass all he was offering me.

I paused, confused by his request. "But I have classes to teach in the fall."

He grabbed me by the shoulders. "But that was before, Miki. Now it's us." His voice was cajoling, beguiling. "Miki, I know a rancher's life isn't as glamorous or exciting as living in town, but it's fulfilling. And the way we ranch, it is a life close to nature." He took a deep breath and spoke again, deeper now. "Damn the Demming curse, Miki! Come with me."

I looked down, searching for the words to explain. I looked up and caressed his bristly cheek. "I spent six months holding my mother's hand while she was dying, unable to stop her pain. She wanted more time and had so many unfulfilled dreams. I bargained with the gods, cursed them, and cried in despair. I realized then that tomorrow is promised to no one. I've worked a dozen years to get this far in my teaching career. That doesn't mean I don't love you. Please, Alex, give me some time."

He glowered. He stepped back and the night air chilled with his anger and frustration. "You want time? I've seen firsthand that there's never enough time for the ones we love. We could lose everyone we cherish in an instant."

I gripped my forehead. I needed to work this out logically, the way I always figured out problems. I lowered my voice. "I've had losses too, Alex. Maybe not as traumatic as yours, but my mother's death made me realize that dreams are just as fragile as life. You've had your career, your adventures. You're ready for a shift into another life. But I'm not. I can't commit to you, not right now." We were both scarred by death, shattered by loss.

Alex stared silently out into the night, seeing nothing, or maybe seeing everything. He turned and asked bluntly, "Miki, will you come with me to Kaua`i?" His voice was hard and demanding.

I shook my head. The evening had turned sour and sad, disappointing and unfulfilling.

We drove home in silence. Before I got out of the car, I leaned over and kissed him on the lips. Then I leapt out and ran up the front steps.

Chapter Fifteen

Ginger Ai'Lee

*F*rom the air, the rounded volcanic peaks of Mauna Loa and Mauna Kea loomed high above the layer of fluffy clouds that shrouded the Big Island of Hawai`i. By the time I walked to the car rental booths, dawn had burnt through the clouds on what promised to be a sunny day.

I did a quick check of all the rental agents. One was a heavyset blond man in a collarless shirt and jacket who spoke with a New York staccato. Another, a twentyish woman who looked like she had never gone out in the sun, glanced up from her physics textbook. In the next, I admired a tanned broad-shouldered man with dark eyes and winning smile who was helping a young couple.

I returned to an older woman dressed in a red and white mu`umu`u with tawny brown skin and thick brown hair pulled back in a bun. A big woman with dark eyes ringed with thick brown lashes and full lips, she was cheerful and chatty. She spoke perfect English to the sweating business-man at her counter. Then she switched to the local pidgin, unintelligible to the tourist she was helping, when she picked up the phone to order his car. When her customer left, I approached. Her name tag said "Irma." She would know what I needed.

"Auntie Irma," I said, in my most "local" pidgin. "I stay looking for my Auntie Ginger and Uncle Jeremiah. I know they stay Hilo. How I find 'em?"

"Aloha." She stretched the word out like a piece of caramel. Her smile was generous and friendly. "You from Honolulu? I can tell by the way you talk. Who's your family?" Someone born and raised in Hawai`i could tell which island, which neighborhood—sometimes which high school—a person came from just by his or her dialect of pidgin.

I told her my Auntie Ginger's maiden name was Ai'Lee, and that she came from Honolulu in 1928 as a new schoolteacher fresh out of teacher's college. She had married in Hilo, to a local fisherman.

Irma leaned forward, her chin in her hand. "Hmm, I was a little girl in school right here in Hilo-town. My sixth grade teacher was a Miss Ginger, but she wasn't an Ai'Lee. Maybe there's another one? Your Auntie Ginger must be in her sixties, almost retired. Her husband might be retired, or maybe not; fishermen never retire." She picked up the phone and dialed. "Mama? This is Irma. Yes, I'm at work. I get one Honolulu girl here from the Ai'Lee family looking for her Auntie Ginger who was a schoolteacher in Hilo. Don't know what grade. You know her? Where? What family? The same one related to Charles and Honey Girl? She's the one get four u`i sons? What's the address?" Irma's face was radiant when she hung up. She looked at me and wiggled her eyebrows with delight. She dialed again. "Nathan? This is Auntie Irma. You come get your cousin Miki. Take her to your Auntie Ginger's."

"No, no." I protested. "I'll rent a car and drive myself."

Irma's eyebrows and arms jiggled when she laughed. "Nah, nah, nah!" She waved away my credit card. "No need!" She pointed to me, then to herself. "Your auntie's husband, Jeremiah, is the son of my sister's husband's cousin. We're family! Nathan will drive you to their house. Got any luggage?"

Besides my purse, all I carried was my briefcase with a notebook and recent photos of the Ai'Lees: Auntie Pua and Uncle Roland and their boys, a black and white of Kam and Ellie with me and Braxton dressed for Easter church service twenty years ago, Auntie Lehua and Uncle Robert with their sons Gordon and Ken at the beach, Auntie Vanda and Uncle Mark at a long-ago family wedding, Uncle Ted in his army uniform with Auntie Verna and their children, and the old family picture that included Gung-Gung Ai'Lee and Auntie Ginger with a big bow in her hair.

I couldn't turn down Irma's hospitality without offending her. So it was settled. "Thank you, Auntie Irma. By the way, you said Auntie Ginger's sons were u`i. What does that mean?"

"U`i means your aunt's sons are handsome and they're built like gods." She straightened her spine and held her hands up to her ample chest. "Muscles like this. They pull the best of their Hawaiian-Chinese-haole blood." She waved her hand in emphasis. "All the girls went crazy for them when they were in school. But your Auntie Ginger is one tough schoolteacher. She made sure studies came first for her boys. Two finished college with scholarships. They're working on the mainland."

A green pickup, rusted and sun-faded, screeched up to Irma's booth. A skinny teenager leapt out of the still-running truck while simultaneously putting on a starched white shirt. "Auntie Irma," he called. "I came for cousin Miki." He was fair, with light green eyes, thick curly brown hair, and a golden tan—an exotic mixture of Caucasian, Asian, and Hawaiian. He had deep dimples in his boyish face and stood a foot taller than I in his bare feet.

"I'm Miki." I held out my hand. "Are you old enough to drive?" I asked cautiously. Nathan would be a heart-breaker when he grew up. His hair was wet and he smelled of the sea, as if he had just leapt from the waves to come and get me.

"I'm sixteen. Got my permit. You're a licensed driver, right?" Nathan showed a shockingly white set of perfect teeth. "Sorry I didn't have time to get dressed. I just got back from swim practice when Auntie Irma called and I'm on my way to school." He buttoned up his shirt and smoothed down his khaki slacks.

"Barefoot?"

He pointed to the leather shoes stuffed with a pair of socks in the bed of the truck. "Didn't have time to put them on. You know real Hawaiians drive barefoot." He pulled out into traffic and we waved good-bye to Auntie Irma.

"I'll see you when you get back," she bellowed as we barreled away.

Nathan and I bumped along the back roads. Mango trees heavy with fruit, hedges of white ginger, and ti plants lined the road. He turned makai, toward the ocean. Here, one-story wood homes, built about four feet off the ground, stood in the center of emerald lawns spotted with plume-ria trees and tall hibiscus shrubs. There were no fences and the lots undulated towards the sea. The homes were on the mauka side of the road.

"Where do you get your green eyes from, if you don't mind me asking?" I asked.

"From my father. He's haole-Hawaiian. My mother is Japanese from Hilo." He smiled shyly. "Everyone asks me that." He had two brothers and a sister, all in college at the University of Hawai`i on the Manoa and Hilo campuses. He was hoping for a swimming scholarship to a mainland school.

Nathan pulled slowly up a dirt driveway that led to a green house where a big blue pickup, its bed loaded with large coolers, was parked in the carport. "This is Auntie Ginger's house, cousin. I'm sure Uncle Jeremiah will take you back to the airport. I have to get to school."

I slipped a twenty in Nathan's pocket before I got out. He protested.

I insisted. "Chinese-style. I must give you good-luck money. This is for your schooling, for your future."

Nathan leaned forward and kissed my cheek. "Mahalo, cousin Miki. A hui hou, see you again." He backed out the dirt driveway and returned the way he had come.

I turned and nervously faced the modest wood house surrounded by four-foot poinsettia bushes. This must be a stunning spot around Christmas when the blooming bracts turned crimson. A short-haired dog, an indeterminate breed locals called a poi dog, ambled from the back of the house. He wagged his tail as if he had expected my arrival. He barked once. I heard a voice inside the house call out "Buster, who's that?" just before the front screen door opened.

I stared at a slender woman in a floral dress and a strand of long white pearls. She looked exactly like Auntie Pua did ten years ago. She was about my height and wore her thick salt-and-pepper hair in an elegant upswept French twist.

"Can I help you?" Her words were distinctly enunciated like Auntie Vanda's. She approached with the same grace and smile of Auntie Lehua.

I took a deep breath and cleared my throat. "Excuse me. Are you Ginger Ai'Lee?"

She slipped on a pair of slippers outside the door and walked down the stairs. Her almond slanted eyes skewered me with a direct and searching gaze. "Yes?" She sounded the way I remembered my schoolteachers, all business on the first day of school.

I held out my hand, nervously, formally. How did one greet an aunt who had been disowned, whose existence I had never known about until now? "Auntie Ginger, my name is Miki Ai'Lee. My father is Kam, my mother was Ellie."

"Ah!" She clapped both cheeks with her hands. She rocked forward, backward, putting a hand to her heart, clasping the pearls circling her neck.

I rushed to catch her.

She waved a hand in front of her. "I'm fine, fine." Her embrace was long and firm. "Come in, Miki Ai'Lee. Come in." She stopped and dabbed at her eyes with a tissue. "Excuse me, I'm in shock. Oh, what a wonderful surprise." She opened her screen door and we stepped into her home.

Her sunny kitchen opened up into a large, comfortably furnished room, which I imagined was the center of family life. Nearest the kitchen was a large wooden dining table with eight chairs. There was a much-used plaid sofa, koa rocking chairs, end tables stacked with books, and an upright piano. In the corner were a couple of guitar cases and canoe paddles. A large window next to the dining room looked out to the front yard, and beyond that, to the sea. The opposing window looked out to a kitchen garden of herbs and vegetables, a swath of green lawn, and a row of trees.

Ginger turned to me with almond eyes as impenetrable as my father's, and asked, "Have you eaten yet? Let me cook you breakfast. Uncle Jeremiah will be back in an hour. Join me in the kitchen." She was an Ai'Lee woman, all right. Within minutes she was preparing eggs from her chickens, chives from her garden, and homemade Portuguese sausages into aromatic omelets. When I offered to help, she selected a ripe papaya from the basket on her kitchen table. I stood at her sink and sliced the papaya, saving the seeds for her garden.

Ginger wasn't shy with her questions. While we ate, I told her that my father had retired shortly after my mother had died eight years ago, that her eldest sister Pua was in the beginning stages of Parkinson's, that her sister Vanda was widowed, and that Ted had returned from the war a quieter man. Her mother Lailee, at ninety-one, was starting to talk about the old days, which is how I had learned about her.

She got up from the table and picked up a few framed photos. "Here are your cousins, Miki." Her eyes softened in happy crinkles when she gazed at each photo. Her sons were handsome boys, even featured, with strong direct gazes and generous Ai'Lee smiles. I recognized the twinkle of Popo Ai'Lee's dark eyes in one, my father's high cheekbones in two, and confident attitudes in all. Her two older boys had graduated from mainland colleges. Her eldest was a doctor at a Los Angeles hospital, married with three girls. Their second son was a businessman in Oregon, married with two sons. After her third son graduated from high school, he decided he wanted to be a fisherman like his father. He married his high school sweetheart and was living in Hilo with their four children.

Her youngest was at the University of Hawai`i Hilo campus. A talented artist, he had been offered a scholarship to the Rhode Island School of Design. "He was our afterthought," she confessed. She lifted an eyebrow and grinned, revealing two deep dimples. "He's kept Uncle Jeremiah and me young." They had hoped to retire and take a trip to the mainland to see their older sons and grandchildren, but not until their youngest graduated from college.

I watched her face with fascination, as if I were watching a younger version of Aunties Pua, Lehua, and Vanda. She had their animation and precise articulation, emphasized by youthful, lilting dark eyes.

"Auntie Ginger, I didn't come to intrude upon your life," I assured her. "When Popo Ai'Lee told me that I had an auntie I had never met, I was ashamed that no one kept in contact with you. The Ai'Lees are such a loving family." I tried to imagine her as the sophisticated flapper my father had described. He said she was the most stylish of his sisters, wearing marcelled waves in her short black hair, and always a long string of pearls.

She looked out the window and sighed. She stood up and replaced each picture, running her fingers lightly along each frame. "You have no idea, Miki, how stifling it was for me to be a woman in a traditional Chinese family in Honolulu. Here I am free. I can teach school and raise my sons in a small, safe community. Your Uncle Jeremiah is easygoing and relaxed. He fishes in the early morning and spends the afternoons with his sons after school. It has been a wholesome, natural way to live."

I was beginning to see the attraction of living far from a big city. I nodded with new understanding. "I brought some pictures for you. Do you want to see them?"

Ginger leaned forward and asked warily. "To see what I've been missing?"

"No," I shook my head. "To see the ones who miss and love you."

She leaned back and clasped her hands on the table. "How I missed them the first few years. At first, I thought of going to Honolulu to see my mother, and sisters, and brothers, even though my mother made it clear I had dishonored not only the Ai'Lees, but my fiancé's family. It must have been terrible for the Ai'Lees; I, an engaged young woman, had suddenly married a man no one knew. Even worse, my mother did not approve of him or his profession." She smiled with the memory of the handsome young fisherman who had captured her heart. "I regret that I've hurt so many people. But I have no regrets about marrying the generous man who has given me a bountiful life and four precious sons." Ginger took a deep breath and gestured proudly at the sea and the mountains, "And a home in the most beautiful setting on earth." She nodded. "Show me those pictures."

I handed her the photos one by one and described the families of Pua, Kam, Lehua, Vanda, and Ted.

"Oh, Pua, her long black hair, her beautiful treasure, has turned white. How does Vanda stay so trim? She still has those long, shapely legs. And Kam is even more handsome now that he's gray." She looked up with tears in her eyes and grabbed another tissue. "Oh, Miki, I'm so sorry you lost your mother. I returned to Honolulu only once, for your parents' wedding. Only your father and mother dared to talk to me." She turned to the next photo. "Lehua and Robert, as youthful as ever. And all these handsome nieces and nephews of mine! So many boys!" As she oohed and aahed, I saw the years slip from her face and body. I could see her as an eager and curious young girl. The last photo I gave her was one that cousin Reginald took of us the day the Ai'Lee ladies had lunch at Auntie Pua's. The only Ai'Lee lady missing was Ginger.

Her tears fell anew the minute she picked up that picture. She touched Lailee's face as if she were caressing her cheek, then Pua, then Lehua, then Vanda. "Forty-two years. Forty-two years of silence." She cried in earnest now. I got up and brought a dish towel to wipe her face. "How much we might have shared." She looked up at me, her eyes swollen and red. "They would have loved my boys, Miki. My mother would have been proud of them."

I got up from the table, found her teapot, and brewed a pot of tea. We continued to talk as we cleared the table and washed the dishes. We moved with the same energy and economy of motion and fell into a comfortable pattern as if we had been doing these chores together all our lives.

We walked out to her garden and chicken coops. My father could have spent hours inspecting her neat rows of fat and leafy Chinese vegetables. Lailee would have been amazed at the quantity of large eggs Ginger's chickens produced, more than enough for their needs.

Her gaze drifted towards the ocean. "Come, Miki. I want to show you something you have never seen."

Buster rose when we passed him on the front porch. He followed us, tail wagging lazily. I followed Ginger across her front lawn to the beach, across the narrow road where wild hens scratched with their chicks.

As far as we could see, the coastline stretched before us in exquisite majesty. White-capped waves crashed upon a coastline of black lava, craggy tidal pools, and stretches of white sand. Beyond the beach, the ocean was deep, dark blue. Above, pure white clouds puffed and stretched across a brilliant wind-swept sky. This was paradise.

"Watch!" Ginger pointed to an outcropping of lava where a dark figure was threatened by waves crashing high over his head.

The man stood motionless, solidly unmovable, as plumes of ocean were pulverized into sprays of white foam. With a graceful motion, he rotated back and cast his net high over his head into the surf. His arms, legs, and torso were knotted with huge muscles, yet he moved as elegantly as a choreographer dancing with the waves. He leaned forward. The surf crashed over him and he was gone. The wave pulled out, came back, pulled out again. Many minutes later, he emerged from a sandy part of the beach through a break in the surf. His net, lively with fish, was slung over one of his massive shoulders. Ginger waved. He beamed. She ran like a little girl to greet him. He put his arm around her waist and they walked back to his cooler under the shade of a coconut tree.

I walked barefoot across the sand to join them. "May I help?" I asked.

"Miki," Ginger grabbed my hand. "Meet your Uncle Jeremiah." She looked up at her husband. "This is our niece, Miki Ai'Lee, my brother Kam's daughter."

I was immediately struck by my uncle's tender smile and sense of peace. If his hands hadn't been full of fish, I was certain he'd have given me a crushing hug.

Up close, I could see his eyes, dark brown with flecks of gold and green, and his eyelashes, enviably long and meltingly lush. He had a kind face framed with brown sun-streaked hair. Water beaded over his deeply tanned skin and dripped from a pair of much-faded swim trunks. I wondered how he could walk barefoot on the lava rock. "Always room for one more pair of hands," he said with a ready smile. "Let's dump the fish in ice." His voice was deep, musical, and gentle.

Together, we slid his catch onto a bed of ice. He had brilliant peach and turquoise parrot fish, bright red snappers, as well as silver mullet, all good-sized. He picked out the smaller ones and, with Buster leaping at his feet, returned those to the sea.

Back at the house, Ginger and Jeremiah packed up most of the catch, enough for all the Ai'Lees, in a large Styrofoam cooler for me to take home. "The gods must have known you were coming. On Sundays, I go surf casting just for fun. Today, the fish were fighting to get into my net!" Jeremiah said. He had rinsed off under the outdoor shower at the back of the house and had returned smelling of Lava soap.

He didn't ask why after forty-two years someone from his wife's family sought her out. He was curious, but I could see he was a patient man. After all, he was a fisherman, reader of tides and currents, of clouds and winds, who could wait out seasons and cycles.

We sat out on the front porch with glasses of guava juice. There was a bench, a couple of koa rockers, and the stairs to sit on. Jeremiah settled on the bench with a ukulele and began to strum. Ginger sat on a koa rocker where she could watch him, her hands unconsciously fingering the pearls in her necklace. I could see how Ginger, a young teacher away from home for the first time, had been captivated. His voice, smooth, rich and powerful, flowed effortlessly. "You like?" he asked.

"Oh yes," I answered. I sat on the steps and leaned back on one of the pillars of the porch. "I can't think of a better way to spend a Sunday."

"Just like your Auntie," he said. "She was so proper and—I hate to offend—so Chinese when she came. She never wore a mu`umu`u, always a dress with matching shoes and hats. And when she taught, she wore a pearl necklace with jade and gold earrings. As you can see, she still wears those pearls. But she learned to relax. This is country compared to Hilo-town."

"Was your father a fisherman?" I asked.

"I never knew him." He put down his ukulele and stared in my eyes as if reading my soul. "I never talk about him. But now, people understand about certain diseases." He paused as if considering what he would say next.

Auntie Ginger rocked in her chair with a smile on her face, as if she had complete confidence that whatever her husband said would be perfect.

His eyes were sad. "My father was sent to Kalaupapa before I was born." Leprosy had appeared in the islands in the 1800s. With no known cure, the government had gathered up the lepers and dumped them in the surf off the isolated north coast peninsula on the island of Moloka`i. The lucky ones made it to shore. Steep cliffs and swift ocean currents kept the lepers, already hindered by their disease, from escaping. In the late 1940s, sulfone drugs brought leprosy under control. But in the early 1900s, Jeremiah's father was banished to a life of isolation, far from his family.

"My mother was left with six children to raise. She sent me, the baby, to live with her `ohana, her family. Maybe that's why I grew up more Hawaiian-style. I lived with my grandparents. We grew our own taro for poi, raised pigs and chickens, and fished every day. Maybe that's why I like fishing rather than politics like the other Demmings on this island. My brother's boy, he's in Honolulu now."

"Christopher Demming?" I asked.

"You know him?" He sounded surprised.

I shook my head. "I met him once."

"That Chris! Smooth-talking, butter-tongued little kid. He'd sell you the shirt off your own back. He's got the Demming temper, but inside, he's soft. He has a good heart."

I stared at this sun-weathered, barefoot man. Everything about him was natural and easy. So I didn't feel uncomfortable asking the obvious question. "Uncle

Jeremiah, I don't understand your genealogy. I was told Arthur Demming's fourth son had five children, not six."

The huge man looked at his wife, then back at me. "I was born a month after my father was sent to Kalaupapa. My mother sent me home to her parents in South Kona, where I was raised by aunties and uncles. No newspapers, no telephone. My older brothers and sisters were going to school in Hilo-town, which was days away by horseback. They had a different lifestyle. Washington and Jefferson aspired to politics. Even hidden in South Kona, I learned there were bad feelings between the Ai'Lees and the Demmings. I heard about the Demmings and the Ai'Lee land, the mysterious Ai'Lee and Demming murders, and the Dr. Ai'Lee who exiled my father to the leper colony of Kalaupapa, where he died. But Ginger and I were willing to put all that behind us. We were in love. I was taught honor, love, and good honest work. I never would have married your auntie if I knew her family was going to dis-own her. Although I cannot imagine life without her."

Ginger rocked with her heels on the wooden porch. "My mother was livid when I told her I had married Jeremiah Demming. If only she had met him, she would have known what a generous, kind man I married." She sounded wistful.

"Not if she's like you." Jeremiah turned his body towards me and jerked his head at his wife. "Your auntie is the smartest lady on this island. But she is so stubborn. Are all the Ai'Lees like that?" His eyes twinkled mischievously.

"No, only the Ai'Lee ladies," I assured him.

So Auntie Ginger's dishonor wasn't just because she married a fisherman, she had married the grandson of Arthur Demming.

Jeremiah picked up his ukulele and sang a naughty song to his wife, complete with winking eyes and wagging head, shifting shoulders and a wiggle of the hips. Ginger clapped her hands and blushed. Obviously, this was one of their favorites. He slipped into some old Hawaiian songs, his bare feet tapping robustly on the wood floor. Buster sat up and wagged his tail.

And this is how we passed our Sunday afternoon, while the breeze blew in with the sweet smell of the ocean and the scent of white gingers growing wild.

—❀—

My father was in his garden when I drove back from the airport. "Where did you go so early?" he asked. A sprinkling of dirt covered his jeans. He had on his baseball cap and in his hands, a trowel. "I got your note that you'd be gone for the day with the car, but you didn't say where you went." He sounded hurt that I hadn't confided in him.

I unlocked the trunk of the Plymouth and lifted out the Styrofoam cooler. I said softly, gently, "This is from your sister Ginger and her husband, Jeremiah Demming."

My father staggered against the wall of the carport. He stared with disbelief at the chest, then at me. "You saw her? My sister? And him?"

I put the chest down on the garage floor and put my hand on his shoulder. "She's happy, Dad. She misses you all, but I don't think she would have given up a minute of her life with Jeremiah and her sons. They sent the Ai'Lees these gifts."

We broke the news to Lailee Ai'Lee first. During the short flight from Hilo to Honolulu, I wondered how I was going to explain to my grandmother that I had disobeyed her. During the drive to her house, it was my father's turn to fret. He wrung his hands and stared nervously at the road.

We carried the fish up my grandmother's concrete stairs. We paused at the landing and put down the ice chest to gather our courage. I took a deep breath. The air was thick with the scent of yellow gingers lining the entire front of the house. Gingers. Auntie Ginger. I bent my head and inhaled their heady sweetness. She may have disowned her youngest daughter, but every time my grandmother opened her front door, she remembered Ginger. My grandmother had planted this reminder.

Auntie Vanda was still at Popo Ai'Lee's when we arrived. Both sat stunned when I told them of my visit. Then they were in tears. Vanda clasped Lailee's hands. "Ma, isn't this wonderful? Ginger has four sons and she's still teaching! It sounds like Jeremiah is a good husband. I can't believe she's still wearing those pearls!" She opened the ice chest. "I'm calling Ted and his family to come over for dinner. After all, Verna can't cook anything, especially fish. Miki, help me choose a few and you take the rest to Pua and Lehua and of course, have your father grill a nice fish dinner for you and Braxton's family."

"I didn't tell her to go," Kam fretted. "She did it on her own."

"That's all right, Kam. It turned out well, didn't it?" Vanda soothed him. She plucked a few fish in a large bowl in preparation for the dinner she was planning for Popo and her brother's family.

My grandmother stopped me on my way out. "Thank you, Miki." Her eyes were swollen and red, her voice choked.

We drove to each of my aunties' and uncles' homes with Ginger's and Jeremiah's gifts of the sea. At our next stop, Auntie Pua held her chest and sobbed her sister's name. Uncle Roland called his boys and their families to come for dinner.

Then we drove to Lehua and Robert's house up the street. Auntie Lehua collapsed in my father's arms. Uncle Robert picked up one of the biggest fish in the pile and cradled it in both hands with awe and admiration. It was a parrotfish, still glossy as if it were freshly plucked from the sea. "Can't catch any this size around Oʻahu anymore," he said. "You think Jeremiah will take me fishing?"

All the while, my father seesawed between the happiness of hearing me retell the story of my visit multiple times to my aunties and uncles, and the deep sadness of loss. The old rivalries and hurts were ingrained heavier on him, the eldest son. Grudgingly, he called Braxton and Sondra and invited them for dinner. "She didn't tell me where she was going. Stubborn and bull-headed, just like her grandmother," he muttered to Braxton on the phone.

That evening, Sondra brought a fruit salad and a hot vegetable dish to accompany the fish my father would grill on the outdoor barbecue. "You all talk while I set the table," she said when she arrived with the twins. She tactfully disappeared into the kitchen after her boys were secure in their high chairs.

Braxton was quiet and thoughtful when I told him about my day. He carefully rolled up the sleeves of his shirt past his elbow and tied on the twins' bibs. A frown creased his smooth high forehead and his dark eyes narrowed. "You know, you shouldn't have gone without asking Popo's permission. She probably would have let you go, but from the story Dad told me, Aunt Ginger was disowned when she married that man."

"Not 'that man.' His name is Jeremiah Demming," I corrected. I watched my father stoke the coals on the grill under the lychee tree. He was a master of the barbecue and enjoyed the building of a fire, the preparation of coals for optimum heat, and the sizzle of a hot, even grill.

"They must really live out in the country, apart from the rest of the Demming clan, if we never heard about him. You know how in Hawai`i everyone knows everything about everyone else."

"He was born after his father was sent to Kalaupapa. You know what a terrible stigma was attached to leprosy in the old days. Jeremiah's mother's Hawaiian family raised him and he learned to live in the old-style. He plays a mean ukulele," I added. It was amazing how those husky fingers were so quick upon the strings.

"How did Popo take it?" Braxton asked.

"She was upset with me. But she was overwhelmed by their generosity. The size and quantity of fish they gave us would have meant a great deal to them. Popo says that none of the Demmings live past the age of sixty. None of the males in that family die a natural death. Ginger's husband is sixty-two now."

"That's a good sign," Braxton said. "One of these days, Popo will forgive you and Ginger and eventually, Jeremiah Demming. She just needs time to change her opinion about him." He carried out the platters for Dad's fish and returned just as Sondra finished setting the table with the rest of the food.

All the fish was meltingly sweet. My father ate very little. He poked at the filet on his plate and nibbled at the edges.

Braxton and Sondra, however, were interested in every detail: how Uncle Jeremiah drove barefoot when he and Ginger took me back to the airport, and how they knew the name of everyone they waved to along the way.

Uncle Jeremiah had wanted to take me to see his fishing boat named Ginger Snap, but we didn't have time. "Next time you come, I'll take you fishing," he had promised. He sniffed back a few tears when he engulfed me in a huge bear hug. He asked me to do him a favor. "I have a grand-aunt on O`ahu, Tutu Maile, who teaches at the Bishop Museum. When you go home, tell her I love her. She's a very wise woman. She's known as a healer, a kahuna of great power."

"Aloha," he and Auntie Ginger called when I walked out on the tarmac. "Malama pono. A hui hou." They stood at the gate and waved until a sudden heavy rain swept across the airport and they dashed inside for cover.

My brother and I cleared the dishes, then washed and dried them the way we used to when we were kids. Except we didn't argue about who was doing which chore. We talked all the while and were surprised when, before we knew it, all the dishes were put away, the kitchen swept, and the garbage taken out.

I kissed Braxton, Sondra, and each of the gurgling twins when they left. My father and I, caught in the emotion of the day, stood in the driveway watching their taillights disappear down the dark street. I felt the trade winds pick up, bringing the scent of the night-blooming flowers. I turned to him. "Everyone enjoyed the fish. They were grilled to perfection," I complimented him. The day had turned out unexpectedly well.

Kam took a deep breath. "Next time you go see her, I'm coming." His voice faltered with emotion. He turned to me and muttered, "Ginger hated fish."

After a steamy shower, I slipped on an oversized T-shirt and slid into bed. I lay awake in the darkness listening to the trade winds flutter through the venetian blinds. I could hear my father's steady snore, a soft rumble in the night. The shadows through the thick-leafed branches of the baklan tree outside my windows became kimono-clad dancers in the moonlight.

When I closed my eyes, I saw twirling hands and swinging silk sleeves. Taiko drums beat their primal heartbeat rhythms. Giant fireballs shot red and yellow flames across the skies of my dreams and exploded, raining fish that swam through the air. I was swimming toward the reef with Alex. Suddenly I was sucked under water. *Shark*, I cried as I sank. My words were caught in bubbles that burbled up in incomprehensible words. Ginger and Jeremiah Demming waded into the surf and cast a huge net into the sea.

My cries for help were soundless. Instead of words, bright yellow o'o feathers flew from my mouth and fluttered to the cold floor. I tried to catch them one by one, to save the endangered bird, but a bodiless hand flicked them just beyond the reach of my fingertips.

The Taiko drums grew louder. My father's voice. Alex's voice. "Miki, get up." Louder. Louder.

I kicked off the covers and lay there, my heart beating so hard I felt a pain in my chest. Was I awake? Asleep? I heard the voice again, "Miki, I'm out here."

I bent an opening in the venetian blinds. "Alex? It's the middle of the night," I groaned. I saw the shadow of his head, backlit by the moon.

"I need to talk to you," he whispered.

I tiptoed barefoot across the polished hardware floors and slipped out the front door. A long time ago, Alex and I would sit on the front steps and talk on Friday or Saturday nights after he brought me home. My curfew had been ten o'clock and this was the only way we had been able to stretch out our time together.

We sat side by side on the steps, arms barely touching. No cars drove on our short street and the night was inky and quiet. We could hear the rustle of the trees in the trade winds, the rushing stream across the street, and an occasional bark from the neighbor's yard.

Alex picked his words carefully, his voice tender with emotion. "Miki, I came to tell you good-bye." He was returning to Kaua`i tomorrow. "I've spent an agonizing day thinking about you. I was pretty cocky wasn't I? Thinking I could overcome a hundred years of rivalries and curses. It's funny, no one talks about the Ai'Lee–Demming feud, but it's still alive." He turned to me, touching me only with his eyes. "I've lived a vagabond life cursed with death and dying. I don't want you tainted by my failures. I was arrogant to think you'd give up your life to follow me."

I touched his rough beard, his sun-weathered cheeks that felt tender to my touch. I leaned against him. When I closed my eyes I could smell the ocean breeze off the beach where his house nestled against the coconut trees behind black lava walls.

He took my hands. "Listen, Miki. I want you to get away from me. Pursue your dreams. Get as far away as you can. Forget me." He bent down. His lips tasted seductively soft and sweet. I put my arms around his shoulders and pulled him so close I could feel his heart quickening. The trees rustled heavily as the winds shifted. Alex held me tight as if he could protect me from the evils of the world. "Good-bye," he whispered. He ran his hands along the length of my bare legs. His fingers continued up the arch of my back and pressed me tighter to him.

I whispered, "I'm not through with you, Alex Demming." The winds picked up and the night rains fell. The silver curtain of rain hid us from the world. These were the gentle tears of our gods.

Silently, I led Alex through the front door and down the dark hallway. In my little-girl room of crisp white eyelet, I slowly pulled off my thin cotton T-shirt. When I faced him naked in the moonlight I was no longer afraid of the Demmings or the Ai'Lees.

I removed Alex's clothes and softly dropped them one by one onto the polished hardwood floor. I pushed him down on the cool sheets and licked the taste of sorrow from the crevices of his neck, from the crease of his legs, and dark hairs of his chest.

We were consumed by the intense passion that follows reconciliation: wanting to forgive, wrapping our hurt in the joy of love.

"Aah!" whispered the gods in the night. Far away, the echo of the Taiko drums, intense thunder-heartbeats of another Obon festival, pulsed through the darkness. In the background, the patter of night rains grew stronger and louder. The rain turned into a roar.

But Alex and I were locked in a dance of our own. We were intertwined like the passionate lovers from the shunga pictures that celebrated the pleasures of love in the seventeenth-century Edo period. As in those erotic illustrations, once banned as pornography in Japan, we explored the enchantment of those sensual pleasures. We melted into the night, the heat of bare skin and intense longing burning to make up for lost years.

In the timelessness of the moment, the trees bowed and rippled with the growing rhythm of the night rains.

"Aah!" the Night Whispers echoed our sighs.

Chapter Sixteen

Hurricane Warnings

"*H*urricane coming!" Auntie Lehua's call startled me awake. "Wake up, Miki! Kam, wake up!" Her knocks on the front door were Taiko drums beating an ancient alarm. "Get up, get up, get up."

I bolted awake, heart pounding, although Alex had discreetly slipped out hours ago.

"Get up, get up," Auntie Lehua called again. We were all early risers, but Auntie Lehua and Uncle Robert habitually rose at five-thirty to get their chores done before the heat of the day. This morning, the sun was already steaming last night's rain off the grass with a zesty smell. With such a clear sky, it seemed improbable that a tropical storm was on its way. The weather service would know by late afternoon if the approaching tropical storm would veer away or keep on its current course towards Honolulu. The meteorologists talked about patterns of highs and lows, the possibility of the storm stalling, dying at sea, or heading towards Kaua`i. Kaua`i, the northernmost of our islands, seemed to be in every hurricane's path.

"You know how everyone panics at the last minute," Auntie Lehua said. She wore a bright yellow T-shirt and shorts that matched her yellow sandals. "They hear the warning. At the last minute, they jam the stores when the sirens go off. Last time, the line to get into Foodland was around the block. We're stocking up on batteries and food. You need anything, Kam?" Uncle Robert, also in a T-shirt and shorts, waited in the car with the engine running.

Hurricane warnings broke up Honolulu's daily weather forecast of "partly cloudy with a chance of showers." Like Auntie Lehua, we prepared for the worst. Luckily, most hurricanes spewed their fury into the sea or lost full power before they hit land.

Instead of flying to Kaua`i as planned, Alex remained on O`ahu to batten down the house in Kailua. I would join him as soon as my father's house was secure.

Violent storms brought excitement to our lives. When we were kids, we looked forward to when the power went out. We lined up knee-to-knee in front of the glass double doors to watch the trees bow to the ground and sheets of lightening scream across the skies. We watched roofs and trees fly by, severed branches whip the power lines, and an occasional foolish driver take a chance to reach his destination. We set out matches and candles and stockpiled water. When the water lines broke we were ready: buckets and bottles of water lined the kitchen counter.

By the time my brother's New Yorker zoomed into the garage, the rice was ready and the chicken wings had been sautéed with bamboo shoots and Chinese mushrooms in a fine sauce laced with whiskey and oyster sauce. While Braxton washed up, I steamed the fish and topped it with a garnish of soy sauce, green onions, and Chinese parsley.

We listened, enthralled, to Braxton's details of the emergency teams he coordinated. Hurricane warnings had been broadcast and the police were already clearing the streets. He had sent Sondra and the twins to her parents until the hurricane passed since he was headed back to the hurricane command center after lunch. We admired the windbreaker he had to wear during this crisis. It read "Ai'Lee, Deputy Commissioner."

Halfway through lunch, Auntie Lehua and Uncle Robert returned in the pouring rain with rolls of masking tape.

"Gee whiz it's cold!" complained Uncle Robert. "Must be sixty degrees." He took off his jacket. I grabbed a large beach towel from the linen closet and wrapped it around his shivering shoulders like a shawl.

Auntie Lehua took off her raincoat and wiped her head and arms with the bath towel I handed her. "We brought the masking tape for your windows," she said.

"If you run out of food, Auntie has pots of rice, beef stew, and potato salad. Come on over, otherwise I'll be eating it for weeks." Uncle Robert groaned good-naturedly.

While the men held the rolls of tape, Auntie Lehua and I applied them on all the windows in the approved safety pattern.

When Braxton and I taped the sliding glass doors, I thought back to the days when we were children. "Braxton, remember how we used to line up like ducks in front of these glass doors to watch the street every time we had a big storm?" I laughed at how innocently we faced disaster.

He shook his head at our naïveté. "It was exhilarating, especially the loud bang of thunder and the lightning that blanketed the skies like a sheet. Now we know that this old untempered glass could have shattered." He tapped the thin glass with his knuckle. Like most Hawaiian homes, our house was designed for a temperate climate, not nature's fury. Large plate-glass windows and double glass doors that welcomed the outdoors became disastrous hazards during these storms.

I looked out at the darkened sky. The wind and rain had picked up.

❧

Another roll of thunder boomed directly overhead when I got to Alex's. The heavens opened the floodgates. Our gods raged, screaming for sacrifice. They shook the skies with the sound of thousands of macadamia nut shells splintered by steel hammers. Sheets of lightning fired the sky. Coconut trees flung their fronds in protest. The low lava rock wall that fronted the Demming house was barely visible through the rain. I gripped the steering wheel and leaned forward, straining to see the gravel driveway bordered by coconut trees.

Alex ran out the front door as soon as my headlights hit his driveway. I could barely hear him through the wind's angry howl. Staggering defiantly against the torrential rains, he guided me into the enclosed garage. We dashed through the garage door into the kitchen.

Alex was shaking—from cold or anger I couldn't tell. "Why did you start out so late? I was worried." He stripped off his clothes and flung them in a sodden pile. "I called your Dad when the sirens went off. You weren't there!"

Grabbing a towel hanging by the door, he buffed dry. "I would have come for you!" Then he saw my face. He pried the car keys from my fingers and hugged me against his body. "You're safe now, Miki."

I patted his bare butt. "If I knew I'd be greeted by a naked man I'd have been here hours ago." I felt his chest, muscled and cool, and the strength of his arms around me. "My father's friend arrived and Braxton had to get back to work," I explained. My father refused to give me the car keys out of concern for my safety. I was finally able to leave when he was distracted by the arrival of Marjorie Chu bearing provisions. After I had washed the lunch dishes, she insisted I try her pineapple upside-down cake, one of my father's favorites. I managed to beg off.

I found the car keys on top of his bureau and snuck out while Marjorie enticed him with pineapple ice cream. I turned on the radio as soon as I got in the car. I knew I had half an hour to get to Alex's house, maybe. The winds buffeted the Plymouth as I drove up the Ko`olau Mountains and through the Pali Tunnel. When I headed down on the windward side, the winds and rains were blinding. If the Civil Defense sirens were wailing then, I couldn't have heard them. I slowed to a crawl. Understandably, there were few cars on the roads, which had turned into rivers of rain. The Plymouth sat up high so it was a target for the powerful winds. But it was also a heavy, well-built old car that grabbed the road and chugged steadily through the storm. When I called to say I had arrived safely at Alex's, my father was so relieved to hear my voice that his anger and frustration dissolved. He warned me to stay where I was until the roads were safe again.

While we still had electricity, Alex, with only a towel around his hips, ground fresh coffee beans and brewed a pot of Kona coffee. He said his father's manager, Eddie Kekaha, had called. They would keep Alex abreast of any changes but they were prepared, for now. William Demming was worried because their home on Oʻahu, where we were, was vulnerable to the high ocean surge expected with the hurricane. They would keep in touch via radio when the phones went out.

When Alex went down the hall to slip on a pair of pants, I walked over to the dining table with its array of radios and equipment. Dials glowed and lights flashed at regular intervals.

A few days ago, Maku had delivered a trunkful of boxes. He promised Alex that once he set up this system, he could be in constant contact with his father, who loathed leaving Kauaʻi. We had laid beach towels and tablecloths over the koa wood dining table that Alex had turned into a command center. After Maku left, Alex precisely lined up the brushed steel radios and amplifiers arrayed with dials and knobs and switches. His worn leather notebook, the same notebook he was writing in the first day I saw him at the Kuan Yin Temple, was open to a page of Maku's detailed diagrams which he consulted as he connected the boxes with thick cables and slender wires. His focused intensity reminded me of those hours we spent in his darkroom and how quietly he worked when he concentrated.

I had touched the distressed leather of his leather-bound book. "It looks like it's been through the war with you." I felt its surface, smooth and mysteriously stained.

"Dr. Xi gave it to me when I started studying with him." Alex's voice had been deep and thoughtful. "I used it to record my research. Dr. Xi used to go through all my expedition notes with me, to make sure I learned the careful analysis and observation required of a cultural anthropologist and archaeologist."

Now Alex's leather journal was on the table, closed and buried under stacks of radio instruction manuals he had tossed aside. I stacked up the manuals up in a neat pile. When I picked up his leather notebook to place it on the top, a much-folded piece of paper fell out. I unfolded it.

Dear Dr. Alexander Demming:

We have heard from colleagues who attended the Art and Archaeology Conference in Chile that you are considering returning to the United States. As you know, our archaeology department at New York University has attracted prominent academicians. We have followed your career with great interest.

I admit I also have a personal interest. Dr. Xi was also my mentor at Harvard. He called me when you began your studies with him and asked me to keep an eye on your career. I mourn his loss and am deeply touched that you were with him when he passed away.

Dr. Harold von Fenster, one of the most published and revered authorities in Southeast Asian archaeology has strongly recommended we secure you for our faculty. We understand that you are interested in the fields of art history, archaeology, and cultural anthropology and we would like to offer you an interdisciplinary position. We are prepared to discuss your terms of acceptance. One of our alumni, who wishes to remain anonymous, has assured our university that her family foundation will offer an endowed chair if you were to accept our offer.

We are especially interested in your work at Angkor. You may have heard of the pending UNESCO project to restore Borobudur, the world's largest Buddhist monument on the island of Java. An international committee of experts will provide technical advice and guidance to restore the twelve-hundred-year-old monument. Work will be carried out by the Dutch consulting engineers, NEDECO, and the Indonesian government.

We realize that you are still in the field. Please contact me at your convenience. I am prepared to discuss the position with you in detail.

I quickly refolded the letter, dated a year before, and laid it on top of Alex's leather book in the middle of the table.

It was early evening, but the islands were plunged into an eerie twilight, as if every building was holding its breath, waiting for the hurricane to arrive. The sky had melted from blue-green to black-gray. The fury we experienced now was only the edge of the storm. The eye was just north of Kaua`i.

The winds and rains were pounding so ominously I didn't hear Alex's footsteps on the thick-planked koa floor. He wrapped me in a light shawl. "My mother's," he whispered. I thanked him. The cotton slacks and blouse I put on after my shower seemed warm enough then, but the temperature was dropping.

I poured two cups of coffee and nestled against Alex on the rattan couch. He had showered and smelled of shampoo and rain. Maybe it was because the air was damp, thick with ominous sounds, that his memories surfaced.

He said that before he walked with Dr. Xi into the Ta Prombh temple, the site of the massacre at Angkor, he had been stopped by a chatty old man dressed like the other Europeans in linen slacks and a short-sleeved shirt. Alex thought he was a German tourist. He looked deceptively fragile, so pale, so colorless, except for those icy blue eyes shaded by a Panama hat. He seemed genuinely interested in what Dr. Xi's research team was doing and the cultural relevance of specific temples out of the over three hundred in the vast complex of Angkor. His voice deepened with ferocity, betraying the shadows of his past.

"I heard rumors about an 'ice-eyed ghost' who haunted these temples: a presence who never appeared the same way twice. Sometimes it was a pale woman in an ivory sari, sometimes a frail Indonesian man in a faded sarong, sometimes a European in light slacks, who blended into the shadows and press of the local crowds. After the horror of the massacre, I forgot about that pale, colorless face. But from time to time, I saw him—that very same face with the deadly cold eyes—near places of archaeological significance. I heard the rumors, saw the Interpol reports, and wondered if he ordered our deaths."

"Why would anyone massacre innocent people to steal a statue?"

"The thrill of possessing what no one else can." Alex gripped his hands tightly, knuckles tense. "Private collectors will pay any price to own a treasure only they can enjoy. They don't care how they get it or where it came from. In London, Tokyo, or Munich, those statues could draw exorbitant prices through private dealers or the underground art market." The pain in his eyes hinted at his private agony.

"You've appreciated art from the pristine safety of museums and galleries, Miki. Your students study cultural treasures in books and projected onto big screens from slides in your air-conditioned lecture halls. How do you think temple carvings and burial jades get to auction houses and private collections? Behind the scenes, there's violence, death, and thievery. No price is too great for some collectors. Thieves are too willing to satisfy them."

I turned away, but Alex touched my arm to command my attention. "You've read how Charles Lang Freer employed armies of Chinese who would gather art throughout China. Freer bought everything, good and bad, so he could pluck the best. The art market has become even more frenzied."

Temple crimes had become one of the most prevalent and unnoticed international crimes sweeping Mexico, South America, and Asia. As a two-billion-dollar-a-year business, art theft was one of the world's most profitable criminal enterprises. Disposition was easy. In Switzerland, goods in storage were treated with the same discretion as bank accounts. An object could come out of bonded free-port warehouses in Zurich or Geneva with clear legal title to the possessor after five years. In Liechtenstein and the Cayman Islands, the term was seven years.

Alex's eyes looked weary, older than his thirty years. I touched his cheek. He held my fingers when I used them to comb his hair away from his eyes. He kissed my palms and held them to his chest. "I have the worst nightmares, Miki. I've relived Angkor every night."

He'd been a man possessed, racing against time to record and preserve the ancient treasures of lost civilizations. He dreamt of exploding temples, their decapitated statuary floating off into the clouds, and priceless friezes of the Ramayana and the life of Buddha splintering into meaningless confetti. In his dreams, he saw his fiancée waving goodbye. He knew he had to end his restless wanderings.

He still yearned for ancient sites like Borobudur and the uncovered ruins of the Prambanan Plain, the most extensive Hindu temple ruins in all Indonesia. Yet he wanted to smell the rich earth of the Demming ranch and return to the exquisite peace and beauty of the land edged by turquoise seas.

"Now, all my dreams end with a vision of you, Miki, swimming towards the reef with me at night, beckoning me to follow."

I leaned my head against his chest and listened to his heartbeat. We startled awake when the Civil Defense sirens sounded again. Residents of low-lying homes were ordered to evacuate. What they feared most was on its way: towering hurricane waves riding the surge would pound the shoreline, wash over the low roads, and raging seas would surge, rushing into homes, indiscriminately sweeping out their contents with a salty flush or lifting wood-frame homes off their foundations. Torrential rains would drown the streets. Storm drains would swell with debris. Police would roadblock the coastal areas in an effort to maintain safety.

Alex immediately radioed Kaua`i to check in with his father and Eddie Kekaha. I left the room, unable to bear the tension in his voice.

I wandered down the hallway, running my fingers lightly along the walls lined with tapa cloth. Memories returned of days when I believed the whole world was open before me, when I naïvely thought that if I listened to my parents and teachers I would automatically make the right choices. But my mother's death revealed the fragility of life: tomorrow was never promised. Auntie Ginger had shown me that some of life's most fulfilling dreams were the ones we didn't expect, and that sometimes they walked out of the surf bearing gifts of love.

A four-poster bed of carved koa wood looked out to the terrace from the master bedroom at the end of the hall. I imagined one could wake up to the view of the beach and, stepping through the doors of that glass wall, dive lazily into the pool. I touched the soft cotton of the blue-on-white Hawaiian quilt finely patterned with tens of thousands of perfect little stitches in undulating waves.

"My mother made that quilt," Alex said from the shadows. I hadn't heard him walk up behind me. "When my father proposed, she said she wouldn't marry until she finished it. It was her wedding present to him." His voice trailed off. He fingered the stitches, then turned away.

I held my breath, not wanting him to know I heard the mourning in his voice.

"Come," he said, taking my hand. "My father said there's nothing else to do until the hurricane passes. Let's eat."

The lights flickered in the kitchen. Alex pulled out a flashlight. The batteries were dead. He took out candles and lined them up on the counter with matches, just in case.

We opened the refrigerator and surveyed the shelves packed with take-out containers and baskets of local fruits. I had skipped dinner and now I was starved.

Alex pulled out a couple of large containers. "When I come home, I eat what I miss the most." He opened a bottle of kim chee and offered it to me. "Smell this!"

I picked out a pungent piece of Napa cabbage dripping with red pepper flakes and licked my fingers appreciatively. Alex plopped the bottle on the counter so we could nibble on the tongue-numbing Korean vegetables while we pulled dinner together. I put on a pot of rice and steamed the laulaus and the kalua pig and cabbage. Alex set the dining table for two and lit a couple of votives. We set out chilled mangoes, lychees, and starfruit in a koa calabash. Soon, the sticky damp smells of rain and sea were overcome by appetizing aromas from the kitchen.

We ate by flickering candlelight to the symphony of unceasing rain. "Just like monsoon season," Alex muttered under his breath, a faraway look in his eyes. In his face I saw visions of distant cities: the crowded back alleys of Hong Kong, the stilt huts of Burma, the fragrant markets of Kampucha, and the fishing villages of Indonesia.

Out of the blue, he asked me why I hadn't married. I didn't know what to say. I concentrated on untying the steaming ti leaves of the laulau on my dinner plate and picked at the salted pork and butterfish with my fingers, licking my fingertips slowly as I ate. I didn't know the answer to Alex's question. Or maybe I knew but didn't want to admit it. Until now, we had carefully avoided the forbidden zone of failures and hurt. These were dark shadows, painful places that we discreetly kept from each other.

"How about you?" I countered. Instantly, I wanted to take back my words. I covered my mouth with the back of my hand as if I could erase my rudeness.

He put down his fork and stared out at the incessant rain. I held my breath, knowing my question had hit home. Most of the time he held his feelings inside and seethed like the molten lava beneath Halema`uma`u Crater. His silence used to terrify me: how quiet he could get when he drew into his own thoughts.

At last, Alex spoke. Haunted by the death of his mother and fiancée at the same time, both tragic, he had become absorbed in living for now, the present. He had always heard rumors of a curse. He didn't want to believe it. Yet, growing up in Hawai`i he knew better than to ignore what he didn't understand. So he lived without ties to keep the ones he loved safe and alive. And this way, he said, he avoided the pain: the pain of love, the pain of loss. Alex found he liked being a shadow, tracking the sacred icons and golden gods, finding clues of the past that told of our future. He touched my hands as if reassuring himself I was still there. "Seeing you was a shock, Miki. A step back into a past I had forgotten. A friend. I didn't have to explain myself to you. I felt drawn back to someone who shared my soul."

We had been best friends in a different time. We had the comfort of not having to explain ourselves when we were with others like us who had grown up in Hawai`i. How could we explain that we local children were like chameleons, able to change our ways, our thoughts, and our speech, depending on who we were talking to and where we were. Among our classmates, we chattered away in colorful pidgin: hybrid English festooned with Chinese, Japanese, Hawaiian, and Portuguese. Filipino, Samoan, and Korean classmates added their own words and customs. On the playground we acted out our heroes: Toshiro Mifune samurai warriors or fantastic Chinese gods from the Run Run Shaw movies. But once we walked back in the classroom, we spoke perfect English and thought in the manner of our Eurocentric textbooks. Our teachers taught us what we needed to live in the American world. We knew the stereotypes that Chinese overachieve, that Hawaiians were considered lazy, that Japanese were masters of imitation. But we needed to understand American ethics if we wanted to succeed.

When we went home we changed again. At home, I was an obedient daughter who was expected to know, honor, and respect the proper customs. Family, honor, and Chinese tradition came first. Filial piety was paramount.

We followed each other's leads in our friends' homes; to sit cross-legged on tatami mats and drink miso soup, to suck fresh opihi from the shell, and speak Japanese, Chinese, or Hawaiian to each other's grandparents. When we went into local shops or chattered with classmates, we talked pidgin with its melodious inflection, Standard English everywhere else. We instinctively knew the customs and mores of our local people, so when a joke was told, we understood the hidden meanings. We hid our secret childhood from outsiders.

While Alex and I talked, the storm raged on with the intensity of New Year's Eve when every Chinese home burned ten thousand firecrackers on the stroke of midnight. We did it to scare away the evil spirits. Perhaps this storm would, too.

The candles burned lower. I heard Alex's stories of restless travels, of the emptiness in his life he yearned to fill. But no exotic city, no treasured site gave him the satisfaction he sought.

He listened to my stories of giving in to my brother, of surrendering to my parents' wishes. I rued that I had believed them, not myself; I accepted their assessment of my deficiencies. That was what I had been taught: to be obedient, to listen, to strive for perfection.

When we ran out of words, Alex rummaged through his sister Casey's old bedroom where his sisters stored the island-style clothes they wore when they returned home. He found me a cotton nightgown and tucked me into the big four-poster koa bed at the end of the hall.

I slept restlessly. Buddhist statues screamed in my nightmares. In my dreams, I reached out furtively, my head tapping the cold floor, and apologized for neglecting what was most important. I jolted awake to the heavy pounding of waves. They lapped louder, closer. The ocean crashed at the steps of the Demming house. I slipped out of bed and stepped down the hallway through the blackness.

Alex sat at the radio connecting him to Kaua`i, head bowed over clasped hands. The light from a single candle flickered across his face, softening the rough furrows etched by the years we had been apart. I had never seen him so tired and worried. As the glow from the flame played against his face, I saw his expression as I had many years ago, when I was not yet sure if he were part of my dreams.

When we were in school, Kelly, Alex, and I had spent the weekend with other classmates at the Malone's beach house. After a full day of surfing and hiking along the beach, we laid out tatamis and old Hawaiian quilts in the screened-in porch. We stretched out—girls on one side, boys on the other—and talked until the only sound was the whir of mosquitoes, the crickets in the grass, and the silence of a dozen exhausted teens. In the middle of the night I awoke. I sensed a presence. Alex sat cross-legged at my side. "Alex?" I had whispered, not sure if he was a dream or real.

"Shh," he said, fingers to his lips.

"What are you doing?" I asked, not sure I was awake.

"Watching you sleep," he whispered.

"Why?"

He shrugged. "Do you know you glow when you're asleep?" Alex bent over and kissed me shyly. There was no moon that night, and the only light came from the stars. Maybe he said he loved me. Maybe I just imagined it. I might have also imagined I kissed his fingers caressing my cheek or that I pulled his hands under my nightgown under the cover of night.

I had forgotten about that vision of him in the starlight until now. I came up behind Alex and wrapped my arms around his chest. I kissed the back of his neck, inhaling him, drawing in the heat of his body. He smelled warm and comforting, like the shirt he threw at me in the photo lab when I stood shivering in a leotard. "Where's the storm now?" I asked sleepily.

"The eye of the hurricane is stalled off Kaua`i. Eddie Kekaha says they're sitting it out now, waiting for the storm to make up its mind which way it wants to go. It has a mind of its own," he answered wearily. Strain cracked his voice.

I reached for Alex's hands. I loved their harshness, rough and weathered, against my skin. Had I really done this before, I wondered. Then I remembered. Long ago, I had placed his hands on my heart and felt his soul melt into mine. Alex was my first love, my true love.

I pulled his T-shirt off and touched the jungle-baked scars on his back. I kissed each one. I imagined the pain they had brought him.

While torrents of rain slammed against the walls, we made love as if our hands and hearts were on fire. We heard ourselves in the wind's ecstatic screams and the roaring voices of the great spirits of the islands. Then we drowned in our passion. Isolated by the storm, we breathed each other's heartbeats with Alex's body wrapped around mine like the protective silk of a cocoon.

Outside, the heavens raged a violent battle with the earth. Forests were reduced to toothpicks by the howling wind ripping horizontally across the sky. Trees groaned and snapped. Even the sea boiled, spitting fish and coral across the land. The hurricane was five hundred miles wide and ten miles high. With the fury of Huracan, the mythical West Indian god of storms, it powered over the islands and rendered us helpless.

Only the radio channel to Kaua`i was silent.

Chapter Seventeen

The Beginning
and the End

The hurricane hovered off our shores for two turbulent days. Masses of churning winds pounded the coastal areas like an army of Taiko drummers. The storm willfully changed direction, threatened to come inland, then scornfully changed its course as if it were waiting, shifting with a purpose.

We heard over the radio that at the storm's peak, sustained winds of 140 miles per hour gusted to 165 when it made landfall on Kaua`i. Alex, in intermittent contact with his father and Eddie Kekaha, agonized over their reports of crushed machinery, blown fences, and flying trees. The storm teased and dallied offshore as if it had a mind of its own. Then it abruptly veered toward the open sea and charged across the Pacific. Early in the morning of the third day, the torrential rains petered out to a light drizzle, sadly caressing the remnants of the storm's destruction. By dawn, the breezes seemed to sigh as if they thought the worst was over.

But it wasn't.

A bleak and cold landscape shocked us when we stepped out to the beach. Coconut fronds littered the grounds, starkly reminiscent of desperate hands reaching for help. Dead fish covered the beach like confetti. A sail-boat rested on its side in the neighbors' yard, the mast snapped in half like a matchstick, the keel buried in the sand. Other boats had been flung awkwardly against homes, trees, or the earth. Roof fragments, couches, remains of lamps and beds posed awkwardly in the sand like a decorator's cruel idea of a joke. Masses of seaweed, flotsam and jetsam, littered the dirty-gray sea. The water smelled fishy, as it always does after a storm when the sea has been churned upside down. In the distance, a lone fig-ure swept the beach with a metal detector, hoping to unearth coins and jewelry ejected from their hiding places.

Phones were out. Downed power lines and fallen trees made coastal roads impassable. Except for Alex's battery-run radios, we were cut off from the rest of the world. Even with the Hawaiian Electric crews working around the clock, power would not be restored to our area for another twenty-four hours. We rationed our meals from the refrig-erator and ice chest.

We started our clean-up by gathering the scores of fish scattered across the property by the high storm surge and burying them in the garden. In a few weeks we would know which plants would survive. Most of the coconut trees had lost their heads. We saved for last the back-breaking task of scooping out the sand and fish in the swimming pool by the bucketful.

The only sounds of civilization we heard all day were the distant digging and hammering as others, like us, salvaged what they could of their homes. So when a military heli-copter hovered overhead around three in the afternoon, we dropped our buckets and scrambled to the beach. We were astounded to see the military craft land with a welcome surprise: my brother Braxton.

He leapt from the chopper dressed in hiking boots, jeans, and his official "Ai'Lee" windbreaker. "Alex! Miki!" he yelled over the sound of the rotors.

Alex and I welcomed a break after two days of storm-watching and an exhausting day of digging out. The old clothes Alex had found for me from the back of Casey's closet—a pair of sneakers, slacks, and a long-sleeved shirt—had been comfortable for heavy outdoor labor. But now our skin was shriveled and we dripped with wet, salty debris.

I threw my arms around my brother. "At last, contact from civilization," I exclaimed. We had not been so happy to see each other in a long time. I was giddy with sisterly love. I anxiously asked about Dad, and Popo Ai'Lee, and Sondra and the twins, and the rest of the family.

"You take a shower," Alex urged. "I'll make us all coffee."

I joined the men after a quick, cold bucket shower wearing one of Casey's faded Tahitian-print pareaus comfortably wrapped once around and tied with a single knot at the neck. The hearty scent of freshly ground Kona coffee, brewed from a portable propane burner Alex had set up on the deck, chased away the smell of dead fish. The air felt lighter, cleaner, refreshed.

We settled in the living room. Braxton said that all the Ai'Lees had weathered the hurricane well with no damage to their property. Power and water had already been restored in the city. William Demming had asked the governor to check on his son after a generator failure on the ranch had pulled him off the air. William wanted to assure Alex that they were fine. He was pleased that they had been able to stay in contact throughout the storm. There had been damage and they would do a complete assessment when Alex got there.

Braxton sipped his coffee and asked how we had fared during the storm. After running through the light damage, mainly to the yard, Alex excused himself to take a shower so my brother and I could talk privately. My brother fidgeted awkwardly. "Miki," he said, "Dad asked me to bring you home."

I looked at Braxton, his clear, high forehead, his earnest, bold gaze. He was a dutiful Chinese son. "Thanks, Braxton," I answered. I reached over and squeezed his hand. "Alex and I are almost done here. The roads will be clear by this evening. I'll drive home."

My brother cleared his throat. He looked out towards the helicopter then back at me. "Are you sure? I bet you'd like a hot shower and a hot meal. Marjorie Chu left a huge pot of curried chicken."

"You bet I would. Tell Dad the Plymouth is safe in the garage and I'll be home tonight."

Braxton nodded. He was relieved to see that both of us were safe. Ever since my trip to Hilo to find Auntie Ginger, my brother had been supportive of my decisions. And for the first time, he saw Alex as an honest man who stood against his own family for what he believed.

Knowing we were starving for information, he handed me both the *Honolulu Advertiser* and the *Honolulu Star-Bulletin* for the past three days. "I took the call from William Demming myself. He congratulated me on my appointment. Said his son told him to quit meddling in politics."

I looked up from the headlines of the paper, shocked by his news. I gasped. "He admitted that to you? He must be a confident man to acknowledge his mistake."

Braxton shook his head and laughed at my incredulous look. "William Demming sounds like a tough old man. I bet he'd do anything for his son. God help him when he meets you."

When Alex reappeared in a clean T-shirt and shorts, my brother updated us on the hurricane damage, which was concentrated primarily on the Wai`anae coastline on O`ahu. A few homes had been picked up and floated a hundred feet across the highway and up the mountain. The wind had stripped off the top floors of Jefferson Demming's five-star hotel. The luxury suites that the Japanese booked months in advance were now exposed to rain and sea. The expensive landscaping, the championship golf course, and the exotic swimming pools were buried under rotting fish and salt water.

We were sad when Braxton had to leave. His helicopter rose like a triumphant bubble as the sun broke through the clouds for the first time in three days. In the distance, a wild peacock trilled and dogs barked once again. Dark clouds billowed away: a sign that through the destruction came new life.

We turned to each other, Alex and I, feeling the warmth of the sun and the sense of renewal it brought. This was a time for new beginnings. After all these years, we were given another chance to start again, with the insights of maturity and compassion.

Alex placed his hard and weathered hands on my neck and ran them down my bare shoulders. His voice was confident. "Miki, I've asked you before, but after all we've been through, will you come to Kaua`i with me?" He talked of the challenges that lay before him. Heavy ranch equipment and buildings had been damaged. William was counting on his son to get the ranch running again and to bring the family operation profitably into the twenty-first century.

I wanted to say *Yes!* But those Chinese rules, the teachings my parents had drilled into my mind over and over, rose up and screamed their warnings. I shook my head. Those rules ordered me to remember family honor.

Alex's eyes darkened to sapphire blue. He picked his words carefully as if he were exposing his vulnerability, something he was not used to doing. His voice was low, reaching for my heart. "I know in my heart you and I are meant to be together. This time I won't let you go. Marry me, Miki. Be with me always." He held my hands to his chest so I could feel the beat of his heart. "I love you, Miki. Always have. I need you."

I felt a rush; I was swimming out on an outgoing tide and a rogue wave crashed down just at that moment, tumbling me end over end. I needed air. I needed to fill my lungs, to breathe. I lifted my arms and cradled his face in my palms. My fingers caressed his stubbled cheeks. I pushed his unruly hair out of his eyes so I could gaze into their azure depths.

Speaking to me through his eyes, Alex undid the tie on my pareau and slowly unwrapped it, letting the soft fabric crumple to the floor. I was naked, revealed to the brilliant sun and the wide-open beach. Alex tenderly ran his hands down my neck, the curve of my breasts, and across my back. "I love you," he repeated, his voice confident and sure. "Marry me."

His touch seemed to melt my skin, releasing the rules that had imprisoned my heart. I grew lightheaded, as if his love had released a heavy weight locked within me. Alex's hands wrapped around my waist. The heat of the sun licked my bare skin as if it, too, was working in collusion with his desire. The pounding of the surf lulled me with its haunting chant of love and forever.

I hung blissfully suspended in time, the power of Alex's love stretching this moment out to eternity.

How could I leave this place where storms moved to the whims of the gods, the trees whispered of love, and the lusty seas lured us for enchanted midnight swims?

How could I leave the one person who had been my friend, who, when we met by chance years later, dared to unfold his love like an exquisitely rare blossom? When we were together, entwined tightly like jungle vines deep in the Ko`olau valley, day turned to night and night back to day, and the Night Whispers cried tears of joy.

Chapter Eighteen

Aftermath of the Storm

*A*s soon as inter-island flights were restored, Alex flew to Kaua`i alone.

Wearing jeans and a button-down shirt, he walked across the tarmac to his plane at the inter-island terminal, leather duffel bag slung casually over his broad shoulders. He carried the much-folded letter I had seen on his dining table tucked in his leather notebook. Before we left his house, he had handwritten a reply, which he sealed with some documents in a long envelope and mailed on the way to the airport. I didn't ask what he had sent. At the cabin door of the airplane he stopped, turned, and threw me a kiss.

I reached up and caught it.

—❀—

When we were children, Mom took us often to the Bishop Museum to view the carved and feathered gods, capes, and other regalia from the time of Kamehameha the Great. Within its dark stone walls, we wandered past monarchical crowns, thrones, and court dress used at `Iolani Palace by

King Kalakaua and his sister, Queen Lili`uokalani. We studied the familiar costumes of the Chinese and Japanese who came to Hawai`i in the 1800s, the artifacts of the early immigrants who made Hawai`i the economic power it was in those days, and the stories of the many people of the islands. So here I returned after I kissed Alex goodbye at the airport.

I crossed the museum lawn to a large tent where groups of children knelt on lauhala mats beating strips of bark with notched rods. A Hawaiian woman knelt in the midst of a class of children. Thick hair laced with strands of white was coiled on her head like a crown. She pounded a muffled pattern while her voice sang out strong and melodiously, "Rhythm, children! Feel it from inside, beat with respect. Like singing a song!" The children imitated her movements and rhythmic tattoo. She walked from group to group with encouragement. "You're softening the bark, asking it for permission to make cloth to clothe your bodies."

When she saw me, she beckoned. "Come. Come closer. Come and watch. The children are making cloth from bark in the old way." Her crimson mu`umu`u brushed the tips of the grass when she stepped toward me in her bare feet. She smelled of sunshine and blossoms. A haku lei of `awapuhi, delicate white gingers, circled her head. She held out both hands. "They call me Tutu Maile. I am Grandmother Maile to everyone. Come, see what my class is doing."

I picked up the sample of the finished Hawaiian cloth and fingered its soft texture. "I've never seen tapa-making before. I've always wondered how the Hawaiians turned bark into cloth," I marveled.

"We have no records of the exact methods the Hawaiians used to make tapa," Tutu Maile said. "When the missionaries came, they made the natives cover up with long mu`umu`us of calico and gingham. So the native art was lost. Au-we! But we have the finished product, and we know how the Hawaiians lived at that time. It has taken a long time for my daughters and me to find the right shape and weight of beater to soften the fibers. See, this is what the bark is like after I soak it for four days in the mountain stream." She unfolded a ti leaf package called pu`olo `la`i, and pulled out the long strip of unbeaten bark.

"Come, you try. You can do this." She flashed a knowing look. "Always room for more. Come. This will be good for you." She led me to a board and beater where a half-beaten length of bark lay. Together we knelt and pounded.

She volunteered to teach school children, Tutu Maile said. To her, it was an honor to help perpetuate the Hawaiian language, culture, and crafts. A backlash of statehood was this resurgence of interest in Hawaiiana. "If I don't find out how our people lived in the past, and teach what I know to our keikis, who are we as Hawaiians? When the New England missionaries arrived in 1820 they banned our hulas, banned our language, and banned our religion to spread the word of their god. We succumbed to the whalers' diseases. Western powers overthrew our beloved monarchy. I will not be here forever, but the Hawaiian culture must live on."

"My Popo Ai'Lee says the same thing. She says we are our culture. It gives us our unique identity." I turned the heavy wood beater in my hands and inspected the precisely carved motif. "What do these lines symbolize?"

Tutu Maile's eyes opened wider. "What do you see in them?"

"I think these curves are the waves of the sea and these angles, shark teeth. Was this a pattern for someone whose `aumakua was the shark?"

She nodded. "Yes, their `aumakua, or guardian spirit, was the shark." She cocked her head and peered at me anew. "Tell me your name and what is it that you do that makes you aware of the symbols and stories others do not see."

I told her my name and my interest in the symbolism and myths in art.

She leaned forward earnestly. "There is so much for you to study here in Hawai`i, Miki Ai'Lee. All these temples, Japanese, Chinese, as well as Hawaiian, are being destroyed by time, neglect, disuse, or theft. Our younger generation takes our culture for granted. Now that we're a state, they aspire to Western values. All this knowledge will go with us to our graves. Your Popo would agree with me."

I looked down at the tapa beater. "Yes, that's what my Popo says."

She looked at me and folded her hands. She sat very still. "You are here for something else."

I sighed, relieved. "Tutu Maile, I came to tell you that Jeremiah Demming says he loves you."

She threw up her hands to the heavens. "Jeremiah! My sweet little boy! Long ago when I lived on the Big Island, his mother brought him to us when he was just days old. Jeremiah is a natural fisherman and hunter. He has such patience. Whenever he casts his net into the sea, fish flock to his nets and leap on his hooks. He has a rare gift, a gentle heart, a forgiving spirit." She eyed me suspiciously. "How do you know Jeremiah?"

"He married my aunt, Ginger Ai'Lee."

"Ah," Auntie Maile closed her eyes and leaned back. She sat still for such a long time one might have thought she had fallen asleep. But I knew she was reconstructing our family genealogy in her head, tracing the names and marriages and children, tracing who married whom to find the connection that tied me to her family. When she opened her eyes, she reached for my hands. I felt her rough palms as she rubbed my fingers between hers.

"There is a terrible curse upon the Demmings. Au-we! But true love and forgiveness will dissolve the anger and hatred that haunts their lives."

"But Ginger and Jeremiah are so deeply in love. Why didn't that end the Demming curse?"

Her huge eyes, a mossy brown flecked with bits of gold, were sad. "Yes, they found love in each other, and all who know them are truly blessed by their generous spirits. But the Ai'Lees never forgave their daughter for marrying Jeremiah Demming. True love and forgiveness, Miki Ai'Lee. Those two qualities will end the curse that plagues the Demmings."

❧ ⚙ ❧

My father visited my mother's grave every week. But whenever I asked to accompany him, he mumbled that I had "other things to do." That was his way of saying that this was his time to be alone with her. While the dew still shone like shimmering pearls on the grass, he gathered stiff sprays of dendrobium orchids from his yard and clipped torch gingers in full bloom. Then he drove toward Diamond Head and turned into the cemetery surrounded by towering oleander bushes. He followed the circular drive and parked. Five steps from the road was my mother's grave with my father's plot reserved at her side.

I coasted up in Alex's old Woody just as Dad unlocked the trunk of the Plymouth to get his flowers. With the comfortable movements of a familiar routine, he filled his bucket at the water tap by the roadside and slowly walked to Ellie's grave. He knelt to pour fresh water over her headstone and washed it carefully with his fingertips. As he picked at weeds from the smooth grass covering her grave, his lips moved to a song, a prayer, a wish.

I crouched beside him.

He said quietly, "You help me with Mother's flowers." Together, we washed the three cylindrical vases at the base of my mother's grave. He cut the twine that bound the stems of the flowers and handed them to me one by one. We arranged them carefully, tenderly. He kept his head down.

"Alex has gone back to Kaua`i," I told him. I knew he was wondering.

My father turned to me. His eyes were cloudy with concern and worry. "And you?"

I looked straight in his dark eyes, a deep liquid brown rich with wisdom. "He asked me to marry him," I answered.

"You throw away your future! What kind of daughter are you?" He clenched his fists. "Cursed Demmings!"

I held his hands in mine and said softly, "Dad, look at me. I'm not a child anymore. Alex loves me. I love him."

I paused for his reaction. He blinked, startled by his tears.

"Alex and I will raise our family on the land that both the Ai'Lees and Demming desired. We will make it a place we all can cherish, a place where our families can be united and together."

"It will never happen. That family is tainted with death. They're cursed," he adamantly argued.

"Dad, don't you think it's time for that curse to end? Forgive them, Dad. Give us your blessing."

My father took a deep breath. His eyes watered. He blinked quickly, as if remembering a trip he took in his youth to meet a long-ago love on another island. A restrained glimmer played across his face.

I had planned a big speech telling him I knew how much he gave up for his family and how Braxton and I always came first with him. I wanted to tell him I was stronger now because of the way he brought me up, and that I loved him. But when I saw the tears in his eyes, I didn't have to say the words. I was his daughter.

He stood up, stumbled, and caught himself. My father put his arms around me and kissed me awkwardly on the cheeks. "My only daughter," he sniffed. "I love you. God bless you, Miki. God bless you and Alex."

❧ ⚙ ❧

A week later, William and Alex Demming flew to Honolulu to meet us. Alex wanted a casual, private dinner so our fathers could relax and get to know each other.

"What do I have to say to William Demming?" my father complained when I told him we had been invited to dinner.

"Remember how Mother used to say it takes less effort to be polite than to be rude? This is the first time William has left Kaua`i since his wife passed away. I'm sure he's as nervous as you are."

When Auntie Lehua and Uncle Robert stopped by on their morning walk around the block, they were skeptical about us meeting William Demming over dinner. They thought he might try to poison us. My grandmother voiced her own opinion when I walked to her house later that day. "Maybe times have changed, Miki. Maybe we should not have cut your Auntie Ginger off like that. Maybe we should have called her once in a while. She sent me pictures. Her sons are big. Not bad looking." Popo held out the long letter from her youngest daughter. She had proudly spread the stack of photographs on her dining table for all to see.

But my father was not so charitable. He wasn't going to give Alex's father the benefit of his courtesy, or his gentlemanly Chinese manners. No, my father was bristly and patriarchal during the entire drive to Kailua. He had carefully chosen a burgundy and emerald Hawaiian print shirt in a powerful print.

Alex met us at the door. He had shaved his beard and his hair was cut short. He was barefoot and wore khaki slacks. Normally he would have chosen a faded Aloha shirt from his closet. But in honor of Dad's visit, he wore a new one, crisp and ironed. He held out his hand to my father, who politely shook it and thanked him for the invitation.

Then Alex hugged me, not too lingering but definitely endearing. Although he had called me every day, my body yearned for him.

Alex's father rushed to the entry with a dishtowel in his hands. "Sorry, I was starting the coals," he said in a deep gruff voice used to commanding men, not apologizing. He was a big, broad man, Alex's height and fifty pounds heavier, with a thickening of the waist that came with age. His flaming red hair had turned pure white. The sad droop of his eyes spoke of his devastating sorrow and the depression that had wracked him when his wife was killed. I felt the roughness of his thick hands and noticed the tremble in the walk of this once powerful man.

Our fathers shook hands with curt formality. William stepped back, at loss for words. Alex ushered us all into the living room where our fathers sat awkwardly, choosing chairs the furthest from each other on opposing sides.

I followed him to the kitchen on the pretext of getting drinks. Evenings in Kailua were cool with the offshore breeze, so I wore a long fitted holoku in pale rose brushed silk.

"I like this," Alex enthused under his breath. He ran his hands down the sleeves that ended in tiny covered buttons at the wrist. "This fabric is as silky as your skin." He bent me back in a long and heated kiss.

I gasped when he finally let me up. "Our fathers are out there," I warned. I ran my fingers lightly along his smooth chin. "As smooth as polished marble."

"Like it?"

"Yes, you look very respectable and clean-cut." I pulled him back in my arms. I tipped my head appraisingly.

"No, I like your roguish look." I laughed at his confusion. "I'll take you any way you are."

"As long as you're where I am," he added. His eyes twinkled blue with green flecks. I laughed. "Sounds like a good idea to me." I looked out at our fathers making cordial small-talk. "Alex, maybe this wasn't a good idea," I whispered. I opened the refrigerator and handed him the fresh-squeezed guava juice. "My father looks like he wants to shoot your father." These two old-timers of Hawai`i eyed each other with generations of distrust. They clearly expected to dislike each other.

Alex filled four tall glasses. "My father's usually congenial and loud. I expect him to crack a joke any minute. He'll think of something to break the ice. Here, try these." He held out a platter of crisp bite-sized fish, fried golden brown.

"Alex, are these `oama?" I plucked one and savored its sweet-salty taste. In the summer between mid-July through August, schools of `oama run close to shore. Locals stand waist-deep in water with a short line and bait to hook these silvery-sweet fish.

It was a mystery to me when I was child, to see groups of tanned adults and children standing shoulder to shoulder, waist-deep in the clear blue-green waters close to shore. They fished quietly, still as statues, barely disturbing the surface of the water with their lines.

"We were lucky they were running. I ran out this afternoon with my bamboo pole and caught a few dozen for pupus," Alex said. He felt like a child again when he stood in the surf, becoming part of the seascape until the fish took his bait. It was a ritual, a quiet meditation that brought back memories of a time when life was simpler.

We each nibbled one of the tasty little fish and nodded our approval. We walked out to the living room with the juice and appetizers and hopeful smiles.

In Hawai`i, the locals always greeted new acquaintances with questions such as what school they went to or who their parents were. In these islands everyone expected to know everyone else or their family, or find out they were related. So within minutes, Kam discovered that William had gone to the University of Hawai`i for a semester with his brother Ted before the war, that William's second cousin on his mother's side had worked for Kam in the engineering department of Honolulu Power and Gas, and that both had mutual acquaintances despite their legendary feud. And of course, Auntie Ginger had married William's first cousin Jeremiah Demming, one of the Big Island Demmings the Kaua`i Demmings had lost contact with two generations ago.

A few minutes later, William asked Kam to help him with the coals. The men walked stiffly out to the grill at the far edge of the patio.

Alex and I set out the plates and silverware and glasses on the dining table in the center of the patio, while keeping a cautious ear on our fathers. I saw Kam turn the coals while William added more in the spots as he directed. The fathers were warming up, keeping a slow but steady conversation while the grill heated evenly under my father's expert eye.

A half-hour later, William Demming turned to where Alex and I were sitting on the far side of the patio. "Alex, why don't you take Mr. Ai'Lee into the kitchen so he can choose the steaks for dinner?" he suggested gruffly.

My father protested that Alex was probably better at choosing them. William insisted. So my father had no choice but to accompany Alex into the house.

William walked haltingly over to where I sat and took the chair Alex had just vacated. His eyes were determined. "Alex tells me he asked you to marry him," he growled.

"That's right, Mr. Demming."

He nodded. His eyes were sad. "I am an old man, Miki. I am ten years younger than your father, but my wife's death has made me look and feel twenty years older. No need to protest. I can see the truth. Eight years ago I was known for my red hair. Now I look like a ghost. I know we Demmings have a bad history with the Ai'Lees. I hope you won't hold that against my son." The sun-baked wrinkles of his face deepened in a smile.

"It wasn't his fault," I said. When I returned his smile, he took a deep breath of relief.

He nodded again and looked out to the ocean. Then he turned to me and leaned forward. "To feel so in love again." He looked towards the house where Alex was holding out a huge silver tray to my father. My father had lifted the lid and both men were laughing. "I never thought Alex would come home after..." he looked down at his hands, "...afterwards. He's driven, like you. I just want to say, that in the whole scheme of life, old family rivalries are pitiful, aren't they? I used to be proud of what the Demmings did to get to where they are. Now I am ashamed for all those we've hurt and the families we've destroyed."

He took my hands. His hands were huge and gnarled, callused and rough. "Alex showed me his plans for the future of the ranch. Ambitious. He will need your help."

He paused, looked down to take a breath, then lifted his head to look straight in my eyes. "My son loves you very much. You will make him a happy man." There were tears in the rough rancher's eyes. He pressed my hands between his. "Love is too precious to waste, Miki Ai'Lee. I am proud to have you as my daughter."

A minute later, Alex and Kam emerged carrying a covered tray out to the barbecue. My father waved me over to the grill with great glee. "Miki, you should see these steaks. Two inches thick. I haven't seen evenly marbled beef like this since before the war."

William stood up, my hands still in his. "Butchered them myself," he said proudly. "I heard you like a thick, juicy steak, Kam. How do you like it cooked?"

"Bloody rare."

William's smile was broad. "Kam, my man, you know how to eat prime grade beef! This will melt in your mouth. Come and help me."

❧

When Alex and I hopped over the seawall after dinner, the two widowers had adjourned to the living room that looked out on the sea through wide plate-glass sliders. Despite their differences, they reminisced about old-time politics, mutual friends from their younger days, and of times long gone. The distrust that separated the men was thawing, so we felt safe in leaving them alone for a while.

We walked hand in hand down the beach, our toes sinking into the soft, clean sand. Millions of stars sprinkled the sky on this moonless night, wrapping the sky like glittering tears. We dug our toes in the sand, which was still warm with the day's heat.

I pointed to two bright stars. "Look, Alex, the stars Altair and Vega. The Cowherd and the Weaving Maid. Did you ever hear that Chinese folktale?" He shook his head. It was one of my mother's favorites. My mother and I would stand in the front yard at night, our bare feet cooling in the grass. She would point out the constellations and the great sweep of stars in the sky. In her soft musical voice, she'd tell me the stories of each, wrapped in Chinese myths and legends.

"See that star?" I pointed above the horizon. "That's the Weaving Maid. Her father was the powerful Emperor of Heaven. All day, she spun exquisite tapestries that were so magical they came alive as soon as she was done. She wove meadows filled with flowers and butterflies, and clear silvery rivers teeming with fish. She wove love and happiness in every picture she created. One day, the Weaving Maid looked up from her loom and saw a very handsome man. He was not dressed in fancy clothes like the others in her father's court. The Cowherd was barefoot and wore simple woven cottons. He did not flatter her or her weaving with the fancy words of her father's courtiers, but spoke to her truthfully, from his heart. The Weaving Maid fell in love with the handsome Cowherd, but this was not the match her parents wished for their only daughter. Her mother, the Empress of the West, was furious. But the lovers refused her demands to separate. The Empress of the West threw the Milky Way between them so that vast river of stars would always be a barrier between them.

Once a year, on the seventh day of the seventh month of the Chinese lunar calendar, the magpies have the power to form a bridge across the river of stars. And on that one night of the year, the lovers are united."

"I know how that Cowherd felt. You were all I thought about for a long time," Alex said. "But you never noticed. I used to wonder what I needed to do to get your attention and reach across the vast divide between us."

I leaned back against his chest. "I never knew. I was too busy trying to fulfill everyone else's expectations."

"You don't have to do that anymore, Miki," he emphasized with a quick squeeze.

"I don't?" I teased. It had taken me twelve years to realize what I truly yearned for. We were both shaped by our childhood experiences, like skipping barefoot through mountain streams and torch-fishing for squid Hawaiian-style. Our legacy was a poi-bowl mix of many traditions.

How quickly they returned, the lessons of who I was and how I should act, especially the words of my mother. The thought of her brought tears to my eyes. I ached with a deep hole in my heart. I loved her so much. I still missed her. Even when she was gone, I clung to the role she set out for me. I never thought that making myself happy was as important as her dreams for me. I had misinterpreted her wishes—for in the end, she wanted me to follow my heart.

Chapter Nineteen

The Hawaiian Wedding

I thought often of my mother in the months that followed. I had moved so far from where she would have wanted to keep me, safe and away from the Demmings. What would she have thought about Alex? And what would she have said about our wedding? It was not the formal church ceremony she had envisioned.

The brilliant Kaua`i sky at Anahola formed the roof of our chapel on a grassy knoll overlooking the Demming ranch. All agreed that this was the most spectacular setting: from the carpet of deep green grass beneath our feet to the lush trees offering shade to the white stretch of sand bordered by the deep blue sea beckoning at the base of the mountain below us. Even the winds that rushed up the mountain were cool and refreshing.

No church could have held all our guests: the Ai'Lee extended family numbering hundreds, the Demmings from throughout the state, including Ginger and Jeremiah Demming and Tutu Maile, paniolos and their families, and friends from throughout the world.

Both Alex, in his formal Hawaiian whites, and I, in a red silk cheong-sam edged in gold, were draped to our toes in maile and pikake leis. Kelly braided sprays of celadon-colored pakalana and orchids in my hair.

Alex and I didn't know if the Demmings and the Ai'Lees would behave; we sensed their caution the minute the first guests arrived. There was a nervous tension rumbling beneath the festivities, the fear that the curse from the past would cast a pall over the newlyweds.

My father, in a formal blue and white print shirt, walked me down an aisle of white ginger blossoms that released their delicate scent with our every step. When we stood before Reverend Chester Aikau, our family minister, he placed my hand in Alex's. Dad looked at me one more time. Then he turned towards his seat and stumbled.

Everyone gasped and collectively rose. There was an audible murmur. William Demming, who stood a step away across the flowered aisle, quickly caught Kam when he faltered and helped him to his seat next to Lailee Ai'Lee.

Reverend Aikau, his weathered face looking up to the sky, held his arms to the heavens in thanks and welcome, then repeated his blessings in Chinese, Hawaiian, and English. His brown eyes softened when he smiled at us. I felt the air thicken with the scent of the sea.

I turned to Alex. He smothered my hands in his. He lifted my fingers to his lips and kissed each one with lips soft and warm. When we faced each other and confidently said our marriage vows, we were surmounting barriers erected generations ago. I watched his eyes deepen as he uttered the promises he had longed to make to me years ago. At last, we turned to our guests as man and wife, Demming and Ai'Lee, finally united.

With a mischievous smile, Alex put his arm around my waist and bent me backwards. I clutched his shoulders and melted into his heart-stopping kiss. I heard the wild peacocks call from across the valley, and the Hawaiian forest birds—`apapane, `i`iwi, and `akepa—sing from the trees surrounding the knoll.

Our friends and family rose and cheered. The clouds danced in exultation while the winds played in the tops of the trees.

Alex and I walked hand and hand back down the aisle, accepting generous hugs and kisses. Behind us, William Demming, Lailee Ai'Lee, and my father led the two clans to a pretty tented pavilion surrounded by towering poles from which long silk banners rippled in the breeze. The three elders sat in the three rattan chairs in the center. I would now perform the traditional tea pouring ceremony, assisted by the Ai'Lee ladies.

According to Chinese tradition, I should serve my husband's family in hierarchical order, from eldest to youngest, males first, symbolizing that now I belonged to their family and was bound to serve them. But in Hawai`i we equalized and simplified the ceremony. My aunties brought me a wicker basket. Within the specially padded basket, an ornately decorated porcelain teapot, in a cylindrical shape from the early 1900s, had been filled with hot tea. The Ai'Lee ladies held out three trays, each with sweetmeats and a single matching teacup. I poured the tea and served my grandmother, symbolizing my respect. I did the same for my father and William Demming. And each handed me a silk jewelry case.

From Lailee Ai'Lee I received a jade bracelet, bright and shiny and heavy. With many oohs and aahs, the Ai'Lee ladies slipped it onto my right wrist. I wept when a pair of jade earrings set in twenty-four-karat Chinese gold, my father's wedding present to my mother decades ago, tumbled out of the silk pouch he placed in my hands. I immediately put them on. But William Demming's present startled us all.

The red silk pouch had the odor of mothballs, the feel of age. I untied the silk tassels. Out rolled a Burmese ruby the size of a thumb surrounded by diamonds and set in the intricate and delicate setting of a previous century.

"It's the legacy of Arthur Demming," Alex's father confirmed in a gravely voice.

We stared from the necklace to him in amazement.

"Alex," I whispered, in awe of the jewels that glowed in the afternoon light like a thousand stars. His astonishment told me he had never seen it before.

William Demming hoisted his huge body up and picked up the necklace. His large, dark hands swallowed the ruby and diamonds. The delicate gold chain caught on his rough calluses as he held it up before me. "May, I, Miki?" he asked gruffly. I turned around. His fingers shook as he clasped it around my neck. Then I felt its weight, heavy and rich. I turned around to face him. I saw a smile wrinkling across his face. He nodded. "It was commissioned as a wedding present a hundred and twenty years ago. At last, it has found its owner."

I touched the blood-red stone. Many cultures associate red with health, strength, sex, passion, and courage. For the Hawaiians, red was the color of the volcano goddess

Pele. For the Chinese, it was the color of good luck. I felt hope and love in this gift created for, but never given to a Kaua`i princess. But its overwhelming emotion was sadness and longing. I stood on my toes and kissed his leathery cheek. "Thank you. I am honored."

"No, young lady. You honor us." For the first time that day, the furrows across his forehead relaxed. He smiled and put his hand on his son's shoulder. He said, "I think Eddie Kekaha is ready to open the imu."

Eddie Kekaha and his paniolos prepared a colossal wedding lu`au under the large tree behind the Demming home. Fragrant steam billowed to the sky when the imu pit was opened and five roast pigs were hauled out, followed by sweet potatoes, and kulolo, all wrapped in delicious sweet limu, the seaweed that Jeremiah Demming had brought with him in his gigantic coolers. The Big Island Demmings brought gallons of fresh opihi, delicious limpets plucked from the dangerous wave-beaten coasts.

The long lu`au tables had been covered with tapa cloth and ferns with centerpieces of dendrobium orchids and plumeria sprays every two feet. Wooden platters of shrimp, sushi, sashimi with soy sauce and wasabi, grilled eels, steamed crabs, and teriyaki steak marched down the center along with calabash bowls of alligator pears, halved pink guavas, wild bananas, and Kahuku watermelon.

Alex and I, too excited to eat, visited each guest sitting at the tables set with bowls of fresh poi and trays of little crabs, coconut cake, and lomi lomi salmon. We heard the Ai'Lees and the Demmings share childhood tales about us and laugh at our embarrassment.

William Demming's boisterous laugh and his gruff voice boomed from where he sat next to Lailee Ai'Lee. My father, quiet and reserved, sat across from them, looking pleased.

When the moon came up, the guests brought out their guitars and ukuleles. We sang and danced until the sun put the moon to bed.

The following day, Alex and I flew off on our honeymoon. We answered hundreds of queries by telling everyone we were going to Paris. "Ah," everyone said, "of course, the two art lovers are going to see the Louvre and Montmarte and walk the Seine."

Chapter Twenty

The Tears
of the Gods

*T*he fine sand was bristling white, the beach empty, the sky sapphire blue. I stared out the door of our beachfront hideaway, tempted to be the first footsteps on the untouched sand that stretched to the lagoon. I glanced back at the bed and the tousled mess of crisp white cotton. I smiled, content and calm. I walked across the polished hardwood floor and lifted the covers.

"Alex, how about a swim?" I leaned down and licked his tummy. Instantly, his hand reached around my waist and tossed me back in bed. I shrieked and tickled him until he surrendered.

"Alex, we can do it on the beach. There's no one on this island. Just us. Haven't you ever fantasized about it?" I asked. I burrowed into his arms, relishing his heat.

"Never! Sand ends up in the worst places," he warned. He slipped his hands under my nightgown and ran his hands down my naked body. "But I've always fantasized about this."

Laughing, I leapt out of bed and tossed off my clothes. I ran out across the empty beach and dove into the sea. Alex sprinted behind me. And when we had swum the lagoon we returned to our cottage by the sea, joyfully content.

We had no sightseeing planned, no museums to visit. Once a day, maids and cooks arrived on a white motorboat. And when they left an hour later, our cottage was immaculate and our kitchen was stocked.

When Alex had suggested this hidden Hawaiian resort, I could barely wait to be there with him. Twelve years was a long time to lose and we had so much to share. So our days and nights rolled into endless waves of quiet talks and lovemaking. We were lulled to sleep by pulsing surf and wakened by the songs of honeycreepers. We luxuriated in the serenity of this island, in its brilliant white sands and lingering sunsets, in the gentle rasping of coconut fronds surrounding a crystalline bay.

Alex spent hours staring out to sea, putting the steamy jungles and desecrated temples behind him. When his silence grew dank and musty like his memories, I slipped away and dove naked among the reefs. I chased brilliantly striped parrotfish across the lagoon and flushed yellow and black butterfly fishes from their hiding places. I swam until Alex broke out of his mood and, swimming out to meet me, would wrap me in a sensual underwater embrace. We curled around each other's bodies, unencumbered by gravity, excited by the erotic pleasures of the sea. We returned to the shore gasping for air, exhausted and satiated.

One day, Alex did not join me. I rose from the water and saw he was still on the lanai of our cottage where I had left him an hour ago. He was standing, one arm on a support column, the other on his hip, watching me. I ran up the beach and put my arms around him.

"Are you all right?" I asked. I placed my palm on his bare chest. His skin was hot with the heat of the sun.

He ran his finger along my chin, then fingered the ruby around my neck. His eyes were troubled pools of blue and green. "Sorry. Here we are on our honeymoon and I'm brooding about our future."

"Hmm," I hummed seductively to soothe him. With my fingertips, I wiped away the crease in his forehead, trying to coax a smile. "Are you worried about the ranch?"

He took my hands in his and shook his head. "It's you I'm worried about. Your happiness is important to me, Miki. You've had a fast-paced, stimulating profession in San Francisco. Are you sure you want to give that all up?"

I had initiated a project with the Bishop Museum to catalog the cultural artifacts of Hawai`i's temples. Besides the detailed documentation, which would take a few years, I would record the rich legends that accompanied these treasures to preserve the memories of the past for future generations. But Alex fretted that it wouldn't be enough. "I'm also worried that you'll feel isolated on Kaua`i, away from your family and friends. I'm taking you away from all the things you love. How long can I make you happy?"

"Happiness comes from within, Alex," I said. I had been listening to my body for a week, feeling it tingle and surge with more than just passion. My figure was still lean and taut, but the changes had begun. "Feel this," I whispered. I held his hands to my face and kissed his palms. With my eyes fixed on his, I covered my breasts with his hands and, relishing the roughness of his palms against my skin, lowered them slowly to my abdomen. "We have a long-term project here. I'm hapai."

One of those rains that falls from a cloudless sunny sky misted around us like liquid sunshine. Then the heavens broke. The rain fell in warm, heavy sheets. Alex threw his arms up to the skies. He danced with me gleefully in the rain, shouting with joy for the new life, for the child to come. We threw our heads back, relishing the feel of the rain against our faces and skin, the soft drips as they fell from our hair, down our cheeks, and slid down our arms.

Then he rocked me in his arms while the rain, the tears of our gods, washed away his sorrows. All we could feel was the power of our love to begin anew.

Author photograph by Al Wright, Raintree Studios

About the Author

Pam Chun was born and raised in Hawai`i. She attended Punahou Academy and graduated from the University of California at Berkeley. Her first novel, *The Money Dragon*, was named one of 2002's Best Books of Hawai`i and received an award for excellence in the 2003 "Ka Palapala Po`okela" book awards. She has one son. She lives in the San Francisco Bay Area with her husband, TransPac sailor Fred J. Joyce III.

Visit Pam's website at www.members.authorsguild.net/pamchun.

Glossary of Hawaiian Terms

A *hui hou* Good-bye, until we meet again.

Ahupua`a A large parcel of land extending from the mountains to the sea.

Aku A fish: bonito, skipjack.

`Aumakua Guardian spirit.

`Awapuhi Delicate white ginger flowers.

Baba Chinese colloquial for "father."

Bagua The "map" of feng shui.

Bai-sun Prayers.

Bento box A fancy, Japanese-style lunchbox.

Bhunti Cantonese from Chungshan County in the Pearl River Delta in China.

Char siu Chinese roast pork.

Cheong-sam Fitted, mandarin-collared Chinese dress.

Ch'i One's energy.

Choy A Chinese cabbage used in many Chinese dishes.

E komo mai A traditional greeting in a society where hospitality is very important. It means "Please come inside."

`Eke huluhulu Soaking-wet burlap bags.

Fop see Buddhist monk.

Gin dui Chinese sweet doughnuts of rice flour fried to the color of gold.

Gouramis Any of numerous African and Asian tropical freshwater fishes.

Gum Sahn Chinese for "Gold Mountain"—a nickname for San Francisco created by Chinese miners.

Gung-Gung The Chinese honorific for grandfather.

Hakka Chinese dialectal group that were primarily mountain dwellers in China.

Haku lei Type of lei in which several types of plant material are braided together.

Haole Caucasian, previously used to denote non-Hawaiians of any race.

Hapa Of mixed blood.

Hapai Pregnant.

Hapi coats Japanese-style cotton robes.

Haupia Hawaiian coconut pudding.

Heiau Sacred site of traditional Hawaiian religion.

Heung Chinese word for "incense."

Holoku Long mu`umu`u .

Hui Society, club, or partnership.

Hula kahiko Ancient Hula.

Imu Underground oven.

"Ipo Lei Manu" A song written by Queen Kapi`olani for David Kâlakaua. The title means "For My Cherished Sweetheart."

Kahili Feather standard, a symbol of the presence of royalty, carried in processions in front of a royal entourage.

Kahuna Expert in any craft or field of knowledge, priest.

Kama`aina Native-born.

Kane Male, husband, man.

Kapakahi Lopsided, crooked, tipped this way and that.

Kapolena Canvas that covers the entire imu.

**Keiki o ka `aina**  The children of Hawai`i.

Keikis Children.

Ki ho`alu Hawaiian slack key. The strings are picked individually and are not chorded.

Kiawe The wood of the kiawe tree is frequently used in barbecues and is also used to make charcoal.

Kim chee A vegetable pickle seasoned with garlic, red pepper, and ginger that is the national dish of Korea.

Koa Largest of native forest trees (*Acacia koa*) with light gray bark, crescent-shaped leaves, and small white flowers.

Koi A carp bred especially in Japan for large size and a variety of colors and often stocked in ornamental ponds.

Kulolo Dessert made of baked, grated taro and coconut milk.

Lanai Porch, patio.

Lauhala Leaves of the Hala tree, used for weaving floor mats, clothing, etc.

Laulau A bundle of food wrapped in ti leaves and steamed, a favorite dish at parties and lu`aus.

Limu Hawaiian word for seaweed, an item in traditional diet.

Lychee Oval fruit of a Chinese tree of the soapberry family, having a hard, scaly reddish outer covering and sweet whitish edible flesh that surrounds a single large seed.

Mahalo Thank you.

Makai Toward the sea.

Malama pono Take care of yourself.

Malasadas Buttery Portuguese doughnuts.

Manapua Hawaiian word for Chinese roast-pork buns.

Mano Shark.

Mao tai Rice wine.

Mauka Toward the mountain.

Mochi Wrapped Japanese desserts shaped like exquisite flowers and fishes made from pounded rice flour.

Mu`umu`u Loose Hawaiian dress.

Mynah A dark brown, slightly crested bird with a white tail tip and wing markings and bright yellow bill and feet.

`Ohana Family.

`Oi`o Procession of ghosts of a departed chief and his company.

Obake A hungry Japanese ghost.

`*Oama* Silvery, sweet fish.

Ohi`a tree Lehua tree.

`*Okolemaluna* A Hawaiian toast meaning "bottoms-up."

`*Ono* Delicious.

`*Opihi* Limpet, shellfish considered a great delicacy.

Pakalana Fragrant lei flower, one of many scented flowers brought to Hawai`i by Chinese immigrants.

Palaka Traditional Hawaiian block-print cotton cloth originally worn on sugar plantations and ranches.

Paniolos Hawaiian cowboys.

Pareau Hawaiian sarong, a traditional Polynesian garment worn as several dress styles, a wrap or as a skirt.

Pikake Jasmine flower, named for Princess Ka`iulani's peacocks.

Pohaku Rock, stone.

Poi Hawaiian staple made by pounding cooked taro root.

Pu`olo la`i A ti-leaf package to store and carry leis.

Pupu Hawaiian word for snacks and appetizers.

Shime-daiko A high-pitched drum.

Shunga pictures Erotic Japanese illustrations which had once been banned as pornography in seventeenth-century Japan, now collected as art.

Taiko Taiko is often used to mean the art of Japanese drum ensembles, but the word actually refers to the taiko drums themselves. Literally, "fat drum."

Tapa Hawaiian cloth made from the bark of trees such as wauke or makami, often scented and elaborately dyed and decorated.

Tatami Straw matting used as a floor covering in a Japanese home.

Tetsu-zutsu A bell-like instrument consisting of three pieces of pipe of differing diameters welded together.

Ti-leaf A tropical palm-like plant of the agave family with leaves in terminal tufts.

Tutu Respectful Hawaiian word for "grandmother."

U'i Youthful, handsome, vigorous, beautiful.

Wahine Woman, wife, lady.

Wiki-wiki Very fast.

Yang The masculine active principle in nature that in Chinese cosmology is exhibited in light, heat, or dryness and that combines with yin to produce all that comes to be.

Yin The feminine passive principle in nature that in Chinese cosmology is exhibited in darkness, cold, or wetness. It combines with yang to produce all that comes to be.

Yukatas Short Japanese wide-sleeved garments suitable for hot evenings.

Zori A flat thonged sandal usually made of straw, cloth, leather, or rubber.

*Glossary compiled by the author using the *Hawaiian Dictionary, Revised and Enlarged*, by Mary Kawenea Pukui and Samuel H. Elbert, and the *Merriam-Webster's Collegiate Dictionary, Eleventh Edition*.